Kentucky Summers 2

Muddied Waters

Kentucky Summers 2: Muddied Waters

Cover design by Shirley Jones

Photography by Tim Callahan

Published in the United States of America

ISBN:9781987709421

1. Southern Fiction / Young Adult, Adult

Kentucky Summers 2

Book 1

Muddied Waters

To Diana,
Spread Kindness,
Blessings,
[signature]
5-2-18

By

Tim Callahan

Other Books

By

Tim Callahan

Kentucky Summer Series:

1. The Cave, the Cabin & the Tattoo Man

2. Coty & the Wolf Pack

3. Dark Days in Morgan County

4. Above Devil's Creek

5. Timmy & Susie & the Bootleggers' Revenge

6. Kentucky Snow & the Crow

7. Red River, Junior & the Witch

8. Follow the Pack

Kentucky Summers Series 2:

1. Muddied Waters

Others:

Sleepy Valley

Come Home, Joe

Nashville Sounds

This book is dedicated to:

my second grandchild, Shelby Jolene.

May God bless her.

Born: August 8, 2017

This book is also dedicated in memory of:

Brenda Lucille Whitt

April 17, 1949 - March 31, 2018

Contents

Chapter 1

First Day of High School

Tuesday, September 3, 1963

"Timmy, Timmy, get up," Mom yelled from the kitchen.

James Ernest opened our bedroom door and said, "He's already up, but I'm not sure where he is. He was gone when I got up."

I heard them from the back porch. I'd had a hard time sleeping during the night; thinking about starting high school was exciting and scary. At five-thirty I had woken up again and decided to get up and go for a walk around the pay lake. I had to talk myself into believing it was senseless to worry about high school, plus there was nothing I could do about it. Most of my friends had been going to the high school, James Ernest went there, and they had assured me that I would like it once I got used to it.

I also knew that the Boys from Blaze would be there and I wondered if they would pick on me. I told myself that since we now had a truce they should leave me alone. After walking around the lake five times I was purty much settled down and now sleepy as all get out. I wanted to go back to bed, but I knew there was no way Mom would allow that to happen.

"Where could he be?" Mom questioned more to herself.

Janie was already up and sitting at the table. She answered, "He's probably in the outhouse. He spends a lot of time in the outhouse." After pausing she said, "I think it's stinky."

I only spent the required amount of time in the outhouse. I thought it was stinky also.

I opened the back door and said, "I'm right here. I'm not in the outhouse."

"Where have you been then?" Janie asked.

"I was standing on the back porch listening to every word. You really need to stop spending time with Delma and Thelma."

"They're my friends."

"They're not friends, they're nuts," I said, and laughed.

"Where have you been?" Mom asked.

"I couldn't sleep. I went for a walk."

"You need to get ready for school. The bus will be here soon."

"Could I skip high school?" I said as I headed to my bedroom.

"You'd better get in there and get ready. Now!"

I saw James Ernest putting his shoes on when I entered the bedroom. "Maybe the Key family is right. There's no reason I need to go school."

The Key family had eight kids and only a few of them had made it through the eighth grade. Their parents left it up to their kids whether to go to school or not. They actually frowned on schooling and thought the kids that did want to continue school were strange. Their twins, Rock and Kenny, who we called Tucky, had gone back to school with our help, and now were going to also start high school today.

I thought it was odd how parents raised their children so differently. I thought about this as I got dressed, knowing I had to go to school. Some parents sent their kids to school, others didn't care about education. James Ernest's parents left him and went off to West Virginia and died when their car plunged off a mountain road. Mom took him in and he now lived with us. I considered him my brother and best friend. My mom moved to Kentucky to keep her family together. I was glad I had my mother even though she was making me go to high school.

We waited on the front porch for the bus to arrive. Janie was all excited about going to a new school and riding the bus. The one-room school we had attended for years closed for good after the school year ended this past spring. All of the students from that school were now going to new schools.

Twenty minutes later the school bus stopped in front of the store. I saw Susie waving from one of the windows near the back of the bus. At least there was one good thing about going to school. I followed James Ernest onto the bus, my first time ever on a school bus. The song popped into my head, *The wheels of the bus go round, round, round.*

The twins, Delma and Thelma, were seated in the front row, probably to direct the bus driver. Janie sat down on the bench opposite them. James Ernest headed toward Raven who was sitting in the seat directly across from Susie. I headed for Susie. Junior and Samantha Washington, Raven's brother and sister, sat together.

I knew most of the kids who were on the bus. I passed Daniel Sugarman who was sitting near the front of the bus. He said, "Hello."

I said hello back to him. I was focused on Susie's smiling face when I tripped over someone's leg and went falling face first toward the dirty bus aisle. I managed to catch hold of the seats and pull myself up before almost landing full face on the floor, as the other kids laughed. Once I was back to a standing position I looked behind me to see Bernice "Skunk" Strunck smirking and hanging her leg out into the aisle to let me know that she was the one who tripped me.

Bernice was one grade ahead of me and had gone to our one-room school in Oak Hills. Eighth grade was a lot nicer than previous years when she attended the school. She had been best friends with Sadie Tuttle before going to high school. I wondered if they would resume their best friends' relationship.

I scowled at her and she mouthed, "This is my bus." I wondered what she meant by that. She was such a hateful, varmint, stupid person. I pondered what her parents were like.

I turned back toward Susie and finally sat down beside her. I saw Brenda, Susie's sister, sitting with Rhonda Blair in the seat behind us.

"That was quite an entrance," Susie said.

"Yeah, thanks to the skunk."

"Well, we've always known what kind of person she is," Susie said.

The bus continued away from the store toward Wrigley. The next bus stop was at the lane leading to the Tuttle's house. I saw Sadie, Randy, Purty, and Francis standing there waiting for the bus. Purty was wearing clothes and throwing rocks at a tree acting as if he was pitching on the mound of Crosley Field in Cincinnati. Sadie was first on the bus and went straight to the seat Bernice had saved for her. That was no surprise. Randy and Purty came on back to the empty seat in front of us. Francis slid in next to one of her friends. Bernice had scooted over for Sadie; therefore she wasn't able to trip Randy or Purty. Randy slid in first and Purty plopped down beside him, but with his head turned toward us.

"What's up, Ladies and Germ?" Without giving us a chance to tell him 'what's up' he continued, "Isn't this great? We're all together again going to the same school. I hated last year with us at the high school and you guys at Oak Hills. The Wolf Pack together again."

"You're forgetting Junior. He'll be at the Junior High," I corrected him.

"Oh, yeah. His loss."

"Will we even see you during the day?" I asked

"Of course you will, between classes, and at lunchtime, and on the bus back home. Just knowing that the two of you are in the same building makes the day okay."

"You know you're a weirdo, don't you?" I asked.

"Yeah, but I wear it well." We all laughed as the bus was coming to a stop in front of the Key house. Purty then saw Rhonda sitting behind us.

"Hello, beautiful," Purty said to Rhonda.

"Hi, Todd," Brenda replied.

"I meant Rhonda."

"Well, that's hurtful," Brenda said. Rhonda just smiled.

Rock and Tucky were waiting on the porch. They jumped off the porch and ran to the bus with brown paper bags in their hands. They sat across from us. We all said hi.

"What's in the bags? Your lunch?" Purty questioned. Before they could answer he continued, "Let me guess, fried possum with a side of turnip greens, or maybe smashed blackened crow with live crawdads on the side. I think I hear them crawling around inside those bags."

Rock looked him in the eyes and said, "You are so funny. We actually have a hearty flattened squirrel and chipmunk stew. What you hear are the fresh tadpoles trying to get out."

"Don't forget the turtle eyes that are in the stew?" Tucky teased.

I hoped he was teasing. You never knew about the Key family. Most of what they ate came from the side of the road after being run down by speeding vehicles. After living in the deep hollers for most of their lives, hunting for their meat, they couldn't believe the smorgasbord of meat they could find left on or along the roads of Morgan County for the taking. Having ten mouths to feed, they needed a lot.

Soon we arrived at the Wrigley school. The kids in first grade to eighth grade would be going into the Wrigley school, and we had to change buses to continue our trip to Morgan County High School in West Liberty.

When we finally arrived at the high school in West Liberty the bus stopped in front of the school to let us unload. I had seen the school before, but this time it seemed so much bigger than I remembered it. There was a stone wall that fronted the school where it seemed like most of the students were hanging out waiting for the bell to ring. The voices and laughter was loud with excitement of school starting again and seeing friends they hadn't seen much of during the summer break. When Raven got off the bus you could hear the laughter die down and see each head turn toward her. I hadn't even thought about how nervous Raven would be. She was the first black student to go to the high school as far as we knew.

All the kids that went to Oak Hills knew her and liked her, but here she was with kids who didn't know her and weren't used to having a black student in their school. I was sure there were kids who wouldn't want her there. I heard one boy yell out; "Go back to Africa where you came from!" Some students laughed and nodded their heads in agreement.

James Ernest took her hand in his and continued his walk toward the stone wall. Susie and I followed closely behind them. Apparently James Ernest was quite popular among the students from the year before. Students stared at the two of them, but no one yelled out anything else after seeing Raven with him. He began introducing Raven, Susie, and me to different students. Out of the corner of my eye I saw a couple of the Boys from Blaze.

I turned and nodded to them and they nodded back. Hopefully our truce with them would continue as it had during the past summer. They turned and headed toward the school entrance. The school was a large two story gray stone building that looked more like a government building than a school. I then heard a bell ringing. James Ernest told us that it meant we had ten minutes to find our homeroom. He led us to the bulletin board which told freshmen where to go for homeroom. Rock and Tucky were with us. Looking at the list we saw that five out of the eight Oak Hills students were in the same homeroom, Room 107, with Mr. Burns. James Ernest pointed in the direction we should go. "You'll find the room number outside the room," he said. He then turned and was gone.

Chapter 2

Mr. Burns Homeroom

Susie and I entered the classroom and saw all the empty desks and a teacher standing at the blackboard writing his name onto it – *Mr. Burns.* As we entered the room the blackboard was on our left where Mr. Burns stood. The door to the room was near the back.

As more kids entered the room he called out, "Take a seat anywhere you'd like. I believe most of the seats should end up being filled." Susie and I found seats across from each other near the windows toward the front of the room. Rock and Tucky sat behind us. Raven sat in front of Susie. She seemed very nervous without James Ernest beside her. I noticed that Daniel Sugarman, Sadie and Rhonda Blair weren't in this homeroom. The teacher was right. All but a couple of the seats were filled by the time the second bell rang.

Once all the students were seated the room became eerily quiet. I figured all of us were new to the school and a little scared of the unknown. James Ernest had told me that each grade averaged around a hundred students. So there must have been two or three more homeroom classes.

Mr. Burns looked at the class and then said, "Welcome to your new school, Morgan County High School. Give yourselves a hand." A couple of students began clapping and then slowly everyone began to join in. I wasn't sure why we were clapping.

"You've made it this far. I hope each of you enjoy your time here for the next four years, some of you, maybe the next five or six years." We all laughed. "And hopefully you will all graduate and continue to college. It's an accomplishment to get this far. Nearly forty percent of students in Kentucky never make it past the eighth grade."

I guess I was actually applauding my mom who made me get up and go to school every day. But it was pretty neat to think I had accomplished something that a lot of kids never did. It wasn't that I didn't like school, it was that I enjoyed doing other stuff more like fishing and exploring the woods.

"Each morning you'll start in here for ten minutes. I'll take roll to see if anyone is absent and go over any announcements and then you'll be off to your first class. But today you'll spend forty-five minutes in here. You'll have ten minutes between classes. That will give you time to do anything you need to do – such as go to the restroom, go to your lockers, or cram for a test – before getting to your next class. You will be marked as tardy if you are not in the classroom before the bell goes off."

A boy in the front row raised his hand and asked, "What happens to us if we're late?"

"Good question Mr.__?" Mr. Burns waited for the boy to tell him his name.

The boy just sat there waiting for Mr. Burns to finish his sentence.

"What is your name, if I may ask?" Mr. Burns asked figuring the boy didn't have a clue.

"Sam Hitchcock," the boy finally told him.

"Well Mr. Hitchcock. If you are tardy too many times, or are disrupting class, or found to be lacking in other social behaviors, you will be given detention." I liked the way Mr. Burns spoke.

Sam raised his hand again.

"I suppose you want to know what detention is. Is that correct?" Mr. Burns asked.

"Yes."

"Yes, what?"

Sam looked confused again and then said, "Yes, I do."

"Mr. Hitchcock, I was looking for you to address me by saying 'Yes, Mr. Burns', or 'Yes, sir.'"

Sam looked at Mr. Burns. Mr. Burns stared back at him. Sam finally realized that it was his turn to speak and blurted out, "Yes, Sir, Mr. Burns."

"One or the other will suffice, Mr. Hitchcock."

I was afraid Sam was going to ask the teacher what suffice meant. But he was probably embarrassed into never raising his hand again during his high school career.

"If you receive detention it means that you will have to stay after school for an hour in the detention room and study and have someone come to the school and pick you up afterwards. It would be best to be on time and not accumulate detentions. Do you agree, Mr. Hitchcock?"

I could see Sam nodding his head in agreement while Mr. Burns stared at him again.

Sam finally took the hint again and answered, "Yes, sir."

I knew I would get along with Sam. He had the guts to ask the questions that most all of us wanted to know. But we were too scared of being made fun of by the other students who didn't know also.

The bell rang. Some of the students began to stand. Mr. Burns called out. "Please remain seated. That is the regular bell for the other grades. I'll release you to your next class in a half an hour."

We heard voices and laughter coming from the hallway outside the door. It was loud. I looked toward the door's window to see if I could spot James Ernest, or Purty, or Randy. I saw none of them. All I saw were strangers passing by the door.

Mr. Burns raised his voice and said, "I will now call out the roster of students that I have listed. Please answer 'Here' when I call your name. Then make your way up here and I will pass out your schedule of classes and a map of the school so you can find your way to your next class. You will also find your locker assignment among the papers. Freshman lockers are all together, so if you don't know where to go just follow each other around the school until you find your storage department. Is this understood?"

"Yes, sir," most of us said while a few of the students said, "Yes, Mr. Burns."

"Let's begin. Miss Lily Ashcroft."

"Here," a tiny voice called out from the back of the room. She then stayed where she was.

"Miss Lily Ashcroft, you are now to come forward as I directed a moment ago."

She quietly got up from her desk and as silent as a mouse made her way to Mr. Burns' desk. Lily was a petite girl with curly black hair. She looked like she should be at the junior high school.

Mr. Burns handed Lily her papers and she very quietly said, "Thank you, Mr. Burns."

I was the fourth student to make my way up front to get papers. One after another, students went forward to get their assignments without incident until Mr. Burns called out,

"Mr. Kenny Key."

"Yep, I'm here," he answered back as he jumped from his desk and made his way up front. As he walked past me I noticed he had already taken off his shoes and socks and was going forward barefoot.

As other kids began to notice they began to snicker. Mr. Burns already looked annoyed by Mr. Kenny Key's reply, but when he saw that Tucky was coming forward without shoes on I thought his head was going to explode. I saw him bow his head and rub his temples as Tucky neared. Tucky stood in front of his desk waiting to be handed his papers as Mr. Burns continued to rub his entire head.

"Mr. Kenny Key. That is an unusual name."

"If you say so, Mr. Burns. My full name is Kenny Tuck Key. My friends call me Tucky."

Mr. Burns stared at him for a good thirty seconds and then said, "For starters, Mr. Key, all I need when I call your name is for you to say 'Here'. I do not need the 'Yep'. You should forgo that. Secondly, where are your shoes, and why do you not have them on?"

"I like going barefoot a lot more."

"If you have shoes, I suggest you wear them. If you do not have shoes I suggest you get some."

"Oh, I have shoes. I just prefer not to wear them. I enjoy letting these piggy's free. It feels good to wiggle these toes. Do you like wiggling your toes, Mr. Burns?"

The class burst into laughter. I wasn't sure if Tucky was serious or just giving Mr. Burns a hard time as Mr. Burns had done Sam Hitchcock.

Mr. Burns started to speak when Tucky asked, "Is not wearing shoes cause for one of them detention things? I do have shoes. I just wanted to take them off, you know, and let them piggy's free, like I said before, Mr. Burns."

"Yes, you could get one of '*them detention things*' if you do not wear shoes in class. Here are your papers. Please return to your desk and put your shoes on, Tucky."

"Yes, sir. But please call me either Kenny or Mr. Key." With that said Tucky turned around and walked back to his desk and put his shoes back on.

I believed in that moment Tucky had just made a lot of new friends.

As Tucky was placing his feet in his shoes Mr. Burns called out, "Miss Rock Key."

"Here." All the heads in the classroom turned toward her. She quickly walked up to the desk.

Mr. Burns asked, "Miss Key, what is your given name?"

"Rock is my given name. My name is Rock Key. I'm Kenny's twin sister."

"Of course you are." He looked down toward her feet. "That's a very unusual name," Mr. Burns said.

"My name is nothing compared to some of my brothers and sisters. We have Monk Key, Adore Key, Chero Key, Sugar Cook Key, Chuck Key and Luck Key."

"Well good, I have more to look forward to."

"I doubt it. Kenny and I are probably the only ones that will make it to high school. They're in that other percentage that we didn't clap for."

Mr. Burns looked down at the roster, hesitated, and then called out, "Mr. Bill Manley." Rock turned away and went back to her desk.

He continued calling out names and handing out papers until he got to the end of the alphabet. The last name he called out was, "Miss Raven Washington."

"Here," Raven answered with her black arm raised. Whispers began among the class.

"No talking," Mr. Burns called out.

When she reached his desk he asked, "Is Raven your given name?"

"Yes sir, it is."

"Okay, Miss Raven Washington, welcome to the class."

The way Mr. Burns said, 'welcome to the class', made me like Mr. Burns a little more. It was almost as if he was telling the other students to welcome her to the school. Raven was smiling as she made her way back to her desk. Maybe Mr. Burns wasn't as bad as he first seemed.

"With the few minutes we have left you can talk among yourselves and look at your schedule and study the map to see where you're to go when I release you. You are to go to your first class. You will have ten minutes to get there. It will last only thirty minutes due to the extended homeroom and then you'll be back on the regular times," Mr. Burns directed.

Susie and I huddled together and studied the map and looked at the schedule to see where we were going first. I had American History and Susie had an English class. The English teacher was Mr. Burns. I had English my third period. I was sad that we didn't have classes together. As we looked at the schedule we saw that the only class we had together was science. It was our last class of the day. We also had study hall together just before Science. At least I would get to see her during the last two hours of each day.

Chapter 3

Roscoe, Roscoe, Roscoe

"Class dismissed," Mr. Burns announced. Everyone rose at the same time and headed for the door. I noticed Susie behind me. I waited for her.

"I thought you stayed with Mr. Burns?" I asked.

"I do, but I've got ten minutes. I'll go with you and find our lockers."

"Okay. Let's go."

Raven and Tucky and Rock yelled out for us to wait for them. They quickly caught up with us.

"I think the lockers are on the second floor," Susie said.

The other kids were scrambling thru the halls like lost puppies either trying to find their locker or their next classroom. The five of us made our way to the stairs. Once we were upstairs we began searching the lockers for our numbers. Our numbers went 225 to 250. I had 228 and Susie 230, one locker between us. We found locker 300 and began following them down the hall. Halfway down the hall we found our lockers. We quickly opened them and put our lunches inside.

"We better get to our classes," Susie said. By the time on the clock in the hallway we only had 2 minutes to make it to our next classroom. Susie turned and backtracked to Mr. Burns' room.

Raven asked me, "What class do you have next?"

"American History in Room 212," I answered.

"Me too," Raven said.

"I have Math class. I've got to go. I may have to take my shoes off in this class so I can count higher," Tucky said.

"Any excuse to take your shoes off," I yelled back as he hurried off. Raven and I were still laughing at Tucky as we found Room 212. We entered the room and found seats near the back beside each other. Students stared at Raven as we made our way to the seats.

The teacher in the front of the room was a short heavy-set lady with her gray hair done up in a bun. She had on a flowered dress that fell almost to the floor. She reminded me of a large tree stump with a head lying on it. The name on the blackboard read Mrs. Hempshaw.

The first bell rang letting kids know they had one minute to be in class before the second bell would ring signaling that they were tardy. After the first bell rang I asked Raven if I could see her schedule. She handed it to me and I saw that we had every class together. I told her what I had found and she smiled and said, "I'm glad. This place scares me."

"You'll be fine once the other kids get to know you."

"I hope so."

I noticed that two of the kids that had been seated near Raven got up and found other seats in the room. The second bell rang. A few stragglers entered after the bell and made their way to empty desks.

Kids were talking among themselves and some were laughing until Mrs. Hempshaw said very loudly, "My name," she hesitated, waiting for complete quiet which happened quickly, "is Mrs. Hempshaw. This class is for freshman American History, except for those who may have flunked the class last year. I see you are back again Bobby Watson for a second go."

Everyone turned their heads to look at the boy Mrs. Hempshaw was looking at. He didn't seem to be embarrassed at all with being called out in front of the class. I would have hid under my desk.

"Those of you who were late will be excused today. But now that you know where the classroom is you will not be excused from now on. Now, I like having my students in alphabetical order in my class. So I will call your name and point to the desk which you will remain for the year. Please come and take your seat quietly. Sally Adams, please take this first seat." She pointed to the front row desk on her right side. Sally Adams made her way up front. The boy sitting in the seat continued sitting there. Mrs. Hempshaw looked down at the boy and asked him, "What is your name young lad?"

"Roscoe Lannister."

"Roscoe Lannister, if I just gave the seat to Sally then that means the seat in which you are sitting in is no longer your seat. Am I correct?"

"Yeah, I guess so." Roscoe continued sitting at the desk.

26

"Roscoe, Roscoe, Roscoe, what do think you need to do?"

"I don't know. You're the teacher."

"Yes, you are right about that. Therefore, I'm going to tell you what you should do. I would like for you to go to the right front corner of the room and put your nose in the corner and stand there until I call your name."

Roscoe stood up and slowly made his way and stood in the corner. Sally Adams took her seat at the desk.

Mrs. Hempshaw then followed along the front row. I ended up in the fourth chair in the first row. From then on students were hopping from their desks very willing to part with them for the student whose name was called. No one else wanted to stand in a corner. Mrs. Hempshaw skipped over the desk that Roscoe would sit in. She continued assigning seats all the way to the back row. Only two students were left for the back row, Bobby Watson, who had flunked the class last year, and Raven Washington.

"Raven Washington, please take this desk and Bobby Watson, please take this one." Raven was given the second desk in the back. Bobby was placed in the fifth desk, the last one in the row. There were two desks between Raven and Bobby.

"I don't want Bobby influencing you," she said looking down at Raven and then over at Bobby. Only then did she call Roscoe's name and let him take the seat at his desk.

She wobbled her way back up to the front of the room and looked out over the class. "Would Tim and Bobby come forward?"

I wondered what I had done. Why was I being brought forward with the boy who had flunked the class?

"Please carry five textbooks at a time and pass them out to the students. Each of you take a row at a time," Mrs. Hempshaw directed. There were six rows of five chairs. Only two seats were empty meaning we had 28 students in the class. The books were stacked along the wall in the front of the room. I picked up the first five and began passing them out to the front row. I gave myself the book I thought was in the best condition. Some on them were pretty ragged. I figured I might as well get something out of all this work.

Bobby and I continued passing the books out until each student had a book.

"Thank you, Bobby and Timmy. Is Timmy okay?" she asked.

"That's what most people call me."

She then directed the class, "Please write your name on the inside of the front cover. Cross out any names that aren't already crossed out. Those are the names of the students who used the book before you." I noticed that I had the book that James Ernest used at one time. I figured Raven would like to have it. I quickly raised my hand.

"Yes, Timmy."

"May I talk to Raven for just one moment?" Raven looked up at me, and I shook my head trying to let her know not to sign the book.

"No, you may not. You can talk to her on your own time."

28

I figured she would say that, but at least I got Raven's attention. I wasn't sure if she got the message or not. I opened the book and pretended to sign it.

"Turn to the first chapter," Mrs. Hempshaw announced, and the real high school began. The first chapter began with the beginning of American history, Christopher Columbus crossing the Atlantic Ocean in search of a new land.

I was already bored.

The bell saved me from drifting off into a deep sleep. I didn't know how I was going to get away with sleeping in the front row. I'd have to find another class to get my nap in.

Mrs. Hempshaw called out, "Read chapter one before tomorrow's class. There may be a test on it." Teacher's always said that to make the students read it.

I met Raven at the door and told her about having James Ernest's book. "Would you like to have it? We can trade."

"I would like it, but I've already signed mine. I was afraid not to."

"That's okay. I can just cross your name out."

"Wait, I signed it with a pencil cause that was all I had. You could just erase it."

"Great," I said as I handed her the book. I looked at the book she handed me and saw that it was probably the most ragged book that had been passed out. It looked as though someone had used it to chop wood, if that was possible. Oh well, it was just a stupid school book.

Chapter 4

Mr. Holbrook's Math Class

I had looked at our next class on the schedule and saw that it was Math class on the first floor, room 114, with a Mr. Earl Holbrook. I wondered if he was related to our teacher at the one-room school, Mrs. Eleanor Holbrook. Raven and I headed for the stairs and found the room near the bottom of the steps. As we headed into the room I saw Tucky coming our way holding his shoes in one hand and his English book in his other hand.

The three of us found seats near each other on the far side of the room. Raven sat in front of me and Tucky beside me. A minute later I saw Rock come through the door and I waved her over. She sat next to Raven. "It would be nice if we could stay seated like this," I told the others. They agreed.

Tucky began slipping his shoes onto his feet but left the laces untied. I figured he would slip them off between classes.

"What class were you two just in?" Raven asked Rock and Tucky.

"I had study hall, but there was nothing to study except the schedule since I hadn't been to a class," Rock told us.

"I had English class with Mr. Burns. Susie was in the class," Tucky said.

The first bell rang and other students began rushing into the classroom. I saw one of the Boys from Blaze walk in. He took a seat in the back of the room. Shortly after, the second bell rung as Lily Ashcroft walked in and took a seat, as quiet as ever.

Mr. Holbrook stood up to address the class. "This is high school Basic Math. I am Mr. Earl Holbrook. If you are in the wrong class you may leave now." The Boy from Blaze rose from his seat and walked out the door with his head hanging down.

"If you do not attend this school you may now leave." Everyone laughed.

"If you want to be here, or are forced to be here by your parents, the school, your grandparents or a command from God, you are welcomed to stay. If none of these apply then you may leave." We laughed and everyone stayed.

"Now, I know some teachers like you seated in order of the first letter in your last name. Some teachers put the bad or mean students in the back and their pets up front. Some teachers may even put the good looking kids in the front and the ugly ones in the back. Hopefully, none of you have been placed in the back of the room and wondered why." The room burst into laughter.

"I, on the other hand, do not care where you sit. You may sit with your friends as long as you don't disrupt my teaching. If that happens, then I will assign you a seat in the back of the room. If you chose to stay where you are seated as of now, then you must always sit at that desk. Therefore, I'll know where to look for you. If you don't like the seat you are sitting in at this time you may switch with someone else who does not like their seat. Raise your hand if that is the case."

A boy in the front row and a girl in the back row raised their hands.

Mr. Holbrook asked the girl, "Would you like to switch seats with him?"

She said, "Yes, Mr. Holbrook."

"And would you, sir, like to switch to the back row," Mr. Holbrook asked the boy.

"Sure would," he said as he gathered his belongings and jumped up.

"They have come to an agreement. All seems to be right in the world now, or at least in this classroom.

"Now, I would like for you one at a time, starting in the back left corner of the room, stand and tell us your name, what school you went to last year, and anything else you think we would like to know about you." He pointed to the boy who had just switched seats and said, "You get to go first."

The boy stood and hesitated before saying, "I'm Frankie Lewis. I went to Wrigley last year. I enjoy hunting squirrels."

One by one, the students stood and told who they were. They were from all different communities in Morgan County. Most everyone told what their favorite thing to do was, spurred on by Frankie Lewis.

It came my turn and I stood and said, "My name is Tim Callahan and I went to Oak Hills last year. I enjoy fishing and doing adventures with the Wolf Pack. That's a club of six guys that I'm part of, plus my dog Coty." I heard whispering all around the room.

Mr. Holbrook walked toward the front of the class from behind his desk and said, "Yes, Timmy Callahan, your reputation comes with you. I've heard of your club's many adventures and heroics. My wife also was your teacher at Oak Hills."

"We loved having Mrs. Holbrook as our teacher. High school is a lot different," I said, and sat back down. I heard other kids murmuring agreement.

"Thank you. I'll past that along. Next."

Tucky stood, "I'm Kenny Tuck Key, and my friends call me Tucky for short. I also went to Oak Hills and I'm a member of the Wolf Pack also."

Six more kids stood before they got to Rock. She stood and said, "I'm Rock Key, Kenny's twin sister. I also went to Oak Hills. I would like to be a member of the Wolf Pack, but it's a boys-only club, so I joined a girls club. I enjoy wading in the creeks near our home."

Raven stood up next and said, "I'm Raven Washington. I also went to Oak Hills last year. I have two brothers and a sister and I belong to a club along with Rock and some other girls called the Bear Troop. I enjoy making wooden baskets."

That past summer the girls got tired of us guys having a club and having all the fun so they started a girls-only club which consisted of Susie, Rock, Raven, Francis and Rhonda. Brenda didn't want to be included, and Sadie wasn't asked to be a member.

The introductions continued along the rows until everyone had their turn. We then were directed to come forward and get a math book a row at a time. He then divided the room into two teams and we had a math contest. One person from each team went to the blackboard. They were given a math problem and the first one to raise their hand and get it right won a point for their team.

There were twenty-six students in the room. Each team had thirteen students. At the beginning the problems were very easy, but they got harder as we went. The first problem was, "What is 12 divided into 144?" Our team member, a girl from the front row, quickly raised her hand and answered 12. We had our first point. Raven, Rock, Tucky and I were all on the same team.

We led 7 to 3 when it was Raven's turn. Mr. Holbrook read the question, "If you have 92 chickens, and seven foxes get into the chicken coop, and each fox eats seven chickens, how many chickens will you have when you gather eggs the next morning?"

The boy going against Raven began figuring on the blackboard. He was multiplying 7 times 7 when Raven raised her hand and answered, "There were 43 chickens left in the coop."

"That's correct." Raven beamed as she made her way back to her seat. It was my turn. Math had always been my best subject. I would show Mr. Holbrook that I was smart and quick. I went up to the board. My opponent was a girl I didn't know. But she wore glasses and looked smart.

Mr. Holbrook began, "You have a tobacco barn." This was already perfect for me.

"The barn has 4 equal sections that hold tobacco when hung. Each section has 24 equal rows where tobacco can be hung." The girl had drawn a barn and put in the sections and all the numbers. I just stood there listening. "Each row can hold 120 tobacco sticks. How many tobacco sticks would you need to fill the barn?"

The girl began figuring. I stood there looking at the ceiling trying to come up with the answer. He said there were 4 sections, but how many rows did each….. The girl with the glasses raised her hand.

"Yes, Jolene. What is the answer?"

"You would need eleven thousand, five hundred, and twenty tobacco sticks," Jolene answered. That couldn't be right, I thought. No one has eleven thousand tobacco sticks!

"That's right. Good job, Jolene," Mr. Holbrook said as I slinked my way back to my desk. "I would suggest next time you use the blackboard, Timmy."

Our team ended up winning 8 to 5, no thanks to me. What a doofus!

The bell rang and we were out the door. I liked Mr. Holbrook even though he made me look like a doofus in front of the class. Raven asked me, as we walked up the stairs toward our lockers, "Why didn't you use the blackboard?"

"I knew every one of the answers before that one without using the board. Who knew I would get a question with eleven thousand different parts to it?" She laughed at me.

Chapter 5

It was worth it.

Our next class was English with Mr. Burns, the homeroom teacher. Rock also was in our English class. Tucky had Phys. Ed. and Health. He took off the other way. Instead of going back up the stairs to put our book in the locker, and then back down, and risk getting a tardy, I suggested we take the math book with us to English class.

We walked down the hall to our class and went in. We found seats in the middle of the room. I noticed Sam Hitchcock walked into the classroom, the boy who asked what would happen to us if we were late and also what detention was. He came over and sat down in front of me.

I tapped him on the shoulder and he turned around. "Yeah?"

"I didn't know what detention was either," I told him.

"I didn't make a very good first impression, did I?"

"Probably not to Mr. Burns, but I would bet most of the kids didn't know what it was. I'm Timmy. These are my friends, Raven and Rock."

He said hello to each of them.

"We went to Oak Hills. What school do you come from?" I asked.

"I live in Stacy Fork, went to Cannel City School last year." The first bell rang and kids began making their way into the classroom. "I've been lost all morning. This is the only room I could find."

"Tomorrow, we'll all be fine," I tried assuring him, and myself. The final bell rang and kids were still filing into the room. Once everyone was seated Mr. Burns introduced himself and said, "I will excuse your tardiness today, in that you are learning your way this first day. But, starting tomorrow you will be marked tardy if you are not in your seat when the second bell rings. If you are tardy too many times you will be given detention. Before any of you raise your hand, Mr. Hitchcock will stand and explain what detention is. Mr. Hitchcock."

I felt sorry for Sam. I thought it was wrong to pick on him because he didn't know what most of us didn't know. Sam slowly stood from his desk. With his head lowered he said, "If you get detention you have to stay after school an extra hour and then find a way home." I thought he would sit down, but he didn't. Instead, Sam continued, "And I would suggest you never ask Mr. Burns a question about something you don't know. This is what will happen to you."

"Mr. Hitchcock - that will be enough! Sit down, now! Tomorrow you will be able to stand in front of your peers and tell them what detention was like. You will report to detention at ten minutes after three today."

I thought of the old saying 'You could hear a pin drop' because it definitely applied to the moment. I'd never heard a room so still and quiet. Mr. Burns looked quite flustered by what had happened. I thought he was to blame. I looked over at Raven and she rolled her eyes.

Mr. Burns, after he took a minute to calm himself, said, "You students shall be seated alphabetically. Please move to your new seat after I assign all the seats. Please remember which seat is yours."

Sam stood from his seat and began walking toward the door.

"Sam, get back to your desk!" Mr. Burns yelled.

Sam yelled back, "I quit. I quit high school. I don't need this bull crap!" I saw tears in his eyes. With that said, he disappeared through the door. I looked toward Mr. Burns; he stood with his mouth agape. I expected him to go after Sam. But he didn't. I froze in my seat for a couple of minutes wondering what to do. Finally I stood and went after Sam. Mr. Burns didn't say anything, at least I didn't hear him if he did.

I saw Sam down the hall leaning against a locker. I walked down the hall toward him. I could tell he was crying. His chest was heaving in and out. Sam had the build of Purty. He was kind of dumpy, but not really fat. He was taller than I was, but not by much. His hair was around an inch long all over his head and lay every which way. He wasn't much to look at is what I'm trying to say, but he had become my friend. And I did feel sorry for him. I felt he was wronged.

I put my hand on his shoulder. He looked up at me with tears rolling down his face. He was the saddest thing I'd ever seen.

"Sam, you can't quit, c'mon," I said to him.

He wiped the tears from his cheeks and said, "My old man told me not to go to high school. He said I was wasting my time. He said I wasn't as smart as our old mule. Perhaps I'm not. I don't know when to keep my mouth shut."

"I feel dumb all the time. You should have seen me in math class. I was a royal clown."

"You're just saying that to make me feel better. Thanks."

"You're right about that, but I really did feel like the court jester in math class. I thought I was so smart and then I fell on my stupid face." Sam laughed even though I knew he didn't want to.

"Me quitting is probably for the best," Sam said.

"Why did you come to high school if quitting is the best thing for you?"

"I wanted to be a veterinarian. I love animals. But I'm not smart enough."

"That's what my girlfriend wants to be. Just because you don't know when to keep your big mouth closed doesn't mean you aren't smart. You can't let some crummy teacher keep you from your dreams."

"If I stay for detention I'll have to walk all the way to Stacy Fork. My old man won't come and get me. He'll say that's what I get for wanting to go get educated."

"I'm pretty sure I'll be in detention also. We can take you home. Come on, Sam. Don't quit. Think of your dreams. Do you really want to work in the coal mines or hoe corn for the rest of your life?"

"No. But I won't go back in that class."

"Let's go to the office. Maybe they can switch you to a different English class. Will you stay then?" I asked.

"Okay, but only if that happens."

We walked on down the hall to the high school office. A small blue devil with a pitchfork stood outside the office. We were the Morgan County Blue Devils. What an awful mascot, I thought.

We went inside and took seats. The school secretary got up from her desk and asked what we needed.

"I need to talk to the principal," I said.

"What is this about?" she asked.

"Changing a class."

"Let me check and see if he can see you. What do you need?" she asked Sam.

"I'm with him," Sam answered.

"How about I go in and talk to him first?" I said.

"That's fine with me. I open my mouth too much anyway."

The lady came back out and said, "Yes. Mr. Davis can see you now."

I got up and followed her to his office. "Isn't your friend coming?" she asked.

"He's going to wait for me. He gets nervous in front of important people."

She gave me a look. I wasn't sure what the look meant.

I entered Principal Davis's office and he motioned for me to take the first of two chairs in front of his large dark wooden desk. He then said, "I hear you want to change classes. What is your name and how can I help you?" he asked. Principal Davis was a huge man, probably in his sixties with white hair like Mamaw. He wore it short and combed straight back. He also wore a gray suit with a blue tie to match the devil I saw outside.

I told him my name and where I was from. He seemed to recognize my name. I then said, "I'm here on behalf of a new friend I met today." I went on and told him everything that had happened up to that point. I tried not to leave anything out. Mr. Davis looked worn out by the time I was done.

"You say he's waiting outside in the office."

"Yes, sir."

Principal Davis got up and went out to the office. When he returned he had Sam with him. He asked Sam to take a seat in the other chair to my right.

Mr. Davis cleared his throat and sat back down behind his desk. "You have quite a friend here, Mr. Hitchcock. He has explained everything, and I mean everything to me. Sometimes we get off on the wrong foot, get out of bed on the wrong side, and stub our toe with our first step. You know what I mean." We both nodded.

41

"Mr. Burns has a certain way about him, but I promise you he is a very fine teacher. Maybe, even, one of our best. I would be very disappointed if you quit school, Sam. I see so many students drop out of high school and end up working the rest of their lives at jobs they don't enjoy. Once in a while, a few of them succeed, but very few. Tim has been a very convincing liaison for you. You can believe that he would be a very good friend. He has battled for your wants."

"Yes, sir, I believe that. He risked getting detention himself for me."

"Here is what I can do. I can have a talk with Mr. Burns about the events. I would like for you to continue in his class because I know you will learn a great deal from him. I would like for you to sleep on it. Come tomorrow morning, if you still feel you want a new homeroom and English class I will grant your wishes, just come to the office first thing in the morning and I'll give you your new assignment. You will need to stay for detention today, but I'm sure it will be the last one you will have. Am I correct?"

"You are if I decide to quit," Sam said. Mr. Davis couldn't help but laugh. "Thank you very much. Can I ask you something?"

"Anything." Oh no. I wondered want Sam was going to ask this time. Had the boy not learned his lesson?

"If I decide to stay in Mr. Burns' class and decide later it isn't going to work, can I change later?"

"Yes, if you're strong enough to try, I'll honor our deal and let you change, Sam," Principal Davis assured him. "We only have a few minutes till lunch. Why don't you wait in the office till the bell rings, and Tim, go back to Mr. Burns' class and see what fate awaits you. Thank you both for coming to me and trying to work this out. It was very mature of the both of you."

"Thank you." I said.

"I really appreciate everything. Thank you, Principal Davis," Sam said.

The principal led us out of his office and Sam took a seat in the office. I said, "See you at lunch, Sam." He nodded, and I hurried back to the English class. I quietly opened the door and walked inside. Mr. Burns was giving the class the homework assignment.

Mr. Burns motioned toward my seat and said, "Please take your seat and see me after the bell rings." The whole class watched me as I sat down. As soon as my butt hit the seat the bell rang. Raven and Rock rushed toward me. "What happened?" Rock asked.

"I'll tell you at lunch time. I've got to go see Mr. Burns. I figure I'll get detention."

I was right. "You earned yourself detention. Is there anything you would like to discuss?"

"No, sir."

"You may pick up an English book and ask your friends about the homework assignment. Be sure to report to detention after school is out," Mr. Burns said.

"Yes, sir. It was worth it," I told him as I turned and picked up a book and left. I hurried toward the stairs and up to my locker. I threw the two books inside and grabbed my lunch. Susie and Raven were waiting for me. Raven was telling Susie about what had happened.

"What did he say?" Raven asked.

"I got detention. I told him it was worth it. Let's go eat."

Chapter 6

Peanut Butter & Detention

During lunch, most of the students went outside and ate either on the wall in front of the school or near the wall. Some went down the street to the Freezer Fresh ice cream stand to get lunch. Some kids who had driven to school took off. Some went behind the school to hang out.

Most of our gang was together and they began asking me about what had happened. I looked around for Sam, but didn't see him. I thought maybe he had gone to the cafeteria. It took me a good twenty minutes to tell them what went down.

"Principal Davis is a good guy. It was smart to go to him," James Ernest said.

"Hey, scumheads, what's going on? I've already got detention," Purty said as he arrived at the scene.

"You didn't take off your clothing did you?" Susie asked him.

"No, of course I didn't disrobe. I'm not crude," Purty said, defending himself.

"Since when?" Raven asked. "Everyone here has seen that dinky thing of yours."

Everyone laughed and agreed with Raven.

"You won't be alone in detention," I said.

Purty pointed at me and said, "You. You got detention also?"

"Yeah."

Purty laughed and said, "I get detention at least once a week. It's not so bad. You can get most of your homework done while you're there."

"How are you going to get home?" I asked Purty.

"Randy can maybe drive back and get us. Or maybe your papaw or mom can pick us up."

"Or we could walk home."

"Are you crazy?" Purty said. I knew walking wouldn't appeal to him. I opened my brown bag and began to eat my peanut butter sandwich. Purty opened his sack and pulled the top off a can of sardines and opened a sleeve of crackers. He began sliding the sardines down his throat one at a time. They smelled.

James Ernest was eating a can of Vienna sausages. I wondered how he got those and I got a peanut butter sandwich.

After eating I asked Susie, "You want to go with me and look for Sam?"

"Okay. Where are we going?"

"I thought he might be in the cafeteria. Do you know where it is?" I asked.

"It's in the basement of that building." She pointed to a building that stood to the south of the school.

We left the gang and headed that way. We went down to the basement and saw a lot of kids eating at tables and some still standing in line to get their food. I searched the group of kids looking for Sam. He was nowhere to be found. I hoped he hadn't changed his mind and was walking home. We left the basement and walked to the back of the school. I saw the football field and the baseball field that was behind the school. Some kids were sitting in the stands. I saw a couple under the stands making out. Behind the school hidden in the corners were kids smoking. They stared at us as we walked by. I didn't much like the back of the school.

I knew we didn't have much time so we headed back to the front of the building. I asked Susie, "What class do you have now?"

"I've got Math class with Mr. Holbrook."

"Did you know that he is Mrs. Holbrook's husband?" I asked.

"Yes. What class are you going to?"

"I've got Phys Ed and Health. By the way, Mr. Holbrook will let you sit in whatever seat you want. So you should sit down with your friends. Do you know who else is in that class? "

"I don't know, maybe no one else."

As we entered the building the five minute warning bell went off. Our classrooms were right next to each other. My class was in 116 and Susie's math class was in 114. As we neared the classrooms I saw Sam walking in front of us. "Do you see that boy that looks like Purty from behind?" I pointed toward him.

Sam turned into room 114.

"Yes. He just went into my class."

"That's Sam. You should try to sit next to him and introduce yourself. Or at least introduce yourself to him."

"See you after class," Susie said as she turned into 114. I entered the next room. Rock and Raven were already seated and waved me over.

We had health class instead of gym class. Mr. Paxton, I thought was the teacher, and he said we would have gym on Mondays, Wednesdays and Fridays and Health on the other two days. The class was boring. I thought I was going to fall asleep, but Raven would poke me in the back whenever she saw my head tilt forward. He talked about what was expected of each student at school. He told us we should smell good, which included our armpits and feet and other body parts that he didn't mention. He said we should bathe or shower often and that no one wanted to sit next to someone who stunk. He also told us what we needed for gym class. He didn't ask who anybody was and didn't seat us in any order. I later learned that we were going to have a lady teacher for the Health class, who was missing that day.

After class was over, Raven and I met Susie in the hall and we walked up the stairs to our lockers. Susie looked so cute. She wore a short sleeve yellow blouse with a blue flared skirt. She had her hair pulled into a ponytail with a yellow bow holding it in place.

Study hall was in room 201 at the end of the hall. We stopped at our lockers and got whichever books we wanted for study hall and strolled down the hall toward 201. The warning bell went off. We found seats together.

"Did you meet Sam?" I asked Susie.

"Yes. He was quiet, but lit up when I told him you were my boyfriend. I told him I hoped he stayed in school. I also told him he was the only person I knew in the class. He seemed nice enough."

The lady who welcomed us said she was a volunteer and that she had all the same authority as the teachers. She said we should study or do homework and that we could softly talk with friends to get help. She took attendance and then went back to reading a book she had brought.

I decided to do my math homework. Susie did the same. I could help her if she needed it. Ended up, she didn't need my help. We compared all our answers and they were all the same. I then asked Raven what our English homework was. She said we were to write a two page essay about starting high school. I decided to read my American History assignment.

The bell rang as I was napping due the boredom of history. Our last class, Science, was in Room 220 at the other end of the hall. We dropped off our books at our lockers and went on to our class. Tucky, Rock and Raven were also in the class with Susie and me.

Mr. Castle was our science teacher. He was a middle-aged, bald, tall man. He seemed very friendly and happy to see us. He opened with, "Everything you see around you was created by some form of science. We will explore the many wonders of science. I hope you're ready for a fun ride. You may stay seated where you are or switch with another if you'd like. Who would like to switch?

Once we're settle they will be your seats till the end of the year. No hands - a good start. Everyone must be happy."

He then took attendance, passed out books, and then he showed us slides of the universe, the moon, the sun, trees, water, icebergs, animals, insects and large buildings in New York City.

"It is all science," he **EMPHASIZED** as the bell rang ending the day. He then said, "No homework this evening except I want you to look up at the stars. Have a great night."

As we headed back to our lockers I asked Susie if she would make sure someone came to get me at four after detention.

"I'll let James Ernest know. I'm sure your mom or papaw with come to get you."

"Great start to high school, huh?"

"You did a good thing," Susie said as she kissed me on the cheek to ease the blow of having to stay an extra hour.

"Hopefully, Mom will see it that way."

I grabbed the books I needed from my locker and walked Susie down the stairs and to the school's exit. I saw kids getting either on the buses or in cars. I walked on to Room 101 where detention took place. The two back rows were already filled with unscrupulous looking pupils. I went forward to the second row and took a seat. I looked to be the youngest one there so far. A minute later Sam walked through the door and looked around until he saw me. He came and sat down beside me.

"Man, I'm sorry I got you in this mess. I shouldn't have walked out of class."

"It's okay. I get to experience I little more of high school than I normally would have. But who knows, I may have done something else to get here," I said to ease his guilt.

"So this is where they send the misfits." I heard a loud familiar voice as he entered the room. The other students laughed at being called misfits. Purty then said, "There's my best buddy, Timmy, one of us misfits. Good to see you here," Purty continued as he made his way up to where we were. He sat behind me.

"Purty, this is Sam. He's a friend I met in homeroom today."

"Hi, Sam. Are you the guy who got Timmy detention?" Purty asked with no tact.

"I'm the guy," Sam said and grinned.

"Good for you. You couldn't have done it to a more deserving guy. He's been a goody-two-shoes for way too long," Purty declared.

"I got detention all by myself. This loudmouth is Todd Tuttle; he's a sophomore if he passed last year. We call him Purty," I stated.

"If you have any questions about detention, I'm an expert. I believe I broke the record last year for the most in one year," Purty bragged.

"Where's the teacher?" I asked.

"One of them will be here as soon as they close up their classroom, the later the better. It's always someone different. They take turns. They all hate doing it. They want to go home as much as we do. You never know who might walk in," Purty explained. We were supposed to be in the room by ten after three and it was already a quarter after. I counted fourteen boys and three girls. It didn't seem fair.

Sam asked Purty, "What did you do to get detention?"

"Nothing compared to what you did. There was a pretty girl sitting behind me with a short skirt on. I mean it was real short, especially when she sat down. I kept dropping my pencil on the floor and then bending down to pick it up and trying to get a peek up her legs. Mrs. Abrams, our teacher, caught me the fourth time. I guess thirty seconds to pick up a pencil was too long. I had to quit. I was getting a headache from bending over so much anyway."

Sam grinned and then asked, "Did you see anything?"

"I saw her upper legs and once I think I saw something white. I'm guessing it was her panties. Mostly I noticed the floor needed to be swept."

"Wow!" Sam said under his breath. "You are now my new hero."

I guess it didn't take much to impress Sam. I thought I was seeing double. I never thought I would ever meet another Purty.

"How purty was she? Did she have purty legs?"

I was ready to move my desk to the back with the deviant kids. I figured I could find more stimulating conversations with them. I looked toward them and two of the guys were playing mumbly-peg with switchblades on the room's wooden floor. I decided to stay where I was. I turned back around before they decided to play mumbly-peg with my face.

I heard footsteps coming toward the door. I saw the boys in the back quickly put their knives away. In walked Principal Davis. The room came to a complete hush. He walked to the front and said sarcastically, "You students have not gotten off to a good start this year. I hope this will be the last time I see you in here this year." A boy in the back of the room snickered.

"Is something funny, Theodore?" Mr. Davis asked. It seemed hard for the others to not laugh at the boy being called Theodore. I learned later he went by Ted.

"No, sir," Theodore answered.

"Everyone please begin doing some school work or at least remain quiet. And Todd, if you continue to get detentions I will expel you from school for a while. You seem to not be able to control yourself."

"Yes, sir, Principal Davis," Purty replied.

I decided to work on my English essay. I got out my paper and stared at it. We were to write about starting high school. What did that mean? I could write about my first day and how the teacher who gave me this assignment was wrong in his dealings with Sam and me. I didn't figure that would go over very well. I could write about what I thought high school would be like. I could write about what I wanted to accomplish in high school. I kept thinking about it and then when I looked up at the clock it was already ten minutes till four. I wasn't going to finish the essay. Shoot, I wasn't even going to start it.

Before the bell rang Principal Davis said we could leave. Maybe there wasn't a four o'clock bell.

Purty, Sam, and I were the last to leave the room. The deviants wasted no time in leaving. I said goodbye to Principal Davis. When we got in the hallway Purty said, "Brown-nose."

I ignored him and we walked together to find Papaw waiting for us.

"Can you give Sam a ride home?" I asked.

Before hopping in the back of the pickup he told Papaw, "I live in Stacy Fork. I can just walk home."

"That's okay, Sam. It's a fine day for a ride. Hop in the cab so you can give me directions to your home." Purty and I hopped in the back and Papaw took off. It was around four or five miles to his house. Papaw drove down a lane to a farm house with a barn. A corn field was on the left of the lane and a tobacco field was on the right.

When Papaw stopped at the side of the house Sam's father came out of the barn. Sam quickly got out and said, "Thanks. I really appreciate the ride."

"Your welcome, Sam," Papaw said.

"See you tomorrow," Purty and I shouted out.

Sam's father was a lean, tall rough-looking fellow. He wiped his hands on his bibbed overalls as he made his way to the truck.

"It's mighty nice of you to bring Sam home."

"No problem. I'm Martin Collins." Papaw stuck his arm out the window to shake hands, but Sam's father ignored it.

"Why wasn't Sam on the bus?"

"From what I gather the boys had a run-in with one of the teachers and got detention. I was happy to bring Sam home. It's a long walk from school."

"No disrespect, Martin, but if it ever comes up again I'd prefer you let him walk home. It might teach him to behave himself. He shouldn't be wasting his time with school no how. He doesn't have the sense that a chicken does," he said as he kicked a hen away from his leg. "I've got plenty of work for him right here to keep him busy."

"Schooling is important these days. The times are changing," Papaw said.

Sam's father huffed and then added, "Just let him walk." With that said he turned around and headed back to the barn. As Papaw was turning around I saw a woman hanging up clothes in the backyard. I waved, but got nothing in return.

"They weren't the friendliest parents I've ever met," I told Purty.

"Purty rude if you ask me."

Purty and I jumped out of the truck bed and into the cab. Papaw drove to Purty's house in silence. I couldn't help but feel sorry for Sam. His dad was a real jerk. I knew how I would feel if Mom told me I didn't have any sense, or was stupid.

Papaw dropped Purty off at his house before taking me to the store. He shut off the engine, Coty ran to me so we could pet him, and then we went inside.

Mom was waiting on Robert and Janice Easterling when we entered the store. They greeted Papaw, and then Robert began, "Detention on the first day of high school. Reminds me of my days in school."

"I never knew you went to school," I countered.

"That smart mouth of yours is probably why you ended up staying after school."

"Unlike you, at least I have a part of me that is smart," I came back as I headed for my bedroom laughing. I heard laughter inside the store.

I left my door cracked open and heard Mom ask Papaw, "So what did he do? James Ernest wouldn't say much when he got home."

"Go easy on him. He was helping a kid who is going through a tough time. Tim didn't do anything wrong. In fact, you should be proud of him," Papaw said. Thank you, Papaw. I heard what he said from my bedroom.

I changed clothes and then went looking for James Ernest. I knew he was probably doing some chore, either getting water or cleaning up around the lake. I went to the back porch, but the water buckets were there. I ran up the hill to the lake. I noticed there was no one fishing, but I saw James Ernest walking along the west side of the lake. I yelled out his name and he turned around and waved. I ran to catch up.

The first thing he said was, "How was detention?"

"Not somewhere I want to go again. There was a gang of boys in the back throwing knives in the floor."

"That doesn't sound good."

"Haven't you had detention before?"

"No, not yet, knock on wood." He reached over and tapped by head twice with his fist.

"Very funny." We walked a ways in silence before I said, "Papaw took Sam home. You wouldn't believe it."

"I wouldn't believe what?"

I went on and told him about Sam's family and what his Dad had said about Sam. I told him how rude Sam's father was and how he wouldn't shake Papaw's hand.

"It reminds me of things my father would say to me when I young."

"Mine wasn't much better, I guess," I said.

"It was good that you helped him. Sounds like he needed a friend."

"Yeah."

We continued around the lake, but there wasn't anything to pick up since fishing had been slow.

Mom never did ask me anything about detention. But she did ask me, Janie, and James Ernest about our first day of school. But the topic of my detention never came up. Janie mainly talked about riding the bus, and the twins, and a boy in her class that got swats for swearing in class.

Janie was now in the second grade. I couldn't believe she was growing up so fast. Shoot, I couldn't believe I was in high school. James Ernest was in the eleventh grade even though he was the same age as me. Purty was in the tenth grade and Randy was a senior. Time flew.

Chapter 7

Adopted

I was lying on the top bunk looking out into the darkness of the hillside. James Ernest was below me reading with his small lamp on before going to sleep. I could hear crickets and tree frogs croaking through the window screen. A partial moon was covered by clouds. I looked for stars, but didn't see many. I completed that homework, I thought. The weatherman said we might have rain during the night, a sixty percent chance. It seemed as though there was always a sixty percent chance the weatherman would be wrong.

"I don't think I like high school," I said.

James Ernest didn't reply right away. I figured he must have fallen asleep with the light on. Sometimes though, he would let me rant without saying anything.

Raindrops began pinging against the tin roof of the house. Good for the weatherman, I thought. I loved hearing the rain fall on the roof, but I knew it would ping me to sleep soon.

"Change takes time to get used to," James Ernest said.

"It sure is different."

"Yeah. We never got detention at the one-room school from Mrs. Holbrook."

"It's just a lot of teachers who don't know you, and a lot of kids I don't know, and the school is so big. It doesn't seem as though it's going to be much fun," I complained.

"You're there to learn," James Ernest told me.

"That doesn't seem right. Who goes to school to learn?"

"I do. Go to sleep."

"Oh, is that what a bed's for, to sleep in? Thanks, I guess you do learn stuff at school. You're so smart."

Suddenly a foot poked me in the butt. I guessed James Ernest wasn't a big fan of sarcasm.

Why did time have to pass by so fast? I wasn't ready to go back to school. I was still in summertime mode. The past summer had gone by way too fast. Randy had gotten a job at the hardware store working for Mr. Cobb. He had stepped down as the Leader of the Pack and we elected James Ernest as our new leader. Randy was remaining a member, but we knew he would find little time to join us.

The rain was still clanging across the roof and I felt my eyelids getting heavy as I thought about the Wolf Pack's past summer adventure.

Monday, June 10th, 1963 - Three months earlier

The alarm clock went off way before any rooster even thought about crowing. James Ernest turned on the light and then jumped up and began getting dressed. I pulled the sheet over my head and closed my eyes. There was nothing exciting about getting up and working in the fields. I felt a headache coming on.

"Get up, dumb butt."

I ignored him – hoping he would go away.

He didn't go away. Suddenly my sheet was jerked off of my bed and I was lying there in nothing but my Fruit-of-the-Loom underwear.

"I have a headache," I moaned.

"You're going to have a headache after I knock you off the bunk and you land on your stupid head."

What happened to brotherly love? Where is that nice, kind person that used to be James Ernest? What happened to sleeping in when school was out for the summer? It would be different if we were going fishin', or canoein', or I was going to see Susie. I would already be up and ready to go. I figured the field would be there whether we arrived at six or eleven.

School had only been out for a week. Doesn't a person deserve a break? I would be starting high school in the fall. I figured I needed a lot of rest before entering high school.

James Ernest grabbed my ankles and began to pull me off the bunk. I quickly gripped the bedpost tightly and held on. "Okay, okay! I'll get up!"

He let go and I jumped down onto his back when he turned around. We ended up in a mass on the floor. It seemed as though we found ourselves on the bedroom floor a lot. James Ernest pushed me off and walked out of the bedroom toward the kitchen. Five minutes later I was outside relieving myself against a tree. I looked over at Coty, who was still in his doghouse. He looked at me like I was out of my mind being up that early. He was right.

When I went back into the kitchen James Ernest was eating a bowl of Rice Krispies and he had set a bowl out for me. After we finished eating we headed up the road toward Susie's house. We were working in the fields for Clayton. I could see fog had settled above Devil's Fork Creek, giving the morning a spooky feel.

"What do you think of Papaw having a gas pump put in at the store?" I asked James Ernest.

"I think it's smart. The store will make some extra money and it will be convenient for the people of the community."

"When is it being put in?"

"I think Martin said they were supposed to be there to start digging tomorrow."

"It will be fun watching them dig that big hole for the tanks."

"You'll only get to watch if we get our work done today."

James Ernest had to ruin it for me. I had to work hard today so I could watch a backhoe dig a big hole. I wasn't sure it was worth it. We could see the sun peeking over the horizon when we got to the top of the hill. Papaw's house stood next to eight giant oak trees with a valley between us and the house. We could cut across the valley to the house and then across another valley to Clayton's or follow the road to Clayton's lane and then down his gravel road. We chose to walk along the road to the lane.

The sunrise colored the wispy clouds that hung in the morning sky with a pink hue. We saw a herd of deer grazing in Papaw's valley. Two fawns were jumping around and chasing each other as though they were playing tag.

"Have you thought about a Wolf Pack adventure this summer?" I asked James Ernest.

"Not really," he answered.

"You're the Leader now. You should come up with something."

"We've always come up with things together as a group," he pointed out.

"Then we need to have a Wolf Pack meeting," I said.

"Okay."

"What do you mean 'Okay'?"

"What do you think 'Okay' means? It means I agree. We'll have a meeting. Are you going stupid?"

"I'm not going stupid. You're going stupid. In fact, you're already there."

We argued and called each other names all the way to Clayton's house. I knew I wouldn't see Susie this morning. She would still be in bed where all sensible people were. Clayton saw us coming and met us on the porch.

"Good mornin' guys," Clayton welcomed us. We returned the greeting and then the screen porch opened and Monie came out.

"You boys look like you could use a sausage sandwich." Before we could answer she was handing each of us a biscuit with a sausage patty inside.

"Thanks," we both said at the same time.

Clayton then led us to the barn where we got the tools we needed and then we headed for the fields. We hoed corn for a few hours until it got really hot and then we repaired fences in the heat of the day. We helped Clayton built a new pen for hogs that he was going to buy later that week. I saw Susie once during the day when we went to the house for lunch. She was riding Mr. Perry, her horse, across a field; both of their ponytails flipping up into the air.

Around six that evening Clayton called it quits. I was dreading the walk home, but Clayton offered to drive us back. "Monie wants to go to the store for a few things." We jumped at the offer. As we were climbing into the bed of the truck Susie ran from the side door toward the truck. She hopped into the back with us and Clayton drove away. I was glad the twins were staying home.

Little did I know that the twins had spent the afternoon at our house playing with Janie. We arrived at the store and when I walked up the front porch steps I was accosted by two sharped-tongued dragons.

The screen door opened and Delma started it, "He looks like something the cat brought home."

"He's smelly, and dirty, and he looks like he can't even make it up the steps," Thelma added.

"Don't forget ugly. He's very ugly."

"Yes, he is," Thelma agreed. "Dad must be awfully hard up to get him to help on the farm."

"I heard Dad say that he felt sorry for the poor boy. Said Timmy doesn't have the smarts to do anything else other than hoe corn."

I stopped short of them and said, "I'm smart enough to know that no other family around here has adopted kids since they saw what Monie and Clayton got stuck with."

The twins stood there with their mouths stuck open. I walked past them and into the store. Finally I heard Delma say, "We are not adopted."

"We are not," Thelma affirmed.

They then ran into the kitchen as I entered my bedroom and I heard them both ask, "Are we adopted?"

Monie laughed and said, "That would certainly explain a lot."

"It's not funny," Delma cried.

"Not funny at all," Thelma cried.

"It is a little funny," Mom said. I could hear Monie and Mom laughing at the girls, which never went over well.

"The whole world is against us, Thelma," Delma said.

"I think everyone is jealous of us," Thelma added.

"That must be it," Delma said.

As they were walking through the living room I heard Delma say, "If anyone was adopted it was stupid Timmy. They had to adopt him from a family of apes in Africa."

"Yes, that would explain a lot about how ugly and stupid he is," Thelma agreed.

"Yes it would, dear sister."

James Ernest said he would try to get a meeting set for Friday night at the cabin. I was already looking forward to it. I changed my clothes and then went out to find Susie. I found her sitting on the front porch listening to the twins giving each other reasons why they thought I was adopted. I took Susie's hand and led her to the lake. Susie and I had been boyfriend and girlfriend on and off for a couple of years. She was the prettiest and nicest girl I had ever known. I couldn't imagine life without her being my girlfriend.

"How was it working for Dad today?"

"It wasn't bad. I enjoyed working on the fences and building the hog pen."

"Did you get done?"

"Yep. Tomorrow they're digging the hole to put in the tanks for the gas pump. I want to watch them dig the hole."

"That should be kind of interesting," Susie said, but I knew she wasn't serious.

"James Ernest and Raven are making baskets. What are you going to do?"

"Don't know."

"We could go swimming tomorrow afternoon."

"That sounds good."

We continued walking around the lake. No one was fishing that evening. Mondays were always slow after crowded weekends.

We walked up and down the two rises of the path making our way to the slanted rock at the back of the lake where we climbed onto the rock and sat down facing the water. Susie tilted toward me and kissed me on the cheek.

"What was that for?" I asked.

"Just because I like you," Susie said grinning. I put my right arm around her shoulders.

"What are your plans for the summer?" I asked.

"Pretty much the same as every summer, I guess. I want to ride Mr. Perry every chance I can. I'll help Mom and Dad around the farm and hang out with you and friends."

"I like the part of you hanging out with me." I laughed.

"What does the Wolf Pack have planned?"

"Nothing yet. We're going to have a meeting this coming Friday evening to talk about it, I think. James Ernest said he would get it together."

"Tell me if you think this is stupid."

"What?"

"I was thinking it might be fun for some of the girls to start a club like the Wolf Pack."

"That would be great."

"I know we wouldn't be able to do all the crazy stuff you guys have done, but we could still have fun and maybe camp out and do some hikes and things," Susie said.

She was right; we had done some crazy things and had some wild adventures since starting the club three years earlier. We had taken a two-day hike and camped next to a graveyard. We had taken a four-day canoe trip down the Red River where we were trapped by a self-claimed witch. We had found a treasure chest in a cave. We had been trapped in a cave for a couple of nights above Devil's Creek. We had also tracked Bigfoot. It seemed we were always in some kind of trouble or dilemma.

"Maybe the two clubs could even do something together," I suggested.

"That would be fun."

A red-tailed hawk swooped down and flew right in front of us at eye level. It continued toward the back of the holler and rose up into the sky high above the ridges and tree line. I marveled at the beauty of its soundless flight past us.

For some reason the hawk's flight that I knew took it up and over the entrance to the cave I had once been trapped in reminded me of the many deaths around me in the past four years. It started with finding our neighbor, Mrs. Robbins, dead on her kitchen floor. Later that summer the Tattoo man, who had killed Mrs. Robbins, would die in the same cave the hawk had flown over, after trying to kill me.

The next summer would come to an end with my father dying unexpectedly, which put in the motions of Mom moving us back to Kentucky permanently. Then last summer Billy Taulbee choked to death while hiding in the woods from the police on a fish bone. He was the worst fisherman in the world. The bone he choked on was probably from the only fish he had caught in his life; a very ironic and sad end to his life.

"It would be fun," I agreed, although hoping a joint adventure wouldn't put the girls in the same dangerous situations we had overcome.

Chapter 8

Uncle Morton KO'd

Friday, June 14

After working all week either at the store or in someone's field or garden I was tired and ready for a little relaxation. It was late Friday afternoon and I asked Mom if we could have bluegill for supper. She told me she would fry them if I would catch and clean them. There was nothing I'd rather do.

It was around five when I headed up to the lake to catch a few fish. I saw Uncle Morton and Mud McCobb sitting on the east side of the lake fishing. As I neared my blind Uncle Morton he said, "That must be Timmy coming to give us a lesson."

I never knew how he always knew who was walking up to him. He was never wrong. He knew things that I knew no blind person should be able to know. But he did.

"How could you know it was me? You're amazing," I said as I stood there looking at him.

"Mud said, 'Here comes Timmy.' That's how I knew," Uncle Morton said, and he and Mud got a big chuckle from it.

"Yeah, but normally you...never mind. Have you two pitiful fishermen caught anything yet?"

"I got one nice bluecat earlier," Mud told me.

"I can't vouch for it. I didn't see it," Uncle Morton teased, and he and Mud laughed again.

"I hear a fishing pole in your hand. Does that mean you're joining us for a spell?" Uncle Morton asked.

"I think I will. Might as well show you how it's done," I said.

I had clipped a long skinny white and green floater to my line with a small size 10 hook and bb sinker. I took a red worm from the bait cup and weaved it unto the hook. I knew the water along that bank was fairly deep so I set the float at five feet and then cast my line into the water.

"What kind of fishing are you doing, Timmy," Mud said, with a puzzled look on his face.

"He must be bluegill fishing," Uncle Morton said.

"I am. We're having fish for dinner. My job is to catch a mess."

"There's nothing better than a mess of fresh caught bluegill with some coleslaw and cornbread," Mud exclaimed.

Uncle Morton began smacking his lips like he was eating the meal right there on the bank. "Is my mouth watering?" Uncle Morton asked as I jerked my pole.

"Just a second and you can eat this one."

"I prefer mine cooked a little longer." We all laughed.

I reeled in an eight-inch bluegill and placed it in the bucket I had brought with me. My worm had survived, so I cast it back into the water. Thirty seconds later a second bluegill was in the bucket.

71

"If you hold your mouth just like this you guys might have a chance of catching a fish," I said as I moved my lips into a weird position.

"You look better that way," blind Uncle Morton teased.

"Now you sound like Delma and Thelma."

"Maybe they're smarter than we give them credit for," my uncle said and laughed. I didn't see anything funny about it.

I weaved another worm onto my hook and placed it in the lake.

"Something is playing with my line. I can feel him nibbling. Come on, you rascal, take it," Uncle Morton urged the fish. After a little coaxing the line finally began to move and tighten. Uncle Morton jerked with all his might and fell backward off the log bench and onto the ground. Apparently the fish had made a quick turn toward Uncle Morton, putting slack in his line. Uncle Morton scrambled to his feet and reeled in his line until it tightened again and then the fight was on.

I looked down at my float and it had disappeared. I jerked and brought in another bluegill as I watched Uncle Morton battle his monster. Mud quickly reeled his line in so not to get it tangled up. Uncle Morton's fish went to the right and then turned and went to the left. It then decided to head for deeper water and began stripping line from Uncle Morton's reel.

"Is your brake on?!" I yelled.

"All the way tight!" he yelled back.

I knew he had a big catfish on the line. I also knew it was doubtful he would ever land the fish. A large bass would have come to the surface and jumped. A large catfish would stay along the bottom to fight.

"You have to hold on and tire him out!" Mud advised.

"What if he tires me out first?" Uncle Morton said as sweat began pouring from his brow.

Mud told him, "I guess you'd have to let me take over."

"I'd rather let him pull me in the lake and drown me first."

"Well, that's a fine how-do-you-do!" Mud huffed.

Uncle Morton's fishing line had all been stripped out and the next step was for the monster catfish to break the line. I could see the line headed toward the back of the lake. I knew soon something had to happen. Uncle Morton couldn't follow the fish down the lake because there were trees between the path and the water. Even if Uncle Morton wasn't blind it would be impossible. Uncle Morton held on for all he had. His pole bent over itself and then suddenly the pole broke in half.

"Who's shooting?" Uncle Morton cried out.

The snap of the broken pole sounded just like a rifle shot. Ten seconds later his line broke and Uncle Morton went tumbling backwards onto his butt again. "I've been shot!" moaned my uncle.

Mud and I hurried to help him up. He was still holding half of his fishing pole and Mud said, "You ain't been shot. You were embarrassed by a fish. That was the worst fight of a big fish I've seen in all my born days. It was like watching a ten-year-old trying to catch a greased pig."

We got Uncle Morton to his feet and helped him to the log bench where he sat. He dropped his broken pole on the ground and wiped his brow with his handkerchief.

"What test line did you have on your pole?" I asked.

"That was forty pound. That fish sure got the best of me. I've never been beaten up by a fish before."

"You lasted a good five rounds before he KO'd you," I tried comforting him.

"I think that might have beaten the time you rolled off the dam into Martin's yard," Mud laughed.

"This certainly wasn't my proudest moment. I'd given ten bucks to have seen that fish."

"Even if you had landed it you wouldn't have seen it," Mud teased.

"I would have seen it in my mind's eye," Uncle Morton said.

I wasn't sure what that meant, but I never doubted anything Uncle Morton said. He was one of the wisest and nicest men I had ever met. I loved him so much.

"I'll go get you another pole. I'll find one that won't let you down next time."

"You're a good kid," Uncle Morton said and smiled.

I ran from the lake down the path to the outdoor shed behind the house. We kept all of our yard tools, the push mower, and fishing supplies inside the shed. I grabbed one of Papaw's best poles and headed back to the lake. Mud was still getting on Uncle Morton about his fighting techniques with the monster fish.

"You wouldn't have done any better, you old buzzard," Uncle Morton told him.

"I would have already had my picture taken with it and skinned and gutted it by now."

"Here's the pole. You need any help? It's already got a hook and sinker on it."

"I'll be fine. Thanks, Timmy."

"You'll be fine as soon as we get those bullet holes tended to," Mud said and laughed so hard he almost fell off the log himself. I couldn't help but laugh myself.

"Go on and laugh. I'll catch that varmint if it's the last thing I do," Uncle Morton proclaimed.

After another twenty minutes I looked down into my bucket and saw that I had around ten big bluegills. I cast my line back into the water. I figured I needed a few more in case Uncle Morton joined us for supper. Within ten minutes I had what I needed so I said, "Be careful. Bye," and left. I headed to an old tree trunk behind the house and began cleaning the fish. There was a small overgrown gulley next to the yard and we always threw the fish heads and guts and scales into the gulley for the possums and raccoons that would come eat them during the night.

I took the fish into the kitchen and placed them on the counter. I continued into the store and saw Mom waiting on a boy and a girl I'd never seen before.

Mom saw me enter and said, "This is my son, Timmy. Timmy this is John and Pricilla James. They're renting the old Cassidy place just beyond Homer and Ruby's farm."

They looked to be about my age. I figured they were brother and sister.

"Do you have other brothers and sisters?" I asked.

Pricilla spoke up and said, "Back in Clay County we do. I've got two brothers and John has one of each."

That meant they weren't brother and sister. I looked at them closer and differently then. I noticed that they had wedding bands on their fingers even though it looked like they were found in a Cracker Jack box.

She continued, "This is our first home together. We were just married not long ago and we've been staying in Winchester with my aunt Gladys."

Apparently Mom hadn't figured that out and she was trying to keep her mouth from gapping open. "You must think we're awful young to be wed. But I turned thirteen in February and John was fifteen when we tied the knot. We just couldn't wait any longer to be man and wife."

Had I fallen asleep at the lake? I had to be dreaming. I tried pinching myself, but it only hurt. Since when did thirteen- and fifteen-year-olds get married and take off on their own.

"You seem so young to be married," Mom finally said once her mouth closed and reopened.

"Well, I was pregnant and I didn't want to place any shame on my family's name," Pricilla told us. Mom's entire jawline sagged toward the floor. I then noticed that Pricilla had a small baby bump.

I was almost a year older than Pricilla. Did this mean that Susie and I could get married if we wanted to?

"Do you have a job, John?" Mom asked once she could close her mouth enough,

Pricilla spoke up, "John is real good with his hands. He's a potter, and I do a little painting. I like painting pretty flowers and old barns and people."

"You're not even old enough to drive," Mom questioned them.

"John has been driving for two years. He hasn't been caught yet. He's very careful." I saw John shoot a look toward Pricilla. I glanced out the window and saw an old blue Volkswagen van. "We don't need a lot of money. We've already started a garden and we're staying at the house for next to nothing. John is going to do some work to it and fix it up. It was part of the deal."

"Are you going to go to school?" I asked.

"No. We dropped out. I had to once I was in a motherly way. And John figured school couldn't help him with his pottery and such. So we decided to get married and start our life together. Today marks our three month anniversary."

I stood there in amazement. How could they be allowed to drop out of school, become parents, and get married at their age? Did I miss something? I was so confused. I knew I was about as uninformed as a turnip, but how could she get pregnant when she wasn't even married yet? I started to ask, but something told me it might not be the best thing to ask with Mom standing there waiting for flies to gather in her mouth.

"Well, well, it's nice having you in the community. Please come to church Sunday. Service begins at ten at Oak Hills Church. It's not far from your house."

"Thank you. We may do that," John said as he picked up his bag of goods and headed for the door. Pricilla leaned over the counter and gave Mom a hug.

"Nice meeting you, Timmy. Come by and visit."

"Okay," was all I could say.

As soon as they were off the porch Mom was picking up the phone and calling Mamaw.

"You won't believe what just ....."

I went back through the living room to the kitchen. I figured Mom would be telling everyone in the community about John and Pricilla. I would have to fry the fish. James Ernest walked through the back door and I asked him to help me. We began fixing supper as I told him about the new members of the county.

Chapter 9

The Meeting

Uncle Morton joined us for dinner. After eating our bluegill dinner with coleslaw and Wonder white bread, Mom was too busy telling the women-folk about John and Pricilla to make cornbread, the Washington family arrived at the store. Not long after, they were followed by Susie and her family, except for Brenda.

James Ernest had set up the Wolf Pack meeting and the girls were joining us to start their own club. We were having the meeting at the usual spot at the old cabin in the woods behind the Tuttle farm. We were camping out all night. The girls had begged and begged and had finally gotten permission to join us. Purty was bringing them their own tent that they borrowed from him. I was sure they wouldn't like the smell of it.

Purty, Francis, Tucky and Rock were going to meet us at the cabin. The rest of us were meeting at the store and walking there together. I had packed up everything I thought we would need, including marshmallows for the fire.

We had to be back by eight the next morning. Most of us had Saturday chores to do. After everyone arrived we gathered on the porch and set off to our first joint meeting of the two clubs.

Besides me, representing the Wolf Pack was James Ernest, Junior, and Coty. Junior was bringing James, his cute beagle. Junior had gotten the beagle last summer and this was the first time he had brought the dog with him. Three girls were there – Susie, Raven, and Rhonda. I knew Purty would be beside himself with excitement to see Rhonda there. I hoped he wouldn't make a fool of himself, but I pretty much knew he would.

"Let's go. We've got a long walk," I said.

Our parents were all on the porch watching and waving as we strolled back the lane toward the quarry. The girls' parents looked the most worried.

I was holding hands with Susie as we began our hike.

"Well, here we go!" James Ernest shouted out. He and Raven were in the lead.

"This is so exciting," Susie said as she turned to look at me.

"It is," I said and grinned.

"I can't believe this is actually happening," Susie said to everyone.

"It already feels like we're starting an adventure," Raven said.

Coty and James were exploring the ditch lines as we made our way toward the crossing.

At the creek crossing James Ernest showed the girls where to step as they crossed the creek. The creek was low in this spot due to the lack of summer rain. We had placed large rocks at even spacing so we could cross without getting our feet wet. James

Ernest crossed first followed by Raven, who had no trouble. The dogs waded through the creek and then shook themselves when they reached the path on the other side. Susie started across but slipped on the third stone and her foot went into the water. Junior and Rhonda made it across with no problems.

"Sorry you slipped in," I told Susie as we continued down the trail.

"It actually felt good. I should have just waded across."

As we continued our hike toward the cabin Rhonda began singing,

> "Nobody knows where my Johnny has gone
>
> Judy left the same time
>
> Why was he holding her hand
>
> When he's supposed to be mine?
>
> It's my party, and I'll cry if I want to
>
> Cry if I want to, cry if I want to
>
> You would cry too if it happened to you."

It wasn't long before Susie and Raven were singing along with the lyrics of the top ten song. It was catchy and I found myself humming the tune along with the girls. I hoped this wouldn't get me kicked out of the Wolf Pack. It wasn't long before Junior joined in and then James Ernest, "You would cry to if it happened to you."

It didn't sound bad.

We made it past the turn off to the Tuttle farm and a little later to the right turn that would take us to the cabin. As we neared, the darkness of the forest was beginning to close in on us. The path was harder to see and the girls stayed closer to the group. I soon saw firelight ahead and knew that Tucky had already started a campfire. The darkness brought dropping temperatures to the evening, and the fire would be a welcomed relief later.

Purty was the first to see us and yelled out, "We thought you guys got lost or eaten by a bear."

"I notice that you weren't out looking for us, scumhead," I said as we came to the fire pit.

"We were waiting for daylight," Purty said and laughed as only Purty could. He started to say something else but then his eyes saw Rhonda. "There she is, the beautiful Miss Rhonda. Come have a seat. I saved you one," he said as he pointed to the empty spot on the log next to him.

Rhonda ignored his greeting and said, "Shouldn't we go put the tent up?"

Susie and Raven agreed and they started toward the spot James Ernest was. He had already begun putting up the Wolf Pack's tent. Purty jumped up and ran to where he had laid his tent. "Here it is. I'll help you. It's purty complicated."

He tripped over a tree root and went head first into the tent bag. No one laughed, even though I wanted to. He was so trying to impress Rhonda that it was too sad to laugh at.

He scampered to his feet with the tent in his hands and asked, "Where do you girls want it?"

"Next to the other one, I guess," Susie answered.

Purty began unpacking the poles and tent and tried putting the tent up. He had pieces flying everywhere. I went over to give him a hand.

"Doesn't this pole go in the middle?" Rhonda asked.

Purty seemed unsure how to answer so I said, "Yeah, I think it does."

After twenty minutes of correcting all of Purty's mistakes the tent was finally up. Purty stood back and said, "See, what did I say? A piece of cake!"

"No. We didn't bring any cake with us," I joked. The rest of the group laughed.

Susie and Rock entered the tent with their packs. Ten seconds later they came out coughing and gagging. "It stinks in there!" Rock screamed out.

"It took Purty a long time to get that smell in there," James Ernest told them.

"I think it actually only took one fart," Tucky said.

"Funny, funny," Purty came back.

"We cannot sleep in there. How's the other one?" Susie asked as she made her way into our tent.

"Don't get any i....," I started to say, but I was too late.

"We'll take this tent. It smells a lot better."

We knew there was no use in arguing. Our fate was sealed. The Wolf Pack would have to sleep in the fart-infested Purty tent. I wondered if I could find an old clothespin somewhere around the cabin for my nose.

The girls took no time in removing Purty's and Tucky's gear from our tent and replacing it with their stuff. None of the guys were dumb enough to argue – not even Purty. Junior and I began cutting marshmallow sticks from nearby saplings. When we returned everyone was sitting around the campfire staying warm. The June weather was unseasonably cool and the overnight temperature was to dip into the 60's. I found that Susie had saved a seat for me between her and Rhonda.

Junior went over and sat by Francis. She was only one grade ahead of him in school. Francis was in the seventh grade and Junior was in the sixth grade, but they were nearly the same age. She was Sadie's younger sister and you would never know they were sisters by their personalities.

Purty grabbed one of the sticks as soon as Junior laid them down and began filling his stick with the creamy white puffs.

As he bent over to cook them he said, "I can't believe you girls were allowed to camp out with us."

"Neither could I," Francis said.

"Mom said that since there were five of us coming she would let me. There's safety in numbers," Susie explained.

"Yeah, but we could do anything we want," Purty said and grinned.

"Keep your clothes on," Raven told him and everyone will be okay.

"We could even play spin-the-bottle," Purty blurted out. We all knew where his mind was. He was hoping this was his opportunity to kiss Rhonda again. I knew it was never going to happen. Poor Purty didn't. He had liked Rhonda for years but she never showed any interest in him. At times I felt sorry for him. He truly loved her and she was just about the only person he ever thought and talked about. It was getting worse as he got older.

"There will be no spinning of the bottle here tonight," Rhonda told Purty.

"So, maybe another night, huh?" Purty said in anticipation.

James Ernest stood up and announced, "As the new Leader of the Pack I am officially calling to order the meeting of the Wolf Pack. Would the members please stand?" When Randy resigned as Leader James Ernest was unanimously voted in as the new Leader of the Pack.

I stood with the other four guys in a tight circle. Coty and James had been lying at my feet. Coty also stood to join us. James followed him. James wouldn't leave the side of Coty. We then chanted, "Forever the Pack" six times and then we howled toward the darkened skies. Coty howled along with us and then began barking. James yelped with delight, like it was a game he could play with everyone. The girls seemed to enjoy our tradition or were making fun of it because they were laughing as we returned to our seats.

James Ernest then continued, "We have been asked to help the girls form their own club and then possibly do some adventures together. Is there any objection by any member of the Wolf Pack?"

No one objected.

"What can we help you do?" James Ernest then asked the girls.

Raven spoke up, "Well, we need to come up with a name for our club. We were wondering what rules you have for members, and what could the two clubs do together?"

"We could play spin-the-bottle."

"Purty, we are never playing spin-the-bottle with the Wolf Pack. If we aren't going to be taken seriously then this was all a big mistake," Raven said, making herself be understood.

"Okay, okay. I was just kidding."

Everyone knew he wasn't kidding, but we let it go.

"As far as rules go it is pretty simple. We agreed that we would never smoke or drink alcohol. We agreed that every decision had to be voted unanimous to apply. We promised to never tell a secret that is told by a member to the club. If someone did they would be kicked out and forever shamed."

"I had forgotten about that rule," Purty said. We ignored him.

James Ernest continued, "We also agreed that the club would not allow girls to become members. We then came up with our club name and a motto."

"What's the club motto?" Rock asked.

Tucky answered, "Forever the Pack."

"We then came up with an initiation," James Ernest added.

"What was it?" Francis asked.

"We all had to tell something we had done that we were totally ashamed of and that we would never want others to know about. That way we could then trust each other with anything," I explained.

"What were the secrets?" Raven pleaded.

"You will never know," Junior said.

"I was just testing you guys," Raven said and everyone laughed.

Purty's marshmallows were burnt to a crisp by now. He removed them from above the flames and offered a couple to Rhonda. She declined his offer but thanked him.

"So, what should we do first?" Rock asked. Rock had been my girlfriend after Susie had broken up with me because she caught three of the Key sisters taking turns giving me mouth-to-mouth resuscitation. All they were really doing was taking turns kissing me. But who was I to stop them from saving my life.

"I think you should elect a leader and then come up with a name for your club, and then you could come up with your rules," James Ernest told them.

"Okay. Who wants to be the leader?" Francis called out.

Girls! Who wants to be the leader? What kind of question is that?

"I think you should have nominations," I said.

"I nominate Susie to be the leader," Raven said.

"I nominate Raven to be the leader," Susie added.

"I nominate Rhonda," Rock said, and then of course Rhonda nominated Rock.

I thought my head might explode. I looked over at Tucky and I actually thought his head had exploded. He was holding his head in his hands which were down between his knees.

Finally Francis said, "I nominate Susie. She has been a great friend to all of us."

Everyone agreed and Susie was the leader of the club.

"Thank you so much. I will do my best. Now we need to come up with a name for our club. Any suggestions? You guys can even suggest names."

It grew quiet around the fire as everyone thought of names.

"How about the 'hen peck'? It's kind of like the Wolf Pack," Purty said laughing. Someone threw a rock at him and hit him in the chest.

"Ouch!" he screamed out like a girl.

"How about the She-Wolf Pack?" Tucky said. Everyone laughed, but I liked it.

All kinds of names were submitted including, Buffalo Gang, Blue Jay Band, Barrel of Monkeys, Flock of Turkeys, Doe Herd, Cow Herd, The Unicorns, and the Timber Rattlers.

My favorites were the Buffalo Gang and the Timber Rattlers. But then Tucky suggested the Coyote Troop, which was cool, but Raven changed it to Bear Troop and they had their name. They voted on it, and it was unanimous. They were officially now the Bear Troop.

They gave Susie the title of Mama Bear. They then voted in the same rules that the Wolf Pack had. But they decided they would have their initiation in private. I reached down and got a stick and everyone else followed my lead and we all roasted marshmallows over the fire. Tucky placed a couple more logs on the fire. The chill was becoming real, and the fire felt good.

"Are we going to do an adventure together?" Junior asked.

"I think that sounds like fun," Francis said. "What could we do?"

The Wolf Pack sat there looking at the fire flames leap into the air. Raven then asked, "What was your first adventure?"

I answered, "We went on an overnight hiking trip up toward Blaze and back. There's a trail. If you take that trail past the cabin it circles around and ends back here." I pointed to a spot south of the cabin.

"We could do that," Francis suggested.

"We've already done it," James Ernest said. "Besides, would you girls be able to stay out overnight?"

"We're doing it tonight," Raven answered.

"I could show you the Big-Butt rock," Purty said proudly, as if it was a national monument. Purty had found a huge boulder rising from a small stream that was shaped just like a butt. We had found him fondling and kissing the rock. What a weirdo!

"I think we could live without seeing that," Rhonda said, and all the girls laughed.

"I've seen it, and it is pretty neat," Susie said.

Coty was lying at my feet. His head would rise when he heard laughter. The beagle would follow his actions.

A lull came to our festivities. We all seemed to be staring into the leaping flames and sparks that were flying off into the night.

I interrupted the quiet and said, "Has anyone else met John and Pricilla James?"

Everyone looked at me. I knew no one else had.

"Who are they – your make-believe friends?" Purty said, trying to put me down, but with no luck. Everyone ignored his comment.

"Who are John and Pricilla?" Rock asked. I was surprised that no one had heard about them. I knew all the women-folk knew about them from Mom and Mamaw.

"They came into the store this afternoon. He's fifteen and she's thirteen."

"Are they brother and sister?" Raven asked.

"That's what I first thought when I met them. But no, they're not."

"Will they be going to school with us?" Purty asked. Then he added, "Is she purty?"

"Sorry, she's already taken. They are married."

"What?"

"Say what?"

"No way!"

"Who are they living with?" James Ernest finally asked.

"They're renting the old Cassidy place just beyond Homer and Ruby's farm. He does pottery and she's an artist."

"I've never heard of a thirteen-year-old girl getting married," Rhonda said. Everyone else agreed with her.

"That's not the only weird thing about it," I said. They all stared at me like I was going to tell them where a treasure was hidden.

"She's pregnant."

Well, that started all the comments again. I had never heard such loud chatter around our campfire.

"And she was already pregnant when she got married. I don't know how that's even possible. It's like the Virgin Mary."

The chatter came to a screeching halt and everyone looked at me. I wasn't sure what they were thinking. I figured they were astounded that a thirteen-year-old girl was pregnant and married.

"What do you mean by 'I don't know how that's even possible.'? Are you serious?" Rhonda asked me.

I sat there with a dumb look on my face. I wanted to crawl into a deep hole, but I wasn't sure why.

"Well, uh, uh, she was pregnant before they got married. Don't you have to be married to get pregnant?" I explained, all the while wanting to stuff the words back down my throat.

"They had S-E-X you knucklehead," Purty spelled it out for me.

I wanted to ask about sex but was afraid to open my mouth again.

"Girls get pregnant all the time by having sex before they get married. That's why the two of them got married, John got Pricilla pregnant. She definitely wasn't a virgin," Rhonda told us. "That's only happened once."

I wanted to ask what sex was. I wanted to ask how sex got her pregnant. I wasn't even sure what a virgin was. I had a million questions looping through my brain, but I did know better than to ask them.

"A lot of folks have sex before they get married," James Ernest said. The talk about John and Pricilla went on and on for the next two hours. The subject of a combined adventure never came up again. The girls decided it was time to go to their tent for the night. Susie gave me a kiss before heading for the tent.

I went into our tent and grabbed my sleeping bag and headed back to the fire. I felt sad and kind of lost – like I was the only one that wasn't privy to an inside joke. I knew nothing about sex. I didn't know what it was. I only knew that it involved a boy and a girl and apparently a girl could get pregnant. My mom or dad had never talked to me about sex. I decided I was going to ask James Ernest about it the next time we were alone. I thought about asking Susie about it, but something told me it wasn't something I should ask her about.

I found a spot near the fire and spread out my sleeping bag. Coty lay beside it. Junior took James inside the tent. I crawled into my bag and then heard footsteps coming toward me.

"Why are you sleeping out here?" James Ernest asked.

"It seemed nice out here."

"Don't get bummed out about the others laughing at you. I'll tell you what I know tomorrow. They probably don't know much about sex either. It's like when Sam asked Mr. Burns what detention was. Most of the kids in the class were wondering the same thing but didn't want to admit it. See you in the morning."

"Thanks," I said. I really was thankful that James Ernest came out and talked to me. It made me feel a whole lot better. What would I do without James Ernest?

I could hear a lot of laughter and giggling coming from the girls' tent. I wondered if I was the reason for it. I finally drifted off to sleep with my arm draped over Coty.

Chapter 10

Dodge Ball

Wednesday, September 4, 1963

I was anxious to hear what Sam decided to do about switching English classes. I laid in bed thinking what I would do in his shoes. I would probably switch classes. The day was gloomy with a heavy cover of clouds. I could hear gentle pings on the tin roof as I laid there dreading getting up. My bed felt good that morning.

"I guess we had better get up," I said to James Ernest.

I got no reply.

"Time to get up, boys," Mom yelled out.

I took my pillow and without looking threw it down toward James Ernest's head. I got no reply. I leaned over the side of the top bunk expecting to get slapped in the face with the pillow. He wasn't there. I grabbed hold of the top railing and did a flip off the top bed and my momentum threw me into the dresser. "Ow!" I yelled out.

No one came to see that I almost killed myself. Maybe they were used to it. I limped into the living room and into the kitchen. Janie was eating cereal at the table. Mom sat beside her drinking coffee. No cooking was going on so I figured cereal was the menu that morning. I limped back through the living room and into the

94

store and grabbed a banana and a crème filled chocolate cake and an RC Cola, a good wholesome breakfast.

I limped back into my bedroom and got dressed as I ate. I finished off my healthy meal and went to the outhouse dodging the drops of rain. When I returned I brushed my teeth on the back porch and petted Coty for a couple of minutes. I checked his food and water bowl and refilled them. I didn't have any scraps for him so it was dog food this morning.

I went inside and got my school books together and Janie and I stood on the front porch waiting for the bus to arrive. I had no idea where James Ernest was. I knew he wouldn't skip school unless something bad happened to him. When the bus pulled into our lot and stopped I saw a window lower near the back of the bus and James Ernest poked his head out and yelled, "Don't get wet, you might melt!"

I let Janie get on the bus first and she sat behind Delma and Thelma. They both gave me a dirty look. Delma stuck out her tongue. I ignored her. I was careful walking down the aisle past Bernice. She gave me a dirty look. I stuck my tongue out at her.

Susie was waving me back to the empty spot next to her. It was so nice to see a smiling, friendly face for a change.

"Good morning, Timmy," she greeted.

"Good morning. It's really good to see you," I said.

James Ernest and Raven were sitting in the seat behind us. I turned and asked, "And where were you this morning? You missed a great breakfast."

"I woke up and went for a walk in the woods and ended up at the Washington's house. Coal made biscuits and gravy and fried eggs with cooked apples."

I didn't even say anything. I just turned around in time to watch Purty fall into the aisle when Bernice tripped him. Most of the kids laughed. Randy was right behind him and then Sadie and Francis and little Billy. The next bus stop would be to pick up Rock and Tucky.

Twenty minutes later we were getting off the bus at the high school. I looked around for Sam, but didn't see him. The school wasn't as intimidating as it was the day before. Susie and I stood outside for a while talking with Rock and Tucky while waiting for the first bell to ring.

It rang and we headed for Mr. Burns' homeroom class. I noticed that Sam was not in his seat when we entered. Ten seconds before the last bell sounded Sam opened the door and hurried to his seat. Once seated, he turned to look at me and smiled. I smiled back. I was glad to see he was giving it another chance. Two students came in late and were marked as tardy by Mr. Burns.

Mr. Burns began calling roll. Everyone was there except one girl. When he called out Sam's name it seemed he wanted to say something to Sam, but he didn't. After calling roll, Mr. Burns said, "Teachers will not be lenient today. They will be marking students tardy if they aren't in their seats when the bell rings. Is that understood?"

"Yes, Mr. Burns," the class answered, nowhere near in unison.

A few minutes later the bell rang and we were off to our first class of the day. The first fifteen minutes were used taking a quiz that she had warned us about. What teacher gives their students a test on the second day of school? There were dates and questions about things I know couldn't have been in the chapter I had read. I did read it in study hall. We had to pass the tests to the student on our right and we graded each other's test as Mrs. Hempshaw provided the answers. I received a 'D' on the test only because she did something called a curve. By the middle of the American History class with Mrs. Hempshaw I was already bored out of my mind.

But then she began attempting to run and was yelling out, "The British are coming. The British are coming." I looked for them out the window but didn't see anyone. Mrs. Hempshaw had on another long flowered dress that hung to the floor. She held a lantern in her right hand and ran across the front of the room screaming about the British coming. I guess she was acting out the dramatic scene. The gray bun on the back of her head was beginning to come apart and droop down and it bounced as she ran, as though she had a squirrel attacking her head. Some of the kids were enjoying the scene, while others were snickering at her. I ended up laughing out loud. It certainly helped the boredom. I looked at Raven and she was smiling.

Later, I found Sam at lunch. I hadn't been able to talk to him all morning.

"So you decided to give Mr. Burns another shot?"

"Yeah, since Mr. Davis told me I could switch classes later if I needed to. Dad tried to keep me home, but Mom finally talked him into letting me come back," Sam told me.

"Did you tell Mr. Davis?"

"I went straight to the office when my bus arrived. He seemed happy with my decision," Sam said.

"I hope it works out."

"Thanks, Timmy."

We went outside and found the gang, and I introduced him to everyone.

While Sam was talking to all my friends I noticed that his left arm was hanging low. He tilted his shoulder down to the left.

I asked him, "Did you hurt your arm, Sam?"

He looked surprised and then said, "Um, I fell on my shoulder last night in the barn. It still hurts a little."

The bell rung and Susie told Sam, "I hope it feels better soon."

"Thanks."

I had to hurry inside to my locker and grab my gym bag, and Susie headed to Mr. Holbrook's math class. Today was Wednesday, so I had gym instead of Health class. We had to report to the gymnasium. Mr. Paxton made the boys sit on the right side of the bleachers and the girls were made to sit on the left, separating us. I saw Raven and Rock sitting among the girls.

He began, "From now on you will go straight to the locker rooms. Once the bell rings, you will have five minutes to be dressed in your gym clothes and sitting in the bleachers as we are now. I suggest you perhaps get here early so you have time to get dressed. You can go ahead now and get dressed and come back out. You have five minutes starting now."

There was a mad scramble to get off the bleachers and into the locker rooms. It was amazing that we didn't have our first injury during the dash.

When I made it to the locker room guys had already chosen lockers and were ripping their clothes off. I tried to get as far away from everyone as possible. This was all new to me. I had never undressed in front of other guys except for James Ernest. It seemed weird. I was very self-conscience. I was still fairly skinny, and I knew I had a couple of holes in my underwear.

Most of the guys were already gone by the time I started getting dressed. I knew I was running out of time. I threw my tee shirt on and slipped my feet back into my sneakers and left without tying them.

I was the last boy out. A couple of girls joined the group after me.

"Today I'd like for everyone to give me four laps around the gym to warm up and then we will play dodgeball. Go."

Most of the kids took off to the right while others went to the left. Mr. Paxton blew his whistle and pointed to the right. I turned around with my other mistaken morons and headed counter clockwise. It didn't take long to run the four laps. I caught up to Rock and Raven during the third lap. After the laps Mr. Paxton divided us into two teams and explained the rules of dodge ball. I had played the game in elementary school in Middletown, Ohio. Most of the kids had never played. Raven ended up on my team while Rock played for the other. Mr. Paxton had us use four balls at a time. A person had to keep their head on a swivel and eyes on the balls.

I used my skinny frame to my advantage while dodging the balls easily when they came my way. Kids were getting knocked out quickly. It seemed like the other team was trying to knock Raven out. But her quickness and staying toward the back had saved her. The biggest and strongest boy on the other team threw a ball at Raven and I manage to move in front of her and catch it, knocking him out of the game. He looked upset.

The other team finally knocked Raven out, and their team cheered. They didn't cheer when they knocked others out. Rock got knocked out early. It came down to me and two other boys on our team against two boys on the other team. I suggested that we get all the balls and at the same time throw them at one of the boys. We did and it worked. We knocked one of them out, but then the only kid left knocked out one of our guys.

We both had a ball and we moved to the center line. I threw high and the other kid was supposed to throw low, but he threw right into the arms of the guy and he caught it. That left me and him. He came toward me and threw the ball hard. It came right at me. I took the ball to the stomach and all I had to do was catch it. The ball bounced off my stomach and hit my hands and popped up into the air. I looked up to catch it and another ball hit me right in the gonads. I fell to the floor in defeat. I was humiliated.

Mr. Paxton said we had enough time to play another game of dodge ball so we changed ends and started another game. It was very obvious from the beginning that the other team again were trying to hit Raven first, picking on her because she was black. I tried again to save her by catching one of the balls, but I misjudged it and it hit me on the foot. I was out. I went to the bleachers and sulked. As the game went on, Raven kept dodging balls, and her teammates kept sending the other team's players to the bleachers. Our team won when Raven hit their last player in the head. Everyone on our team ran to congratulate Raven. It was one way she had gotten acceptance at the school, and I then realized she didn't really need protecting all the time. She did a good job on her own.

When school ended for the day I was heading for the bus when I ran into Purty going the opposite way.

"The bus is this way," I said.

"I have detention again," he said and laughed. I laughed also, but I wasn't surprised.

Chapter 11

Night Crawler Sex Ed

Saturday, June 15, 1963

The Wolf Pack and the Bear Troop walked back to the store that morning after the first joint meeting the night before. James Ernest and I had chores to do that morning and we needed to help pump gas now that the gas pump was working. I knew that the pump meant more work for us at the store, but we needed the extra income and it was kind of fun pumping gas and cleaning windows.

Walking back to the store were Henry Jr., Susie, Rhonda, and Raven. As we walked into the gravel lot I saw Clayton pull his truck up next to the gas pump. I hurried over to pump his gas. He opened his door and got out and said, "Fill her up, Timmy."

"Yes, sir," I said as I stuck the nozzle into the tank and began pumping the gas. I picked up the squeegee and began washing his front windows.

"How was the overnight campout?" Clayton asked me.

"It was fun. The girls formed their club. They called the club the Bear Troop and Susie was named their leader. Her title is Mama Bear." Clayton chuckled.

"So, what is their first adventure?"

"They haven't decided yet. We want to do a joint adventure with the two clubs," I said

102

"I have plenty of projects to do on the farm. You all could have a big adventure there," Clayton said with a grin.

"We may pass on that one. That might turn into more than fun," I said.

"Haven't all your others also?" Clayton reminded me.

"I guess you're right."

I took the nozzle out and placed it back on the pump and told Clayton, "It took 15.2 gallons and the total came to $4.86."

"Gas is getting so expensive these days," Clayton said as he pulled his truck up to the porch.

There were quite a few cars and trucks parked along the side of the lot which I knew were fishermen this morning. Saturday mornings were always our busiest.

When I went inside the store most of the kids were drinking pop and standing around the store telling Mamaw and Papaw about the night we had. I knew Mom had planned an early shopping trip to Ashland with Miss Rebecca, Pastor White's wife. Miss Rebecca had given birth to a baby girl in April and I was sure they were going to buy supplies and frilly baby clothes for little Marie. They named the little girl after my Mom, whose middle name was Marie. Mom and Miss Rebecca had become best friends.

I went to the cooler and pulled out an RC Cola and opened the bottle with the opener that was attached on the front counter. I watched the cap fall into the metal container under it. Papaw was standing behind the counter in his usual spot and Mamaw was standing in front of it with her hair up in a bun and an apron covering her large stomach. She was laughing about Susie being called Mama Bear.

I heard another vehicle pull into the lot and up to the porch. A minute later the screen door opened and John and Pricilla walked into the store.

"Good morning, everyone," Pricilla said smiling. John nodded at us. Since I was the only one to have met them before I figured I should introduce them to everyone. I went around the room making introductions. I noticed a lot of the girls were glancing at Pricilla's stomach trying to see if her baby bump was showing. It was still only showing a little.

"We're so glad to meet everyone. It's been a little lonely. We would love for y'all to come visit us. We could eat and play games and have such a good time."

"That would be fun," Susie politely said.

Pricilla turned to face Papaw and said, "We've been told that you give credit to folks in the community. Would you do the same for us? We promise we'll pay you."

Papaw looked at Mamaw and then said to John, "John, could we talk in private?" Papaw led John through the house and onto the back porch.

"Is Raven your given name or a nickname?" Pricilla asked.

"It's my given name."

"It's so pretty and unusual. I love it."

"Thank you, Pricilla," Raven said smiling.

"I'm surprised to see that a colored family is living here in Morgan County. Are there many black families in the area?"

"We're the only colored family around these parts that I know of. Are you upset by us living here?" Raven questioned her.

"No. No. Not at all. I was just surprised. I hope you don't take offense for me asking. I was just curious. We're not in position to judge anyone. And I don't believe anyone has the right to judge someone because of their skin color. Please forgive me if I offended you."

Mamaw spoke up, "We have a very loving community as you will see the longer you live here. I'm sure you and John will be welcomed here just as Raven, Henry Jr. and their family were also welcomed."

"Thank you, Mrs. Collins. That is so good to hear," Pricilla said.

Papaw and John returned and Papaw reached under the counter and got a pad and wrote James family on it and placed it on top of the other family pads of credit behind him on one of the shelves.

"Thank you so much, Mr. Collins," Pricilla said. "Do you mind if we get some supplies now?"

"Help yourselves."

"We'll help you. What do you need?" I said.

"We need sugar, Martha White flour, white bread and a pound of bologna and salt."

I grabbed the sugar. James Ernest got the flour. Papaw began cutting the meat. Susie got the salt and took it to the counter.

As they were leaving Mamaw reminded them that church started in the morning at ten.

"We will see you then," Pricilla said and smiled.

Junior watched them through the window as they drove away and said, "I's sure thought you needed to be sixteen to drive."

"That's what we all thought," Mamaw said. "But we also thought you had to be adults to get married and have babies."

Soon after, everyone was gone and James Ernest and I spent the day pumping gas, doing chores, and running snacks and food to the fishermen at the lake. Mom returned home around three that afternoon and Mamaw filled her in on the reappearance of John and Pricilla. Mom just shook her head.

Around eight that evening James Ernest and I decided to make a trip around the lake to pick up the trash left behind by the fishermen. Then we placed the garbage bag on the dam and walked back to the slanted rock. It was my favorite place on our property to be at sundown. We could watch the ducks heading to their nests near the shallows of the hollow and watch the owls fly from tree to tree overhead.

Deer and other animals would come down to get their nightly drinks before settling in for the night. The twilight scene dancing across the waters was always beautiful. It looked like a scene that some famous painter should have captured and hung in a fancy art museum next to *Mona Lisa* or Vincent van Gogh's *Starry Night*.

We were both lying with our backs against the slanted rock. I could have easily gone to sleep as the gentle breeze blew down the lake rustling the leaves of the overhead limbs. I asked James Ernest, "Do you know much about sex?"

"Some. I'm not an expert, and before you ask, I've never had sex."

"Tell me what you know."

James Ernest laughed.

"Stop laughing at me. I'm tired of kids laughing at me because I don't know anything about sex."

"Who was laughing at you?" James Ernest asked.

"Last night everyone was. I heard the girls giggling about me in their tent. I know they were laughing about me."

"Girls laugh and giggle about everything."

"Are you going to tell me or not?" I said heatedly.

"Okay. Okay. Tell me what you know."

"I don't know anything. I don't know what sex really is. I don't know how it's done. I think it's how people have babies, but I'm not sure. No one has ever told me any of this stuff."

In those days we didn't have the internet or scenes on TV where we might learn things on our own. We could only learn this type of stuff from another person. Rob and Laurie slept in separate beds on the *Dick Van Dyke Show* as did most married couples on TV. On the *Andy Griffith Show* the most we would see was Barney holding hands or kissing Thelma Lou on the cheek, and Andy would tease Barney over that. There was no John and Pricilla getting pregnant on TV.

"Well, have you ever seen two animals having sex?"

"I'm not sure."

"When you find two nightcrawlers connected to each other they are having sex. When you see a horse or a pig on top of another one that's what they are doing."

"I still don't understand. What are they doing to each other?"

"The male horse is placing his penis inside the female horse. That is what sex is."

"Inside what?" I asked flabbergasted.

"Inside the female horse's vagina."

"How do you know this stuff, and what is a vagina?"

"That's all I know and all I'm going to tell you. If you want to know more, ask your mom or Papaw. Or you could pay attention in health class. The teacher will go over the male and female sex organs."

"How did you learn this stuff?"

"By reading the encyclopedia. Pick up a book every once in a while," James Ernest answered before closing his eyes.

Who knew I had a sex organ? I still didn't understand how that made a baby. I was more confused than before we started talking. The whole thing seemed pretty yucky.

James Ernest seemed to be asleep. I was thinking about all the things he had filled my head with. We laid there another half hour before heading back to the store. As we were stepping off the slanted rock I said, "Are you sure nightcrawlers have a wiener? I've never seen a wiener on a nightcrawler."

James Ernest continued to shake his head all the way home.

We made it back to the house in time to watch *Have Gun – Will Travel* and *Gunsmoke* - two of my favorite shows. They made me forget my worries about my shortcomings in knowledge.

Sunday, June 16, 1963

Sunday morning came and Mom woke us up early so we could make a trip to the spring for water before getting ready for church. "You guys need a bath this morning before we go to church," Mom said as we were making our way out of bed.

We quickly put on shorts and shoes. I grabbed a bar of soap and a couple of towels and James Ernest got the two buckets for water. We dropped the soap and towels off at a deep pool of water in the creek and continued to the spring. We stopped on our way back to the store at the pool and stripped off our clothes and jumped into the water. It was so much easier to take a bath in the creek than it was in the winter in a wash tub.

As we were rinsing off the soap from our bodies and hair we heard, "Hello, boys."

I looked up and saw Chero and Sugar Cook watching us from the bank of the creek. I was glad the water was up past my waistline. James Ernest was taller than me and he had to dip down to hide his privates.

"We heard splashing and came down to investigate," Sugar Cook said. She was the oldest daughter of the Key family. "We could join you guys in the water."

James Ernest looked over at me with a smile on his face and whispered, "This is your chance to learn more." He then laughed.

The last time I had seen these girls in the creek they took turns giving me CPR by doing nothing but taking turns kissing me. Later they claimed to have saved my life. Susie had witnessed it and broke up with me for a while.

"We were just leaving. Mom is waiting for us. You want to go to church with us?" I asked them. What a silly thing to say. They were wanting to skinny dip with us and I was asking them to church.

"We'll wait here and walk back to the store with you," Sugar Cook said. I noticed they were standing next to our towels and shorts.

"You can go on and we'll catch up," I suggested. They didn't take my suggestion. Instead they sat down right next to our stuff and Sugar even picked up my towel and held it out for me.

"Just toss it to me," I begged.

James Ernest walked out of the water with his hands covering his junk and grabbed his shorts. He then turned and walked behind a tree and put them on. I knew then I was going to have to do the same thing. As I was walking up the bank I stumbled and threw my hands out to catch myself, exposing myself to the girls. The girls laughed at my blunder. I quickly covered myself and grabbed my shorts and did the same as James Ernest had.

We then got our towels and began drying the rest of our bodies. We got the buckets of waters and the girls offered to help carry them. I knew my face had turned red from embarrassment.

"No need to be embarrassed, we see our brothers naked all the time. We're pretty used to it," Sugar Cook said. She helped James Ernest with his bucket while Chero helped me. We finally made it back to the store and the girls continued down the road toward their house.

When we finally made our way into the church I was worn out. I knew it would be hard to stay awake. I was hoping for lively music and a rip-roaring sermon. Preceding the sermon we sang a slow version of *Amazing Grace*. Then Pastor White began his sermon. I looked around the congregation and saw that John and Pricilla were sitting near the back of the church. Midway through his sermon he read Leviticus Chapter 18 which was all about sex. I was awake! But it was all about who a man shouldn't have sexual encounters with. I was shocked as he read it, but it did keep me awake.

After the invitation and before Pastor White dismissed everyone, he had John and Pricilla stand and had the congregation welcome them to the church by applause. A few minutes later they stood next to the pastor, grinned, and shook hands with the people as they exited the building.

Chapter 12

Where's Sam?

Friday, September 13, 1963

Almost two whole weeks had gone by and I was getting use to high school. I was enjoying most of my classes. My favorite teachers were Mr. Holbrook and Mrs. Hempshaw, she was always coming up with something to lighten and enlighten the class, but at the same time we learned all the boring History stuff. Mr. Holbrook was just a nice man who seemed to really care about his students.

I entered homeroom already anxious for the day to be over and the weekend to begin. Even though I knew I had nothing special going on over the weekend it would still better than school. I settled into my desk and watched as other kids came lumbering in, some with smiles and others with sleep in their eyes. I looked back at Susie and she smiled at me. It was almost time for the final bell to ring and I saw that Sam Hitchcock still hadn't made it into the classroom.

I sat there watching and hoping he would make it to his seat before the bell rung. *Ring, Ring, Ring!* It was too late for hoping. Mr. Burns began taking role. When he called Sam's name he looked up to see the empty seat. With a slight grin on his face he went on to the next name on his list. It wasn't unusual for a kid to miss school, especially high school in Morgan County. There were always reasons to miss school. Besides sickness, there was work around the farm that needed to be done, taking care of a sick younger sibling so their mother and father could go to work, or just playing hooky. But I couldn't stop worrying about Sam.

One day I had noticed Sam was favoring his left shoulder and I wondered if maybe his dad had done something to him. I figured his dad was capable of anything; among them was beating on Sam and Sam's mom. I hoped I was wrong in my thinking.

After home room was over Raven and I headed for Mrs. Hempshaw's American History class. We walked in to find Mrs. Hempshaw dressed in a red, white, and blue striped dress with fifty white stars covering the stripes. She made sure we knew she had fifty stars by saying, "There are exactly fifty stars on me. Would anyone like to come up and count them?"

We all took her word for it. I couldn't imagine someone wanting to go up and count the stars around her body and between her bosoms', except for maybe Purty, but he wasn't there. She made sure we knew there were now fifty stars instead of forty-eight. Alaska and Hawaii had become states in 1959, four years earlier. Mrs. Hempshaw was hilarious and a bit out there, but I'll never forget how many states there are or how many stars are on the flag and dress. She was a great teacher.

The clock seemed to stand still the rest of the day except for gym class in which we played dodge ball again. Mr. Paxton just sat in the bleachers and watched us pound each other with the rubber balls. What a job he had.

Finally the day was over and I headed to the bus with a couple of books in hand. As I headed to the back of the bus excitedly Bernice tripped me again and I and my books went flying into the aisle. I wanted to get up and smack her, but I would never hit a girl, even though I wasn't positive Bernice was a girl. Purty and Tucky laughed at me. When I finally made my seat Purty said, "I guess riding the bus home is a lot more fun than detention. I didn't know what I was missing."

In the nine days of school, so far Purty had detention six of the days. Mr. Tuttle, Purty's father, told him that if he got anymore detentions he would not be able to go on the next Wolf Pack adventure or to any meetings. I knew that would probably mean the Wolf Pack would be down a member.

Monday, September 16

I was back on the bus on the way to school. The only thing good about it - I was sitting next to Susie. She looked awfully pretty with her hair pulled back in a ponytail and her freckles and face shining in the morning light.

Purty was behind us jabbering on and on to Rhonda about how he had taken out the biggest jock in the sophomore class in dodgeball. From what I had heard he was hiding behind the largest kid in the class and happened to reach down and picked up a ball next to him. He threw high in the air while still hiding and the ball hit the poor guy. He never saw it coming. According to Purty though he faced off against the guy, each of them will a ball. They both threw the ball at the same time and Purty said he jumped four feet high to avoid the ball while the other guy took his ball in the face. No one on the bus believed his story, but it was entertaining as always.

"Four feet high, huh! Are you expecting us to believe you jumped four feet high? Are you a freaking kangaroo? I would believe you may have jumped four inches from fright," Rhonda teased. We all laughed, including Purty.

We arrived at the school and I looked at Susie and said, "I'm worried about Sam." As I said it I was looking for him in front of the school among all the kids.

"Why?" Susie asked.

"Remember, last week when he was holding his shoulder like he had hurt it and then he missed school on Friday," I told her.

"Yes, but kids miss school all the time."

"I just have a weird feeling about it."

"How come?"

"I met his dad," I said.

We stood outside with our friends until the first bell rung. The whole time I was scanning the crowd for Sam. We walked into home room just before the tardy bell rung and I saw that Sam's seat was empty again. Hopefully he hadn't gave up and dropped out of school. I decided I needed to talk to Principal Davis.

Mr. Burns took roll call and gave announcements and then the bell rung. I told Raven I would see her later in Mrs. Hempshaw's American History class. I turned and headed for the office.

115

"I need to see Principal Davis if possible," I told the school secretary. Principal Davis must have heard me and he came out of his office.

"How can I help you, Tim?"

"I need to talk to you about Sam, but I've got class in a couple of minutes."

"Come on in. I'll write you a tardy excuse. Whose class are you late for?"

"Mrs. Hempshaw."

"She'll be fine. How do like her class?"

'We all like it. She's very colorful and a great teacher."

"We agree. Have a seat and tell me about Sam."

I went into detail about meeting Sam's dad and about what I'd observed last week and how Sam had missed the last two days. "I'm just worried about him. Do you know anything about what's going on?"

"First, you're a good friend. Second, as principal I've learned that with farm kids I have to expect them to miss school fairly often. Between you and me, I also have concerns about Sam's father. That's all I can say. Sorry."

"But what if something is wrong? What if Sam is being made to stay home? That's not right. He should get to come to school if he wants to. Doesn't a kid have some rights? What if his dad is beating him?"

"Unfortunately, at this time there's nothing I can do, Tim. Once he's been absent for five straight days I can send someone to their home to check on him."

"Okay. Thank you for talking to me," I said as I started to get up from the chair.

Principal Davis came out from behind his desk and patting me on my shoulder and said. "I'm sure Sam is fine," not very convincingly.

"Oh, wait a moment, Tim. I'll write you a tardy note."

"Thank you. I didn't much like detention."

"Glad to hear it," Principal Davis said and laughed.

I was off quickly to my History class. I quietly opened the door and slipped into class. Mrs. Hempshaw was putting on a dramatic interpretation of a Revolutionary War battle. She had an old musket in her hands and was marching toward the British. Soon she was shot and lying on the floor. Despite her dramatic death the class was roaring with laughter as she lay there silently on the wooden floor. She continued to lie on the floor without moving for another ten minutes making some of us wonder if maybe she had actually died of a heart attack. She finally rose when a girl approached her to check.

Mrs. Hempshaw explained that men were actually dying for our country and that they were giving up their lives forever. It wasn't just for ten minutes, but forever they were lost. It sunk in.

I waited until after class to give Mrs. Hempshaw my tardy note.

"Is everything okay, Timmy?" she asked.

"Yes, I hope so," I said. I then hurried to catch up with Raven and then head to Mr. Holbrook's math class.

That evening at home I talked to Mom and James Ernest about Sam before going to bed.

"What exactly are you worried about?" Mom asked.

"I'm worried that Sam's dad might be beating him, or hitting him. If you had seen the way he talked about Sam the day we took him home. It was like he was talking about one of his hogs. I think his dad is capable of anything."

"I'm sure you're overreacting. He may have had a bad day. Burdens have a way of mounting up on a person."

"His wife looked as though she was scared to death of him. She didn't say a word," I offered in explanation.

"Maybe we should go check on him after school tomorrow if he's absent again," James Ernest suggested.

"No. No. I think you should stay away from their place. If what you say is true you could be putting yourselves in danger," Mom demanded.

"Okay. I'm going to bed. But I doubt I'll be able to sleep," I said dramatically. Maybe Mrs. Hempshaw was rubbing off on me.

I laid there on the top bunk thinking about Sam and his dad.

"Go to sleep," James Ernest said from the bottom bunk. Your squirming is keeping me awake."

"I can't help it. My head's full of thoughts and I can't get comfortable."

"Go try the couch."

"That's not very brotherly. What do you do when you can't get to sleep?" I asked.

"I go for a walk in the woods."

"Maybe I'll do that."

"Maybe a bear or coyote will eat you," James Ernest said.

I ignored his nonsense and said, "I think we should go check on Sam."

"Okay," was the last thing I heard him say before he drifted off to sleep.

Chapter 13

Wading Licking Creek

Monday, June 24, 1963

The members of the Wolf Pack and the Bear Troop decided for our first joint adventure we would wade down Licking Creek toward the quarry and back. Today was the day. It would give us a chance to see how the two clubs would do together and it wouldn't be an overnight trip.

It had rained a bit the day before but not enough to make the creeks muddy or dangerously high. It was almost perfect conditions.

Everyone began gathering at the store around seven-thirty. We were leaving at eight. We each were responsible for bringing our own food and anything else we wanted to bring on the trip. James Ernest and I decided to eat a big breakfast and skip eating until we returned that evening, therefore not having to carry anything on the creek trip.

Coty was being allowed to follow us. He didn't like the water, but he would be able to follow us along the road which paralleled the creek. I put some treats in a plastic bag for him in the pocket of my shorts. The girls began arriving with bags of food and Rhonda even brought a blanket for a picnic. 'Girls.' The last member to arrive was Purty and he had the biggest backpack I had ever seen stuffed with food and stuff. 'Purty.'

The Wolf Pack all wore tee shirts and shorts with sneakers. Susie and Rhonda wore swimming suits with shorts cover-ups. Francis just had on her swimming suit. Raven and Rock wore tee shirts and shorts. James Ernest, Raven, Susie and I had walking sticks. No one else did.

Purty and Francis each brought an inner tube for floating down the creek. It actually was a good ideal – must have been Francis's.

"I'm not sure we need the blanket. It will be hard to carry," James Ernest spoke up.

"I wasn't sure. I can leave it here," Rhonda said.

Papaw, Mamaw and Mom were there to see us off. Clayton and Monie had stayed after bringing Rhonda, Raven and Susie to the store. They all waved from the front porch as we began our trek across the road and over the bank and into the creek.

"If you get lost just follow Coty back home!" Papaw yelled out. Coty barked hearing his name.

"You don't think they'll get lost, do you?" I heard Mom ask.

"I don't see how. Following a creek down and back isn't too difficult," Clayton said.

"But, then again, it is the Wolf Pack," Mamaw said as she turned back into the store.

I heard laughter coming from the store.

Although the temperature was already in the mid-seventies the water was chilly as we step off the bank. It took a few seconds to get used to it. I knew that later on the water would feel great. Rhonda had the hardest time stepping into the water. Susie had to coax her in. Soon we all were wading down the creek. It was fairly shallow where we began, only six to twelve inches. Later on we would come across spots that would be over our heads. We would have to either swim or walk around those holes.

"This is going to be so much fun," Francis Tuttle said. Eleven-year-old Francis was Purty's sister and the youngest member of the Bear Troop. I always thought she was the kindest of the Tuttle family and a complete opposite of her sister Sadie, who none of us got along with. Sadie was a self-centered, egotistical beauty who thought she was destined for fame and fortune. She had few friends, her main one being Bernice Strunck, who we called Skunk because of the streak of white in her black hair and her personality. The two of them were inseparable and intolerable, thus the reason they weren't invited to become members of the Bear Troop.

"What are we going to do?" Rhonda asked as she was still getting accustomed to the water. She held her hands away from the water as though the water might bite.

'What do you mean? This is it. We're going to wade down river and then back," I answered.

Rhonda stood there as if she was expecting more. I wasn't sure what she thought wading down the creek meant to her. Apparently it didn't mean the same to her as it did me.

"I'm not sure about this. I'll freeze before we're done. This doesn't seem like it would be a lot of fun," Rhonda complained.

"I can keep you warm," Purty suggested. Rhonda shot him a dirty look. I thought Rhonda was going to climb the bank and head back to store right then. To her credit she didn't.

"You'll get used to it, Rhonda. We'll find fun things to do on the way. You'll see," Susie told her.

"It will be a blast," Rock chimed in.

I stuck up behind Susie and began splashing her back. She screamed and turned around and returned fire. Within seconds we were in a water battle –Wolf Pack against the Bear Troop with Rhonda trying to stay as dry as possible, but soon all nine of us turned on her and she soon was soaked from the top of her head down.

"I hate all of you," Rhonda teased with a grin after the water fight. She never uttered a complaining word about the trip after that.

A while later I began to recognize large boulders that Papaw and I had fished from over the years as we passed them. The boulders stood ten to fifteen feet above the water, but could be accessed from the road. We were entering deeper holes of water as we waded down river. Purty was floating on his tube. Tucky was using Francis's tube. Junior was walking along side Susie and I.

"I think this is so much fun," Junior said. I knew Junior had a crush on Francis. They were the same age, but he was a year behind her in school. Francis would be entering the seventh grade while Junior would be in sixth.

I looked at Junior and said, "This is your chance to get to know Francis better. Why don't you go walk and talk with her?"

"I don't know what to say."

"Just say hello," I said.

"Ask her if you can walk with her," Susie suggested.

Junior slowly made his way through the water toward Francis. Susie and I watched him say hello as Francis turned to him. She smiled and began talking to him. Junior always seemed a little self-conscience since he was black and all his friends were white. Everyone liked Junior. He was always smiling and happy and just a nice kid. I knew I would probably feel the same if I lived in an all-black community.

Suddenly, there was a scream and we saw Rhonda disappear under the water. James Ernest and Raven were the nearest to her and hurried over to help her up.

"Those rocks are slippery," James Ernest told her after getting her back on her feet.

"I'm surprised I haven't fallen before now," Rhonda said as she wrung the water from her long hair.

"A walking stick would help steady you," James Ernest suggested.

"I don't happen to see any floating by," Rhonda said frustrated.

"I'll get you one," James Ernest headed for the shore. I followed, with Tucky close behind. We ended up cutting sticks for everyone that didn't have them already.

We continued our trip down the creek. The creek was edged by stone overhangs in spots along the way. Sycamores, red buds, oaks, dogwoods and many other types of trees soared high into the sky on both sides of the water. Coty followed on the road and when the bank flattened out he would come down to the water to drink and get a friendly pat on the head from us.

We came upon a shallow spot in the creek covered with flat rocks that I knew would hide many crawdads. I bent down and tilted a rock up and waited for the disturbed water to clear and there would be a big crawdad looking up at his raised hiding spot. I stuck my right hand to his rear and quickly grabbed him up. Susie was busy talking with Rhonda and Raven so I came up behind her and placed the crawdad near her ponytail and the crawfish opened his pincher and attached to the ponytail. I let go of it and Susie suddenly felt the added weight to her hair. She turned to look at me and saw me smiling.

"What did you do?"

"I didn't do anything," I lied.

When she turned the other girls saw the crawdad and screamed. Rhonda yelled out, "There's a crawdad on your ponytail."

Susie calmly asked, "Will you please take it off?"

Raven waded over to her and grabbed the crawdad and pulled it until it slid off the end of the ponytail.

"Let me have it," Susie said. She took the mud bug and started toward me and I ran through the water as she chased me. My foot hit a slippery rock and I ended up on my back in the middle of the creek. Susie jumped on top on me and straddled me.

"Get his arms," she yelled out. Raven grabbed my right arm and Rhonda my left. I was just able to keep my face above the water to breathe. She began her torture by bringing the pinchers close to my lips and then toward my eyes. The other kids were gathering around us and laughing.

"Help!" I yelled out. I was being betrayed by my fellow Wolf Pack members.

Susie then said, "Open your mouth."

"No," I mumbled through my closed lips.

"Okay then girls, let's pull his pants down. I know where I want to attach this thing," Susie said.

I started kicking my legs. I knew I didn't want the crawdad attached to any part of my privates. Rock and Francis started moving closer to me and I screamed, "Help, guys!"

"You can attach it to me!" Purty shouted out.

Everyone turned toward Purty to see him standing there with his pants down. He was standing in water that was up to his waist, thank goodness, but you could still tell his pants were down around his ankles. Three years earlier we had become friends with Purty and Randy when their family moved to the community. We soon found out that Purty loved being naked any chance he got. He hated wearing clothes. I had finally convinced him that it was wrong and explained why, but his olds ways had never completely died.

The girls shrieked at the sight of Purty and jumped off of me to get as far away from Purty as they could. I quickly got to my feet. Tucky hurried over in front of Purty to block the view and told him, "Pull your pants back up. You're crazier than a horse covered with black flies."

Purty smiled and then reached down and pulled his pants back up.

Rhonda made her way over near Purty and said, "Purty, that is totally inappropriate. You will never have a chance to have a nice girlfriend doing things like that." Purty looked embarrassed and seem to take her words to heart.

Finally everything settled down and we continued our wade down the creek. I was glad to have been rescued by Purty's antics, but I knew it upset everyone at the same time.

Susie walked over to me and grabbed hold of my hand. She smiled at me and said, "I wasn't really going to let the girls pull your pants down. I was just having fun."

"It's okay. I deserved it. I remembered the first time you got a crawdad stuck in your hair and thought it would be funny to relive it." Four years earlier Susie had fallen in the creek while she was helping me look for crawdads and when she had risen from the water a crawdad was attached to her hair. I didn't tell her it was there and she didn't realize it was there until her father told her it was attached at the dinner table.

We continued going under the wooden bridge that led to Mrs. Robinson's home that the Tuttle's had bought. We also waded past

Pastor White's house and the place where Raven and Junior had lived when they first moved to the area. It was getting to be about noon and we were still a ways from our destination which was the rock quarry.

James Ernest and Raven made their way over to us and James Ernest said, "Up ahead is the rope and a good place to stop and rest."

I knew where he was talking about and agreed it would be the perfect spot. We were there within five minutes, and we followed a path that had been cut through the brush onto a huge flat rock that hung over the creek. It overlooked a deep pool of water and there was a rope hanging down from a limb that stretched nearly all the way across the creek. The flat rock was around eight feet above the water and it was large enough to hold all ten of us plus Coty.

As the girls and Purty were unloading their food for the picnic, Tucky grabbed the rope and pulled on it to make sure it was still solid. He backed up on the rock and ran for the edge. He jumped off and swung out over the deep pool and flipped off the rope and splashed into the water. The rope swung back to where James Ernest could grab it.

"Who's next?" he called out. Junior raised his hand and went to get the rope. He backed up and then ran. When he reached the middle he let go and did a three-sixty twist and went feet first into the creek.

Susie and Rhonda took off their shorts cover ups to reveal their full swimming suits. I couldn't help but notice what a great figure Susie had. Not that I hadn't already noticed it, but seeing her in the swimming suit was way different. Purty couldn't take his eyes off of Rhonda. It almost became creepy. I guess it wasn't almost creepy – it was really creepy.

I walked over to Purty and quietly said, "Stop staring at Rhonda. You're making her feel uncomfortable. It's weird."

"Isn't she beautiful? I can't help it, Timmy."

"Well try before she punches you in the nose," I said. "Let's swing off the rope."

Purty walked over and grabbed the rope as he continued looking at Rhonda, who was lying on the rock getting a tan. He began running toward the edge but didn't notice when he got to it because he was still gawking at Rhonda. He stepping off the rock and went straight down along the rock and into the water. Everyone burst out in laughter.

Rock was next off the rock and then everyone began taking turns except Rhonda who said she didn't really want to. After spending nearly an hour on the rock we decided we had better continue the trip. James Ernest suggested that the backpacks could be left there and picked up on the way back. They were glad to be rid on them. James Ernest found a hiding spot under the rock.

Ten minutes further down the creek we came upon a blockage of trees and limbs that went across the creek. Some of us climbed over it while Purty led others around it by climbing the bank and taking the road around the snarl. We all met back up a hundred yards north of the logjam. While we waded up the creek I kept seeing spots that I thought would be great fishing holes. I tried to remember where they were by looking at the road and trying to find something to identify the spots.

At times we would have to take a route that led us into deep mud and silt. The girls complained about their shoes getting filled with the sludge. At one spot Francis lost a shoe that came off in the mud. We had to search the mud in the area where she thought she was standing. We dug and dug with our hands until Junior finally came up with it. He washed it out and handed it to her and she kissed him on the creek in return. I swear his black face turned red within seconds. It was my favorite moment of the trip.

We had a blast just talking and joking with other as we waded on down the creek. The hills around us began to change. Instead of forest and trees, surrounding us now were tall rock walls soaring into the sky a couple of hundred feet high. I knew we were getting closer to the rock quarry. We could hear the noise of heavy duty equipment in the distance. We had heard the trucks driving by on the road as we had waded during the day, but this was different.

"How much further are we going?" Rhonda asked.

James Ernest answered, "It's nearly two now. We probably should head back soon. Let's just go around the bend. I'd like to see the other side of this cliff."

We made our way another fifteen minutes to where James Ernest wanted to go. The stone wall rose from the edge of the creek. It was very overwhelming looking up at it. It made me feel so small.

"Aaaahh! Aaaahh!"

We all turned to see Francis staring at the creek bank and screaming bloody murder. We ran to her as she continued screaming. When we saw what she saw, the other girls and Purty also began screaming. The body of a young man was lying there dead. His body looked broken and bent. It was lying with his lower half in the water, the top half of his body laid on a flat rock out of the water. He was lying on his stomach. James Ernest and Tucky walked over to the body and looked at his face.

"Don't recognize him," James Ernest said, and Tucky seconded it.

"You think he drowned?" Raven asked.

James Ernest looked straight up along the stone wall in front of us and said, "I think he fell or was pushed off this mountain."

"So you're saying he was either very clumsy or he was murdered," Rock said.

"Looks that way to me," James Ernest confirmed.

I never doubted anything that James Ernest said. He was by far the smartest person I had ever known. But what would a person be doing out in the middle of nowhere on the edge of a cliff. I didn't think there were any roads near the top of the wall. That side of the creek was nothing but wilderness.

"What are we going to do?" Purty said through his tears. Some of the girls were also crying, mainly Francis and Raven.

"I'll go find someone at the quarry; I guess they'll call Sheriff Cane. Some of you need to stay with the body and others can go with me," James Ernest explained.

I stayed with the body. Susie, Tucky and Rock stayed with me. The rest of the gang went with James Ernest.

"I can't believe we found a body on our first adventure," Rock said.

"Yeah, lucky us," Susie said sarcastically.

"This poor fellow wasn't so lucky," Tucky offered.

"No, he wasn't," I said. I couldn't help but think that the man was thrown off the mountain. I wondered what he did to get himself thrown from a mountainside. We took seats on the ground not far from the body as we waited for James Ernest to return.

"What do you think he did?" I asked.

"What do you mean?" Susie asked.

"I mean if he was thrown off the mountain he had to have done something to someone."

Susie and Rock both looked at me as if I was crazy. Tucky knew what I meant and said, "Maybe he double-crossed the Kentucky mafia and they snuffed him out."

"The Kentucky mafia?" Susie questioned. We ignored her as we were guessing his demise.

"Or maybe he stole someone's horse and they caught him and threw him off the mountain," I proposed.

"Don't they hang horse thieves?" Rock asked.

"That was out west," I answered.

"Maybe he cheated on his wife, and she pushed him off," Tucky said.

"Maybe he was part of the Hatfield and McCoy family feud and the other family had him snuffed out. That feud isn't that far from here," I told them.

"Who said he was murdered?" Susie said.

"How else would you fall off a mountain?" I asked.

"He could have slipped, or stumbled, or tripped, or been drunk and staggered off the edge," Susie explained.

"I guess any of those things could have happened. But I agree with Timmy, he was definitely murdered," Tucky said.

"That solves it," I quickly said.

"You two are so stupid," Rock told us.

We all laughed, even though a dead man was lying twenty feet from us. We meant no disrespect.

Chapter 14

330

Around an hour later we heard voices nearing us. I recognized Sheriff Hagar Cane's voice. He would soon be my stepfather. He was engaged to my mother.

James Ernest, the sheriff, and a deputy I had never seen stood at the top of the opposite creek bank. The sheriff and the deputy both had on hip boots so they could cross the creek. The deputy was carrying what I figured was a stretcher. James Ernest hopped off the bank into the water. The sheriff held on to tree branches as he scrambled over the ledge, as did the deputy.

They waded over to where the body laid. Sheriff Cane said, "Hi, Timmy, Susie."

I nodded and Susie greeted back, "Hello, Sheriff Cane."

"This is Deputy Sonny Hughes," the sheriff introduced as he made his way to the body. Sheriff Cane bent down and looked at the face of the corpse. The deputy did the same. "Do any of you recognize him?" the sheriff asked.

We all said no together.

Sheriff Cane started to turn the body over but stopped and said, "You may want to turn away."

Susie did, but Tucky, Rock, James Ernest and I stood still as we watched him place the body on its back. I could see that the left side of his head was caved in, apparently from smacking against the rock. I almost wished I had turned away. He had dark brown hair, medium length, not long, but scraggly, but it could have been from lying dead in a creek. He had a goatee but no mustache. His entire looks gave you the ideal he wasn't a model citizen. I couldn't help but think of the 'Kentucky mafia' term Tucky had used earlier.

The sheriff checked the corpse's pockets for any clues as to who the fellow was. All he found were a few coins in his right front pocket and a white handkerchief in a back pocket. The dead man had on Converse Chuck Taylor black and white sneakers.

"I would guess he probably died last night. He hasn't been here all that long," Sheriff Cane told us. I heard a siren coming down the road. "James, will you run up and wave down the ambulance."

James Ernest high-tailed it across the creek and climbed the bank like a billy goat and stopped the ambulance just as it got there. As they loaded the body into the ambulance, or as Tucky called it, "the meat wagon", the sheriff and the deputy began searching the entire area looking for clues. Sheriff Cane said we could help look for clues.

Susie and I searched the creek thinking that something could have fallen from his pants on the way down from the mountaintop. The creek was shallow in this area and we could easily see the bottom and anything that looked like it wouldn't belong there. I did see something that glittered gold. I got down on my hands and knees and looked closer. It was a gold key. I reached into the water and pulled it out. It definitely wasn't real gold because it was rusty with just a glint of the gold finish still on it.

Soon the sheriff called off the search and asked if anyone had found anything. I showed him the key I had found. He examined it and determined that it was nothing, saying, "It looks like it's been in water for quite a while. I don't believe it belonged to the corpse." He handed it back to me. I wasn't sure what I was going to do with the old key, but I stuck in my pocket instead of littering the creek with the metal.

A foreman from the quarry had given the others a ride back to the store. We rode back with Sheriff Cane.

On the way, Rock asked, "Sheriff Cane, do you think the man was murdered?"

"Well, I'm not sure about that. His face could have been bashed in and then left there. He could have fallen by accident and died, or he could have committed suicide. The coroner will be able to tell me if he died from a fall or not. Right now I'm not ruling anything out."

Susie spoke up next, "Timmy and Tucky have some interesting theories." We shot her a look.

"Oh yeah, what are they," Sheriff Cane asked.

"We were just messing around. Nothing serious," I said trying to defuse the conversation.

Susie continued, "There were speculations that he was a member of the Kentucky mafia and had double crossed them and was thrown from the mountain. Also, he had cheated on his wife and she pushed him off the mountain. Maybe he was a horse thief and was killed instead of hung because they only hang them out west. The best one was that he was a member of either the Hatfield's or McCoy's and was killed because of the feud."

"They are all definitely interesting theories," Sheriff Cane said. I could see him snickering from the back seat. "I would bet that if he did die from a fall he either fell accidentally, or it was a suicide."

I asked Sheriff Cane to stop at the rope swing so I could gather up the backpacks we had left there, five minutes later we had arrived back at the store. Everyone was there. All of the families of the kids who had gone on the trip were there. It was nearly six in the evening.

Delma and Thelma were standing on the porch just waiting for me to get near enough for me to hear them. "There's comes the Prince of Death," Delma led out.

"The poor guy probably saw Timmy's face and instantly died," Thelma added.

"Everywhere you go tragedy happens."

"It happens every time."

"He sure is *some* kind of hero," Delma said as I passed them on the porch.

"A fool's hero," Thelma echoed.

I had never considered myself any kind of hero and ignored their insults. Usually that drove them crazier than arguing with them. A man had died and I didn't feel like fooling around with them. It didn't matter to me how he died, he was still a human who was lying there in the creek with his head smashed into the rock.

Mom came over and hugged me when we entered the store. "Are you okay?" she asked.

"I'm fine, Mom," I said knowing this was something all mothers would ask their child. She walked over and also hugged James Ernest, although I don't believe she asked him if he was okay. Sheriff Cane quickly said he needed to go back to town to talk to the coroner. He kissed Mom on the cheek and left.

"Did Hagar know who the man was?" Susie's father, Clayton, asked.

"No. He asked us if we recognized him," I answered.

"It feels kinda strange that he died right across from where I work and no one knew nothin' about it," Mr. Washington said.

"Have you ever seen anyone up on the top of those stone walls?" I asked.

"Never have," Mr. Washington said. "Why do you ask?"

"Just wondering how a person could get up on top of there. Would there be a road from Blaze that goes near there or maybe from Morehead?" I said.

Mr. Washington just shook his head and then said, "I can ask at work if anyone knows."

I turned to Papaw, who was standing behind the store's counter. He said, "I don't have a clue how one would get near there. That's out in the middle of nowhere."

The tall stone walls went on and on down along the creek. I also was baffled. But I knew deep in my heart that the man had fallen from on top. Whether he was pushed, had slipped, had been thrown off, or jumped, I had no idea.

Later in the evening, after everyone had left and darkness was overcoming the store, I was sitting with Papaw on the front store porch. Mom was inside with Janie. James Ernest had went home with the Washington's and said he would be back in the morning.

"So another big escapade," Papaw said.

"I guess so. It was really scary finding a body like that."

"What did the sheriff think happened to the guy?"

"He either didn't know or didn't want to tell us what he thought."

"What do you think?" Papaw asked me.

"I think he came off that mountaintop. No one knows how that happened. But I get a feeling he was pushed or thrown off the top."

"Your gut is usually right." When Papaw said that, it made me feel really good.

Later that evening I was lying in my top bunk wishing James Ernest was in the bottom bunk. I really wanted to talk to him. I was going over everything we had seen at the spot of the death. The only possible clue we had found was the key I had found in the water. I jumped out of bed and removed it from my pants pocket that was lying on the floor. I turned on the lamp my James Ernest pillow and looked at the key more carefully. It still looked the same.

139

As I rubbed it to get some of the rust off I felt something near the middle of the head of the key. I padded into the store trying not to wake Mom or Janie. I looked under the counter and found the three-in-one oil can. I took it back to my room with a rag I had also found and then placed some of the oil on the rag and then rubbed it on the key. Soon I was able to make out that there was a number on the key. I rubbed the other side but there nothing there. I turned it back over and rubbed it some more until I was able to make out the number - **330**.

Did it mean anything?

Chapter 15

Civil War in the Classroom

Friday, September 20. 1963

"Here," I called out after Mr. Burns had said my name during roll call. He continued calling out names as I turned and saw that Sam Hitchcock was again absent. He had missed the entire week. I wanted to go check on him, but Mom and Papaw suggested I stay out of it. Mr. Hitchcock had made it very clear he didn't like people interfering with his family or his way of thinking.

"I'm worried about Sam," I said to Susie as I left home room heading for our next class. Susie had walked into the hallway with me after I motioned for her to follow me. She had Mr. Burns for first period English while I would be entertained by Mrs. Hempshaw, our American History teacher.

"I am too, after what you told me about his father," Susie said.

"But maybe he decided he didn't want to fight his father on coming to high school and dropped out."

"Let's hope not. Maybe you should talk to one of the teachers or the principal," Susie suggested. She was right. I would think about who to talk to while I was in my next class.

"See you later," I said as I hurried to History. On my way up the crowded stairwell to class someone punched me in the arm on their way down. I turned to see who it was and saw Purty grinning back. He waved and stumbled and almost took out the entire group of kids in front of him. I heard them yelling at him as I topped the stairs and turned toward room 212.

Raven was already seated at her desk in the back of the room. I felt sorry for her. Because her last name, Washington, started with a w she found herself seated in the back of many of the classes. It had to make her feel she was there because of the color of her skin. I hoped she didn't think that.

I took my seat as the bell was ringing.

Mrs. Hempshaw stood and moved to the center of room in front of her desk and said, "In 1861 a war began in this country that lasted 4 years and left around 650,000 dead. Who can tell me what war this was?'

Hands shot up all across the room. "Johnny."

Johnny, who was seated in the first row, answered, "World War 1." He seemed very proud of himself, which was silly, because he was only 50 years or so wrong.

"That, I assume, was a wild guess, Johnny,"

"Yes, Ma'am," Johnny replied.

"Does anyone else have a wild guess?" Mrs. Hempshaw asked the class.

"Raven Washington. Would you like to tell the class?"

"Yes'm, I believe it was the Civil War." It was the first time I could remember that Raven had been called upon in a class.

"That is correct. And would you please stand and tell us what the Civil War means to you." Mrs. Hempshaw continued. The whole class turned their heads toward the back of the room to hear Raven's answer.

Raven stood and hesitated before answering, as though thinking about her answer. She then said, "It meant that people cared about the way blacks were treated as slaves. It was hope for freedom for my ancestors. Speaking for myself, it's hard to believe so many men died for us."

"Thank you, Raven. That was very well said. More men died in the Civil War than all our other wars put together. Seven southern states declared their secession from the U.S. to form the Confederate States of America. The Confederacy grew to eleven states. This is probably the most important era of American History and is what we are going to be studying for the next few weeks. Would anyone else like to state their opinion on the Civil War?"

Bobby Watson, who had flunked the class the year before and who sat in the back row with Raven, raised his hand.

"Yes, Bobby."

Bobby stood up and said, "I think the war was stupid. My dad said that the reason the nig…, uh, the blacks were brought here was to be slaves and men shouldn't have died freeing them. I agree with my dad."

I saw Raven shoot darts at Bobby with her eyes. Other kids were agreeing with Bobby. One girl named Sandy yelled out, "You and your dad are stupid."

Bobby yelled back, "No one calls me and my family stupid," and he started to march forward through the desks toward the girl. Mrs. Hempshaw waddled hurriedly down the aisle trying to intercept the beginning of another Civil War right there in our classroom. Most of the kids were screaming at the opposite side. Some were on their feet pointing fingers. I sat there wondering how many would die in this war.

As Bobby was making his way toward the girl, Lenny Muncie stood and punched Bobby in the nose. Bobby stopped and held his nose with his two hands and blood began running through his hands and dripping onto the floor and the students nearby. They began screaming and moving out of the way which caused extreme panic. A few of the boys began pushing each other. Mrs. Hempshaw was moving around the room in extreme terror trying to stop all the bedlam.

Mr. Castle, whose science room was just down the hall, burst into the classroom and climbed onto the desk and yelled out, "Stop it. Right now! Stop!"

It worked, because the fighting suddenly came to a halt. Everyone turned to see who was yelling. At that moment our principal, Mr. Davis, ran into the room. Everyone quickly returned to their seats. I was already in my seat because I had never left it. I had been watching out for Raven. I was going to run to her if I saw anyone going for her. No one had. Their arguments were with each other.

"What's going on in here?" Mr. Davis nearly screamed at Mrs. Hempshaw.

"We were recreating the reasons the Civil War had been fought. We had differing opinions on the matter of slavery. I believe everyone now sees how the war began and the reason for it," Mrs. Hempshaw said the best she could while almost out of breath.

"And that's why we have a boy with a bloodied face and blood on the floor?" Mr. Davis asked.

"A lot of blood was shed in the fighting of the war. Men believed one way and other men believed another and they went to war to fight for what they believed in," Mrs. Hempshaw explained.

Mr. Davis just stood there and shook his head and then said, "I expect to see a list of names of the students on my desk by lunchtime. They will be given detention and possibly be expelled. Do you understand?" He stared at Mrs. Hempshaw.

She stared back and said, "Yes, Principal Davis."

As he was heading to the door with Mr. Castle he stopped and turned around and said. "I don't want to hear another outburst ever in this class or we'll see about finding a new teacher or students." He stormed out of the class and I could swear I saw steam coming from his head.

The class all watched Mrs. Hempshaw to see what she would do next. "We can have different opinions and ideas without the name calling and fighting. This is probably what happened in 1861 and it led to war. Kentucky was on the border of the Confederacy and the Union. Families were split on the war. Even brothers fought for different sides. Now, I believe some of you owe others an apology. Bobby, I'm sorry you got a busted nose, but I believe Lenny was just trying to protect Sandra. I will not give our principal a list of names as long as nothing else occurs out of this misunderstanding."

She came closer to our desks and said, "My teaching method is, I guess you could say, a bit unorthodox, or different than others. I believe I might be at fault for starting this."

Bobby Watson stood as soon as she stopped talking and said, "I apologize, Mrs. Hempshaw. I don't want you to get in trouble. You're my favorite teacher. I'll take the detention." A lot of the other students nodded in agreement.

"I appreciate that, Bobby, and everyone else." I thought she was going to cry. "Uh, class, I would like for you to begin reading Chapter 4 in your class text book for the rest of our time together. Your homework is reading the entire chapter before Monday. We will have a quiz."

Mrs. Hempshaw then went to her desk and she started writing something on a pad of paper. I figured it was to Principal Davis.

When the bell rung Raven and I headed for Math class with Mr. Holbrook. I wanted to hurry because I wanted to talk to him before class started. "That was something," Raven said as we headed back down the stairs to Room 114. I saw James Ernest and Randy on the way down. I waved through the crowd.

Mr. Holbrook was standing outside his classroom when we walked up. Raven continued inside and I asked, "Could I talk to you for a minute, Mr. Holbrook."

"Of course, Timmy. How can I help you?"

It was very noisy in the hallway and I asked if we could go somewhere quiet. We went down to the hall and found an empty room and went inside.

"Do you know Sam Hitchcock? I think he's in your fourth period class, after lunch."

"Yes. I know who he is. He's been absent all week."

"That's what I wanted to talk to you about. I'm worried about him and didn't know who to talk to, so I came to you."

"Why are you worried, Timmy?"

I explained to Mr. Holbrook Sam's situation at home with his father not wanting him to come to school, and how he talked down to Sam. "Mom and Papaw think we should stay out of it because Sam's dad made it very clear to stay out of it. I want to help him, but I don't have any ideas as to how to do that," I explained.

"I'm sure the truant officer will be checking on him soon. If his father doesn't send him to school there's not much the school can do about it. Kids drop out of school all the time at this age. It really is a shame," Mr. Holbrook said.

"But he wants to come to school. He told me that. Is it okay for a parent to stop a kid from coming to school? That doesn't seem right," I said.

"I agree. But sometimes it's out of our control."

"I saw a big bruise on his arm last Friday and asked him about it."

"What did he say?

"I forget. He said something about falling down or running into something. But I think his father might be beating him to stop him from coming to school," I told him.

"Let me talk to Principal Davis and see what he can do. Why did you come to me?"

"I like you and trust you, and I thought you would do something."

Mr. Holbrook put his hand on my shoulder and said, "I wish there was more I could do, Timmy. I will talk to Mr. Davis this afternoon. Let's get to class, before we get detention." He laughed, and the bell rung and we were already late. When we entered the room together the other kids in the class watched me as I took my seat."

The rest of the day was pretty boring. The afternoon seemed so long. Gym class helped with the boredom. We went outside and ran around the track, and then we were timed in the hundred yard dash. I didn't understand why we were timed. Mr. Paxton did say we would be timed again at the end of the school year to see how much faster we were. I figured I could have run faster if we hadn't run around the track first. I was tired by then.

Chapter 16

Sadie and an Old Cat

Tuesday, June 25, 1963

Mom let us sleep in. I guess she thought we needed it after the trauma we had endured the day before. At least she thought we had endured trauma. I was actually getting used to seeing dead bodies. They seemed to pop up around me all the time.

After looking down over the side of my top bunk I noticed that no one was in the bottom bunk. I had forgotten that James Ernest had spent the night at the Washington house. I then heard his voice coming from the store. He was talking to Uncle Morton. I hopped out of bed and quickly dressed. I loved Uncle Morton and knew he would be asking about the body.

When I walked into the store Uncle Morton said to me, "James Ernest was just filling me in on the body."

"Do you know who he was?" I asked him.

"What do you mean? I didn't see him," said my blind Uncle Morton.

"You always know who people are without seeing them. You knew who I was when I just walked into the room. I thought you could probably tell us who the dead man was without seeing him."

"Very funny. I can tell who most people are by the sound of their walk. Since I didn't get to hear him walk or talk I guess I know less than you do. Do you two have a clue as to who he was?"

"Not really," James Ernest answered.

"I might have a clue," I said, hesitating.

"Tell us," Uncle Morton said.

"We were helping the sheriff search the area for clues and I found an old rusty key in the water close to where the body fell. I showed it to Sheriff Cane, but he didn't think it was anything important since it was so rusty, so he handed it back to me. He figured it had been in the creek for a long time. I kept it."

"Why do you think it might be important?" Uncle Morton asked.

"Well, who's to say the key wasn't already rusty when it fell from the man's pocket as he fell from the mountain. It was only a few feet from the body and last night I discovered a number on it."

"What kind of number?" James Ernest asked. I had gotten his interest.

"I was looking at it last night and I decided to try and clean it up some. I was rubbing off the rust when I felt something, so I went and got the three-in-one oil and a rag and rubbed the oil on it. I then could make out a number. It was 3 3 0."

"Can I see it?" James Ernest asked.

"I'd like to see it also."

"I'm sure you would," I said to my blind uncle. He laughed.

I turned and went back into my bedroom and found the key where I had left it, and quickly returned. James Ernest looked at it first.

He described it to Uncle Morton, "It's a gold color with a rounded head. The rust is mostly on the head, with a little rust around the edges of the key. I can faintly see a number where the most rust is." He then handed the key to Uncle Morton.

He took the key in his hands and rubbed the outline of the key and then felt the spot where the numbers were. He then held it in his palm and moved his hand up and down a few times. "Well, we know it's not real gold. Gold doesn't rust and it's a lot lighter than gold. You are right about the number. What do you think it might go to?" he asked.

"How do you know I'm right about the number?" I asked.

"I read braille. It's pretty much the same thing," he explained.

"I don't know. Maybe a safety deposit box at the bank," I ventured a guess.

"A good guess. I've never seen one. Never had anything of such value I needed one. It would be easy to find out. Take it into town and ask Mr. Harney, the banker," Uncle Morton suggested.

"It could be to a post office box," James Ernest said. "They have numbers."

"We could check there at the same time." I said.

"What else could it be to?" Uncle Morton said.

"What about a hotel room? Room keys have numbers on them," I said.

"The three would mean it would be on the third floor. We would have to go to Lexington to find a hotel with a third floor," James Ernest reasoned.

"You're right," Uncle Morton said. He then added, "There are some storage units popping up around these parts. It could be a key to a storage unit. They would have numbers."

The three of us stood there thinking about the different possibilities when a car pulled up to the gas pump. "The key could be just an old key that's been lying in the creek for years like the sheriff said." I said this and then left them standing there while I went out to pump gas for Robert Easterling, my cousin.

"Fill her up. I hear you're playing with dead bodies again," Robert said.

"I wasn't exactly playing with it. He was in no shape to play anything except possum," I said. Coty must have heard my voice from the back yard. He appeared by my side. I reached down to pet him.

"Nobody knew who he was?"

"Nope."

"There's always the possibility that the Wolf Pack killed him. He dropped dead when he saw all the ugliness."

"And he could have been so upset that he wasn't this good-looking that he jumped off the top of the cliff and committed suicide," I countered.

"I don't believe that's it," Robert joked.

I finished pumping and Robert followed me into the store and handed James Ernest the money for the gas. James Ernest gave him his change. "Good morning, Morton."

"Good morning, Robert."

"It's amazing how these boys can always find trouble, isn't it?" Robert said.

"It is amazing how they come across it. Probably because they're more active than any of us old fogies," Uncle Morton said. Robert chatted for a while and got all the details of the body we could give him.

"I gotta go. Oh, hey, you didn't clean my windshields," Robert said as he opened the front screen door on his way out.

"Clean them yourself. I would have been happy to until you called me ugly," I said.

"A person can't take a joke any longer. What's the world coming to when a person can't take a joke?" Robert mumbled to himself as he walked to his car.

"Are you fishing today? I thought I saw your pole leaning against the front porch," I asked.

"Yes. I'm going to catch that big one that got away if it's the last thing I ever do," Uncle Morton declared.

"I'll walk you up there. You need bait?" I asked.

"Give me a dozen nightcrawlers and a box of chicken livers," he said.

I went to the old refrigerator on the back porch and got the bait. I said good morning to Mom on the way through the kitchen. On the way back she said, "I heard you talking to Uncle Morton. Do you guys want me to fix breakfast?" she asked.

"I don't think Uncle Morton wants any. He's on his way to the lake, but I'd like some," I said excitedly.

"In that case you and James can grab some cereal. You and James Ernest need to watch the store this morning. I'm going to West Liberty and Morehead with Rebecca this morning. We need water from the spring, and the grass needs mowing."

I dejectedly left the kitchen and went back into the store. I told James Ernest what Mom had said. "I'll go to the lake with Uncle Morton and clean up the lake while I'm there if you'll watch the store."

"That's fine. I'll go get the water after you get back," James Ernest said. We had to walk about a quarter mile up the road toward the quarry to a spring to get fresh water. It was almost a daily chore. I followed Uncle Morton out the door and got him settled on a bench in the same spot he had hooked the big one earlier.

"Good luck, Uncle Morton." I then walked on around the lake going counter clockwise picking up any garbage I came across. There was quite a bit to pick up from the weekend since we didn't get a chance to do it the day before.

When I returned from the lake I saw Clayton's truck in the parking lot. Susie was standing in the store with Mom, her dad, and

James Ernest. Susie had on an old tee shirt and cut off bibbed overalls. She still looked as pretty as ever.

We chatted for a few minutes. Clayton picked up a few items to buy that Monie needed. Janie came into the store and said, "I'm ready."

"What are you ready for?" I asked.

"I'm spending the day with Delma and Thelma."

"You poor child. What is Mom doing to you? What did you do to deserve such a horrible punishment?" I said.

"Did Betty hear you cussing a blue streak?" Clayton teased.

"I don't cuss a blue streak. I wanted to go play with them. They're my friends," she said.

"I can go out in the parking lot and find a couple of rocks to play with. They would be better than the twins."

"Very funny. You're as weird as they say you are," Janie cut me.

Everyone laughed. Clayton finished paying for the items and said, "Well, I guess we'll mosey on back to the farm if you're ready young lady." Janie had her favorite doll in her arms.

"Why don't you spend the day here at the store with us?" I asked Susie.

"I can't. I'm helping Dad with some farm work today. That's why I'm dressed like this."

"I guess I'm stuck here alone with James Ernest then," I said.

Mom followed Clayton out the door and we were left alone. James Ernest told me he was heading to the spring for the water. I saw him grab two buckets and walk up the road with Coty by his side.

During the morning many people came into the store or pulled up at the pump for gas. The conversation always ended up talking around the body we had found the day before. Randy, Todd, and Sadie came to the store with their mother, Loraine. I know Loraine talked for a good ten minutes without stopping. She covered every topic she could think of during those ten minutes. She talked about the body, the Bear Troop, poor Francis having to endure finding the body, the weather, the farm, Mom and Miss Rebecca going to town, the church, how she thought she might need glasses, their chickens, her husband, the Key family, needing Sugar to bake, various other random thoughts, and her headache.

I then had a headache, a terrible headache.

Sadie offered to stay with me at the store to keep me company. I didn't know quite what to say. I tried my best to think of a reason she couldn't, but the headache her mom had given me kept me from thinking.

Sadie quickly asked, "Is it okay if I stay here for a while, Mom? I'll walk home later."

"Of course you can. I'm sure Timmy would love to have some company. I'd better get on home. I have so much to do. I couldn't possibly tell you what all I have to do. I have washing, dishes, sweeping the floors, dusting, make some cookies, shake the rugs, fix lunch, get ready for supper, take a nap if I have the time and I'd like to finish that awful book I'm reading. It is just horrible, but I hate to start a book and not finish it, just like I hate to start telling someone something and not finish it."

I couldn't wait for her to finish. Please quit talking and go home, I thought. My headache was getting worse with each syllable. What was I getting into? Sadie was spending time with me alone at the store. Susie would be furious if you knew. Hopefully, James Ernest would be back soon. Sadie was a really pretty girl and much more advanced in her desires. She knew what she wanted and did everything she could to get what she wanted. She wanted fame and fortune. She wanted certain boyfriends. At one time it was me. Then it was James Ernest. She had French kissed James Ernest and he told me about how she had stuck her tongue in his mouth like a frog.

The biggest problem with Sadie was her personality. She treated people bad unless she wanted something from them, and almost all the other girls disliked her. Her only real friend that we knew of was Bernice, the skunk.

Loraine finally left. I moved to behind the counter and Sadie came over and leaned over the counter and smiled at me. She had on a low cut top. I tried not to look, but I would sneak a peek. I think she was doing it on purpose.

"What do you want to talk about?" she asked.

"I don't know. You were the one that wanted to stay."

"Purty told me that you don't know anything about sex."

What! Did Sadie want to stay at the store to teach me about sex? Yes, I wanted to know more about sex. What James Ernest

157

told me left me more confused than I was beforehand. As much as I wanted to hear what she had to tell me I knew this was wrong. It felt wrong. I'm sure it had to be wrong. I thought, how would I tell Susie that Sadie taught me about sex. I knew that wouldn't be a good conversation. I had learned a few things in my short life.

"I know plenty," I told her.

"Oh yeah, tell me what you know."

I wanted to tell her about the nightcrawlers. I wanted to tell her I knew nothing and please tell me. I wanted her to leave. I wanted her to explain it. I needed for her to leave. My head and heart and stupid self were battling each other.

"I know that a man and woman have to have sex to have a baby." I thought that should put an end to this misery. I was wrong.

"And how do they do that?"

"How do they do what?" I said.

"How do a man and woman have sex?"

"Just like nightcrawlers," I declared just as I heard a large truck pull up to the gas pump. Thank God I could leave for a while. I heard Sadie laughing as I jumped off the porch and headed for the pump. I saw Mud McCobb climbing down from the big dump truck that he drove for the quarry. We were getting a lot of gas business from the truckers since Papaw put in the pump.

"Fill her up, Timmy," Mud told me. I noticed that Sadie had come out onto the porch and taken a seat in one of the rocking chairs. Mud had turned his head toward the porch when he heard the screen door shut.

158

"You and Susie on the outs," Mud asked.

"No."

"Then why are you keeping time with her?"

"I'm not keeping time with her. Her mother wanted to get rid of her and pawned her off on me here at the store. Now I have to put with her nonsense. Besides, what do you care? Do you have your eyes on her?"

"No. No. No. I'm happily married," said the middle aged man. I figured Mud had to be getting close to fifty if he hadn't already gotten there.

"Well, I happily have Susie as my girlfriend."

"Touchy. Touchy," Mud exclaimed.

"I don't want her here, and I don't know how to get rid of her. Any ideas?" I asked.

The gas pump continued to pump. It was already up to nearly six dollars. It sure took a lot of diesel fuel to fill one of the dump trucks.

"You could shoot her with that rock salt filled cutoff shotgun you have behind the counter. You're good at that."

"Hopefully it won't come to that, but it's not that bad an idea." At one time I did have to shoot a robber who was trying to hold up the store. The guys bring it up to me all the time now. The tank finally was filled and Mud followed me into the store. James Ernest entered from the back at the same time. Sadie also followed us.

"Put the gas on the quarry tab," Mud said and then proceeded to get a grape soda from the metal pop tank and a moon pie cake.

"How are you, James Ernest?" Sadie asked.

"I'm fine. What are you doing here?"

"I'm spending some time with Timmy. I was teaching him about sex. He seems to think it has something to do with nightcrawlers."

Mud stood there with his mouth open. He then said, "Sounds pretty kinky to me," before hurrying for the door.

There was an awkward silence after Mud left. James Ernest looked at me and then he looked at Sadie.

"If you'll watch the store I'll go out and mow the grass," I said. I left before James Ernest could object to my plan. I literally ran out the front door. I didn't really enjoy pushing the old push reel mower, but it was a lot more fun than the torture I was going through with Sadie. I took my time and even pulled some weeds along the side of the house, the shed, and the outhouse. I then decided to straighten up the shed.

As I was beginning to unload the shed I heard James Ernest say from the back porch, "You're safe now. Sadie went home."

I quickly threw the stuff back into the shed and went to the back porch and washed my hands. As I was walking through the living room toward the store I yelled out, "How did you get rid of her?"

I entered the store and there stood Sadie next to the counter. I closed my eyes and scratched the top of my head. "How did you get rid of that cat that had been hanging around, James Ernest?" I thought it was pretty fast thinking. I was about to pat myself on my back when Sadie burst into a tirade.

"I stay to keep you company and you run away from me and then you're so happy that James Ernest got rid of me. How dare you!"

"I didn't mean you." I knew as I was saying it that I wouldn't even have believed it, but I stuck with it. "We had an old cat that had been hanging around on the back porch. Coty hated that thing. Maybe Coty got rid of her."

Sadie just stared at me. She then walked over to me as I inched backward. She poked her finger into my chest and said, "I offered to teach you a few things. Apparently others have done a pitiful job of it if you believe it is anything like nightcrawlers, or whatever. You are a terrible, terrible friend."

She turned and grabbed an orange soda from the case and left out the screen door.

"That went well," James Ernest said and smiled.

"I never knew me and her were friends. And you told me she had left."

"She came back to get an orange soda, I guess," James Ernest said with the grin still spread across his face. "So, she wanted to teach you about the birds and the bees."

"I guess so. Apparently she wasn't too fond of the worms and the nightcrawlers."

"It was nice of her to offer," James Ernest said as Tucky and Rock entered the store.

"Hi guys. Any word on the dead guy," Tucky greeted us. "He was deader than a rabbit smashed by a dump truck."

"You have a way with words," James Ernest said.

"Thank you," Tucky said.

"We haven't heard anything yet," I answered.

"We saw Sadie storming up the road to her lane. What was she mad about?" Rock asked.

"She looked madder than an old wet hen, madder than an old wasp getting sprayed by water, madder than hog without slop, madder than chicken with his head cut off. Stop me whenever you want. I could go on forever," Tucky said. It was the most words I had ever heard him say at once.

"I guess we could assume she was mad. She wanted to teach Timmy a few things but he wasn't to obliging," James Ernest explained.

"Do you have to tell everyone everything you know?" I said.

"I do when it's hilarious," James Ernest told me.

"That was pretty forward of her," Rock stated.

"Please don't say anything to Susie about it. I did everything I could to get rid of her."

"We won't tell her if you - teach us everything you know about sex," Tucky said grinning.

"It won't take long. Watch nightcrawlers," I said.

Chapter 17

The Chair

Thursday, June 27, 1963

I awoke and James Ernest was gone again. He had gone to bed early the night before and I knew that when he went to bed early he was usually planning to do one of his night hikes through the woods. He had told me he was planning to spend the day at the Washington's farm. He had planted another garden there this past spring and he took good care of it. He also said he was going to do some farm work for Mr. Washington.

He asked me to bring Susie and meet him and Raven around six that evening. I wasn't sure what he had planned. I spent the day doing my chores and helping in the store and pumping gas. I told Mom that I needed to go the meet James Ernest later and she said it would be fine.

Mamaw and Papaw came to the store around five and brought fried chicken, mashed potatoes and white creamed corn. The meal was delicious. Then she surprised me with cherry dumplings, my favorite. I needed a nap after the meal. Papaw said he would be happy to take Susie and me to the Washington's. We picked Susie up and soon we were there. Papaw got out and visited with the family for a while.

The four of us walked down the lane toward the main road. I knew we all were wondering where we were going. I finally asked, "Where are you taking us?"

"I thought we should go visit John and Pricilla. They're probably lonely, and I would like to see their pottery and paintings," he explained.

We all thought it was a good idea. I had wanted to do the same thing since I met them. As we walked James Ernest began, "I went for a long walk last night. I made my way up to Blaze and found a road called Callahan Road. You think it might have been named after your dad's family?"

I shrugged my shoulders and said, "I have no idea."

"It runs from Blaze back toward the quarry and then it just stops. It's all rutted out and would be hard to drive on."

"It does sound like it could have been named after Dad's family," I said, only half joking.

"I followed it to its end and then continued through the woods to the top of the cliff overlooking Licking Creek."

"So there is a way to get to the spot we think he fell from," Susie said.

"Could you see anything?" Raven asked as we walked down the road.

"Not too much in the dark."

"We need to go check it out in the daylight," I said excitedly.

"I thought maybe we could go on Sunday afternoon if we all can get away," James Ernest said. We all nodded in agreement.

"Should we see if the other members of the Wolf Pack and Bear Troop want to go?" Susie asked.

"I think it should just be us four. A lot of people trampling around could mess up any clues we might find," James Ernest said. We quickly agreed.

"That was a long walk," I said.

"I left the house around midnight. It took some time."

I marveled at how James Ernest could spend the night walking the different animal trials and make friends with animals. I felt as though I would be scared to death of everything if I was alone in the woods at night. He loved it. He was a strange and wonderful person.

We talked about a lot of different topics as we walked. After thirty minutes we arrived at the lane to their house. We saw smoke rising from somewhere near the house. I was worried that maybe the house was on fire. But then we saw John outside and he didn't seem to be panicking. As we near the house he turned and saw us coming and waved.

"What brings you around here?" John asked us.

"We wanted to come say hello and see how you're doing and I would love to see some of your and Pricilla's work," James Ernest said. We all nodded in agreement.

"It's nice of you guys to stop by. Come on, I'll give you the tour."

"What's the smoke from? I was worried the house was on fire," I said.

"The smoke is coming from the kiln. That's where I have to fire the pottery. It hardens the clay and brings out the colors of the piece. I have five pieces in there right now."

It looked like he had built a kiln out of bricks. It had a narrow passageway leading to a dome looking housing that held the pottery pieces. He said he had to maintain a steady fire for nearly four hours and had to control the temperature the best he could or the pieces would overheat and be ruined. It looked like quite a hard process.

"I've been shaping the pottery in the barn. I've got a stall all set up for me to do the work. It's been pretty good."

Pricilla walked out onto the back porch as John was telling us about his work. She motioned for the girls to come inside.

Susie told me later that Pricilla showed them some of her paintings. Susie said they were bad, something a six-year-old might have done. She said Pricilla called it folk art. She said they ended up in the living room and they had a flowered couch and a nice padded chair.

"Let's sit for a spell and talk," Pricilla said as she pointed to the couch. When Susie and Raven started to sit on the couch Pricilla said, "Raven, I think you might be more comfortable sitting in this chair."

"This is fine, Pricilla. You needn't to go to any bother for me. Take care of yourself and that baby."

Susie said Pricilla went to the old worn kitchen table and picked out the worst looking chair she had and dragged it into the living room. She said it had a cane bottom that had the cane ripping out of it. One of its legs was definitely longer than the other three and the back of the chair was split.

"I would rather you sit here. It might be more what you're used to," Pricilla said with a devilish smile.

Susie said she abruptly stood up from the couch and told Pricilla, "I think our time here is over. Thank you for showing us your childish paintings, but I will not sit by and have you insult Raven like you just did. I don't know why you think you're so much better than anyone else."

"Well, I didn't mean to insult Raven. I just thought the couch seats might be too comfortable for her. It's not like I'm a bigot or something," Pricilla tried to explain.

As James Ernest and I were entering the house with John I heard Pricilla say. "I've never had a colored person in my house before. I didn't know how I should treat her."

"You treat her like you would want to be treated. She's just like you only a lot kinder and not two-faced," Susie said and then stormed by us and out the door.

We quickly turned and followed her lead. I heard John say loudly, "What did you do, Pricilla?"

Within twenty seconds we were out of their yard and halfway down the lane toward the main road. It was hard keeping up with Susie. We then heard John yelling and saw him running toward us. He stopped short of us and tried to catch his breath. He then said, "Raven, I am so sorry that Pricilla treated you that way. She grew up in a very fine home and her parents were very snobbish and prejudice, and not just with blacks, but anyone who wasn't in their so-called social standing. This isn't my way of making an excuse for Pricilla's actions but to explain why it happened. I truly apologize and hope someday you will forgive her. She's not all bad and I believe she will change over time. I'm hoping that church will be the start of it."

"I understand. I hope Jesus can change her. Thank you for apologizing," Raven said.

"I'm sorry guys. I was so much enjoying your visit. You were the first visitors we've had," John said.

"We'll see you later," James Ernest said. We turned away and continued our walk home. Susie told us what had happened.

"That's awful. She seemed so nice at the store. I think we may have found a friend for Sadie," I said. I then realized I should not have brought up Sadie's name. I sure was hoping James Ernest wouldn't mention her visit. I looked at him and he smiled, knowing what I was thinking.

James Ernest reached for Raven's hand and held it and said, "I'm sorry that happened to you. That was awful."

"I had forgotten how that felt. Everyone has been so nice to me and I've been treated like I was one of you. I used to be treated bad like that all the time. I'll be fine. Hopefully God can change her heart."

"You are one of us," I said.

"I wanted to change her heart right then. From inside her body to my right hand," Susie said angrily. We all looked at Susie and then at each other. Raven couldn't help but laugh at her hurt friend. We all ended up laughing at her statement.

It was nearly sundown by the time we got to the Washington's farm. Raven asked us not to mention what had happened to her parents. We agreed not to. Mr. Washington offered to drive us home.

"So how was your visit to see John and Pricilla?" Henry asked us as he drove us home.

"John makes some really nice pottery. He built his own kiln. He's very talented," James Ernest answered. Susie and I remained quiet.

Mr. Washington paused and then asked, "Did something happen while you were there?"

We all remained silent, not wanting to lie to Mr. Washington. He decided to drop the questioning. I'm sure he figured out something did happen, but not quite what.

Later that evening, after grabbing bologna sandwiches and drinks, James Ernest and I were sitting on the front porch listening to the crickets and tree frogs sing. It was late and I was tired, almost falling asleep in the rocker. Coty was lying by my feet.

James Ernest got my attention when he said, "I think we should go up on top of the cliff and see if we can tell where the guy fell from. Maybe look for clues."

"Should we tell Sheriff Cane?" I asked.

169

"No need to unless we find something."

"When?" I was excited.

"We had talked about going Sunday after church."

"That wouldn't give us a lot of time, would it? It's a long walk up to Blaze and back."

"Maybe we could get someone to give us a ride up there. We could say we're taking a small Wolf Pack hike."

"Are we going to ask the entire pack to go?"

"Anyone who wants to."

"Sounds like a plan," I said.

"I'm ready for bed," he suggested.

"Sounds like an even better plan," I said.

Chapter 18

The Fight in the Bleachers

Friday, September 20, 1963

The Morgan County high school football team had a home game that Friday evening and James Ernest and I decided to go to the game and watch Randy play. He was doing real well this season. He played tight end and had caught two touchdowns so far this season. He also played on the defensive line. Susie, Raven and Junior were going with us. Papaw agreed to take us and was going to stay and watch the game.

I asked Susie to go with me and James Ernest invited Raven to go. Junior had never seen a football game and asked if he could go with us. Of course, we said yes. Almost immediately as we unloaded from the pickup a group of people began throwing around racial slurs. We were out of the safety of Oak Hills or the inside of a school building. Most of the slurs came from people who didn't know Raven and Junior.

They just saw colored people and their prejudice came flowing from their mouths. Seldom did Mr. Washington take the kids outside of the community where we lived because he didn't want them facing the abuse he had faced most of his life. We tried to find a spot in the stands where we wouldn't be so noticeable. Papaw sat nearby with a couple of men he knew. Junior sat in awe of the game as he watched the runners and the quarterbacks throw the ball down the field. We saw Purty and Sadie sitting with their family. They were there watching Randy play.

"I want to do that one day," Junior said with a smile across his face. I knew he would be a terrific football player if given the chance. When we played games he was always the fastest and quickest among all the boys.

A couple minutes later a couple of young men came up the stadium stairs toward us. I knew this would be trouble by the looks on their faces. I saw the young women they had been sitting with watching them and giggling. The men stopped at the end of bleacher row where we were sitting and the largest one said, "I believe you two are breaking the law."

James Ernest looked up at them and said, "What law is that?"

The man answered, "I don't believe I was talking to you. I was talking to the two spooks."

James Ernest started to stand but Raven grabbed his arm. The other young man, I guessed he was around twenty, said, "Coloreds aren't allowed to sit in the bleachers. If you have to be here, you all have to sit in the grass beyond the fences. But it would be better if you just stayed away all together."

At that moment Papaw arrived on the step above the two men. "Is there a problem here?" Papaw asked.

The bigger of the two men turned to face Papaw and said, "Yes there is. I think you'd agree that coloreds aren't allowed in these bleachers. They're reserved for white folks. There's no place here for spooks."

By then, the whole section of people were turned watching the altercation.

"I believe you two are mistaken. They have every right to be here. How about you two idiots should go back to your seats before real trouble starts?"

"Old man, I think you ought to mind your own business and leave."

I saw a smirk come across Papaw's face. I knew the look. Papaw could become angry and combative when someone crossed him. I hadn't seen it often, but this was one of those moments. James Ernest removed Raven's hand from his arm and stood. I followed his lead and stood, ready for the fight. Papaw wouldn't be fighting them alone.

I looked down to see one of Sheriff Cane's deputies hurrying up the steps toward us. The two young men followed my eyes and turned to see the deputy bounding the stairs. The deputy arrived and asked, "What's the problem here?"

The game was continuing on the field and folks were applauding a defensive stance by the Morgan County home team.

"There's no problem here deputy. We were just welcoming the two spooks to the game."

Papaw jumped from the above row and landed on the man and they fell onto the wooden stairs and began rolling down the steps. The deputy was trying to stop them from rolling all the way down the stairs to the field. He managed to stop them after rolling nearly ten rows. The man Papaw had jumped on was screaming as though he had broken his back. By then, the game was halted and the entire fan base was standing watching the deputy, Papaw, and the fellow Papaw had jumped on. James Ernest and I had scurried down the stairs trying to help Papaw.

The deputy was pulling Papaw off the man when we arrived. The young man lay there on the steps holding his head while blood ran down his face. Papaw had scrapes on his arms and a scratch on his forehead. The deputy looked at Papaw and the young man as if he didn't know what to do.

The man looked up from the steps and said, "You're going to be sorry you ever saw me, old man."

The deputy then decided what to do. He told Papaw, "Go back to your seat, Martin. You and your friend can come with me."

The man looked up at him and said, "That crazy old man attacked me. You should be arresting him." Blood was dripping off his chin.

"Get up. Let's go," the deputy told him.

The man finally was able to stand and the deputy led them away. Around fifty percent of the fans applauded as they were taken away. Their female companions weren't sure what to do. They just sat there watching the men as they disappeared from their sight.

The game resumed and the people again took their seats. I noticed Papaw limping as he made his way back up the steps to his seat. Papaw had always been my hero. I loved everything about the man. I didn't think my respect for him could ever rise any higher, but it did that evening.

The Morgan County Blue Devils won the game 28-14. Nothing was said to us as we walked away after the game toward the truck. I was walking beside Papaw and I noticed him still limping. I asked, "Are you okay?"

"I'm fine, Tim," Papaw assured me, even though I wasn't assured.

When Papaw got into the cab Raven walked to the window and said, "Thank you for taking care of us. You're a good man."

Papaw nodded as his eyes began to water. I believed then that one thing a man needed was to know someone appreciated him. I believed a man needed to work, but also a man needed to know they were loved and valued for their hard work to provide.

Papaw dropped James Ernest and I off at the store and then took Raven, Junior and Susie home. By the time we got home Janie was already in bed and Mom was up watching the news.

"How was the game?" Mom asked.

"We won and Randy played well," James Ernest answered.

"Everything went well?" Mom asked. I knew then she knew about the fight, but how? Then I knew that Sheriff Cane had found out about it and called Mom to tell her.

"Papaw is okay. He has a couple of scrapes and a limp, but he's fine," I said.

"What exactly happened?" Mom asked.

James Ernest and I sat down and told her what had happened. Mom nearly jumped from her seat when we told her about papaw rolling down the steps attached to the young man. When we finished with the story she said, "Poor Raven and Junior. Why can't people just let each other be? I'm surprised you two weren't rolling down the steps."

I laughed and said, "Papaw beat us to it."

Mom got up and went for the phone. I knew she was calling Mamaw to make sure Papaw was okay. James Ernest and I headed for bed knowing we would have an early wake up and a busy day when we arose.

Chapter 19

In a Box

Sunday, June 30. 1963

It was Sunday morning and I was anxious to start our trip to Blaze. But first we had to go to church. I sat with Susie during church. She even held my hand during the service. James Ernest sang a solo at the beginning of the service. He was fantastic as usual. The twins, Delma and Thelma were asked to pass the plates for the collection of tithes and offerings. If the twins saw the plate pass by someone without them giving they would stare at them. Some of the people changed their minds and reached for their money so the twins would stop giving them the evil eye. I dropped a dime in the plate so they wouldn't glare at me.

Pastor White preached a sermon about the second coming of Christ. It was interesting and I sat there and wondered how long it would be before He came back again. Was Pastor White talking about next week, next month, next year or a hundred years from now? He didn't know the date and didn't speculate. I assumed it was okay to take the hike that afternoon and we wouldn't miss it.

We decided to invite everyone who had gone on the creek trip which was the Wolf Pack and the Bear Troop. The girls decided not to go. Junior couldn't go because he was helping his dad on the farm. Tucky and Purty were riding back with us after church. Papaw had agreed to drive us up the point where he would drop us off.

Papaw drove us in his pickup to Blaze. He turned onto Callahan Road and followed it as far as he could. We jumped out of the back and waved goodbye as Papaw left us there.

Purty reached into his backpack and pulled out a Milky Way candy bar and began eating it before we had even started walking.

"You hungry?" I asked.

"We didn't have lunch," Purty said.

"We each had a bologna sandwich and a snack cake before we left the store," I said.

"That's no real lunch. That was just a snack," Purty whined.

We each turned and began the walk toward the top of the cliff. James Ernest said it was probably less than a mile to the spot we wanted to search. The forest was sparse with trees but scattered with large rocks and boulders, which we had to walk around. James Ernest seemed to keep his bearings and was leading us. I figured if he could find it in the dark he could definitely find the spot in the daylight.

We heard a caw coming from the top of a tree. I looked up by habit seeing if the bird could possibly be Bo. I had a pet crow for quite a while that would land on my shoulder and follow us wherever we went. A year or so ago he disappeared. We hadn't seen him since. Every time I now heard a crow I would look for it hoping he had returned. Coty stopped his sniffing and also looked toward the sound. I knew Coty missed his friend. At times Coty would let Bo ride on his back – a strange duo.

The crow flew away followed by other crows from nearby trees. Squirrels would scamper up trees as we walked by. Chickadees and wrens flew from limb to limb as though they were interested in what we were doing in their territory. It was a warm day in the mid-eighties, but the top of the mountain and the forest cooled off the heat for us.

Purty was trailing behind us. Suddenly he yelled out, "Wait for me guys. I've gotta poop."

Tucky yelled at him, "You shouldn't eat so dang much."

"Don't leave me behind. I'd never find my way out of here."

We for sure didn't want to be too close to Purty as he was doing his business. I just hoped he didn't wipe with poison oak like he had done on a hike we had taken years earlier. We waited for him to finish. It took a while and we could hear him grunting. It made me a little sick to my stomach. Coty ran away.

After nearly ten minutes he stepped out from behind a huge boulder and said, "That was a good one. I feel a lot better now."

"Sounded like you were giving birth to a ten pound baby," Tucky said.

"It was no baby, but it might have been ten pounds," Purty said proudly.

"Too much information," I said, grimacing.

James Ernest shook his head in disbelief and began walking away. We followed. Purty quickly caught up – much lighter on his feet.

"What are we hoping to find?" Purty asked.

"I think the most we can hope to find is proof that the man fell from up here to the creek," James Ernest said.

"Maybe we'll find a suicide note nailed to a tree," Purty said.

"Possibly, but not too probable," James Ernest said almost laughing.

"Maybe the murderer left a confession note explaining why he pushed the corpse from the mountain," Tucky said laughing.

"That would be neat," Purty said.

"It would sure make this a lot easier," I said.

The route got steeper as we neared the edge of the cliff. "We're getting close. Make sure you keep your eyes open for any clues. Something maybe dropped on the ground, footprints, suicide notes attached to trees, or confessions," James Ernest told us.

We walked slowly around ten feet apart and kept our eyes to the ground. I thought our best chance at any proof was footprints. It had rained some the day before we waded down the creek and I thought if we could find two sets of prints then we had proof the dead man had been up here with someone else who may have pushed him over the ledge. Coty was sniffing the ground as though he too was searching for the man's smell.

We weren't sure if this was the path they would have taken. We weren't even sure the man had been up here at all. We could be on a wild goose chase. After fifteen minutes of going slow James Ernest yelled out, "Up ahead is the ledge."

We looked up to see the opening as though the world just stopped and fell away. Beyond the trees was nothing but blue sky. We were less than a hundred yards from the ledge. I searched harder for footprints as we neared the edge. Soon we were standing near the ledge looking out at the far ridge and the quarry on the other side of the creek. "Is this right over the spot he was laying?" I asked.

James Ernest got down on his hands and knees and crawled to the edge. Tucky was right beside him. Purty and I waited for their report. I could hear the two of them talking, but I couldn't make out what they were saying.

They crawled away from the ledge and then sat up. James Ernest said, "We're close. We need to go fifty yards that way." He pointed downriver. They stood and we all continued the search as we moved along the ledge to the spot the man may have fallen from to his death. It seemed to me that it would be strange for a person or persons to have been this far off the road in this wilderness. How would a man be lured to this spot to be murdered? If it had been suicide, there would have been a lot simpler places to do that.

As we neared the final location I looked all around and saw a small clearing that had some shrubs and wildflowers. I walked toward it as the other three Wolf Pack members crawled to the rim of the cliff. I looked down and there they were - two sets of shoe prints in the bare ground. It looked like they had stepped in the wet dirt. The prints were heading in the direction of my friends. I studied the prints. They were definitely different people making the prints. One set were much bigger than the other. The bigger prints looked to be boot prints while the other may have been sneakers. I followed the prints until the clearing ended and the prints faded away.

My friends eased away from the edge of the cliff and stood. They all agreed that it was the spot. I stayed in the clearing and called out, "I found something."

They all hurried to the spot where I was standing. "Stop there," I ordered.

"What is it?" Purty asked.

"Be careful. I found two sets of prints in this clearing," I told them.

They looked surprised and Purty started to step into the clearing, "Stop, Purty," I yelled.

"What?"

"We don't want to disturb the prints. Come around to this side and ease into here and I'll show you."

They did as I directed and they came to my side. I pointed toward the best prints I had found.

"As you can see, there are two sets of prints. One set is a lot bigger than the other set." I looked each of them in the eyes and then said, "There were definitely two men up here. I believe he was murdered."

"Wow," was all Purty could say.

I went on, "It had rained some the day before we went wading down the creek. That's how there were prints left behind. If there were two men here and one accidently fell off the cliff, the other man would have reported it. Therefore, I believe he was pushed or thrown."

James Ernest got down on his hands and knees and crawled to the prints and studied them. He followed beside them all the way to where they ended. "I agree," was all he said after he stood. A minute later he said, "One set are large boot prints and the other set are sneaker prints."

"The man in the creek had on Converse Chuck Taylor's," I said.

"We need to search the edge for clues as to exactly where he went off the mountain."

"I'm going to look back here in the direction they were walking," I said. The other three headed back to the ledge and continued their search.

Coty was sniffing something ahead of me in the direction I was heading. "What did you find?"

I got to him and saw his nose next to a leather billfold. I bent over and picked it up. I opened it and inside I found a driver's license. There was a picture of the man we had found bashed on the rocks. His name was Thomas Back. It was a Michigan driver's license. I found a nearby stick lying on the ground and stuck it into the dirt where the billfold had been lying. I continued searching the billfold as I walked toward my friends. Coty was walking beside me as though he was saying, "Hey, I found that. It's mine."

I bent over and petted his head and said, "Good boy." He barked.

Inside the billfold were some large bills. It looked to be nine or ten hundreds and some lesser bills. In one of the pockets I found a receipt. I stopped to study it. It appeared to be from a storage unit rental called *Secure Storage*. The address was in Morehead. It was dated June 21st, 1963, three days before we found him lying in the creek.

I made my way on over to the guys. They were discussing something they had found. They turned when they heard me. Purty said, "This is the spot where he was thrown from to his horrible death."

"How do you know?" I asked.

Tucky spoke up, "James Ernest found a limb that was hanging off the edge of the cliff and it looks like all the leaves were pulled off. He thinks the man must have grabbed the limb as he was being thrown off the edge trying to save himself."

"Plus, it looks like there was a scuffle on the ground at that point," James Ernest added.

"The dead man's name was Thomas Back."

"Wait, how do you know that?" Tucky asked.

I lifted the billfold into the air and said, "Coty and I found this not far from the clearing."

"Wow!" Purty said, adding a lot to the conversation.

We found a spot to sit. There was a log and the three of them took seats on it. I sat on the ground with Coty in front of them. I took the driver's license from the wallet and handed it to James Ernest. He studied it and passed it on to Tucky.

Purty then looked at it and said, "It looks like him if his head was half caved in, I guess."

He then asked, "Was there any money in the wallet?"

"Yeah, about a thousand dollars." I held up the money for all of them to see.

"We're rich," Purty announced.

"It's not our money," I said.

"But we found it," he started to argue.

"Actually, I found it. So if it's anyone's, it's mine."

"But we share things," Purty said.

"It's evidence in a murder case. We have to turn it over to Sheriff Cane," James Ernest said.

"But the money doesn't matter," Purty continued.

"We are not keeping the money, Purty. Why would a man have a thousand dollars in his wallet? It's a clue as to why he was killed," I said.

"Can I at least hold it for a minute? I've never held anywhere close to that amount of money."

"Sure," I said as I handed him the money. I watched to make sure he didn't try to get up and make a run for it. He wouldn't get very far anyway, before he ran out of gas and collapsed.

"I doubt if all four of us together have ever held that much money," Tucky said as Purty was rubbing the money on his face and smelling it. No telling how many germs were jumping onto his face and head.

"Someday I want to be rich. I'll be so happy," Purty said.

We all stared at him. We knew there was no reason to remind him that money didn't make a person happy, because at that moment, he was more than joyful.

I wasn't sure if I should tell them about the receipt I had found. James Ernest knew about the key, but none of the other Wolf Pack members knew about it. I decided to keep it to myself until I had a chance to get James Ernest alone. I couldn't help but wonder if the key did go to the storage unit lock and what might be in the unit. Perhaps Uncle Morton was right. He had suggested that the key might be from a lock on a storage unit.

"I think we've found all we wanted to and more than we thought we would. We had better head back home. It's a long walk," James Ernest said.

We got up and began our hike back home. I took the money back from Purty and put the wallet in my back pocket.

"What's the best way back?" Tucky asked.

James Ernest explained, "I think the quickest way would be back to Callahan Road. We can follow it to the end and then we'll be able to go down the hillside to the creek and cross over to the quarry road."

Sounded like a plan since I had no idea how to get back without going the way Papaw had brought us along the road. We all were in a great mood, having thought we had pieced together how Thomas Back was killed. All we had to do was call Sheriff Cane and tell him what we found and lead him back up to the spot.

When we got near to the spot on Callahan Road where Papaw had dropped us off, we saw a vehicle sitting on the road. We were hopeful.

"Maybe someone decided to come back for us so we don't have to walk all the way back," I said.

We were laughing as we stepped out of the woods and onto the road. The two doors of the sedan opened and two men stepped out of the car. The man on the passenger side held a rifle in his hands. The driver of the car was a large man with a full beard and a ball cap covering the top of his head. He must have been six foot two and two hundred and seventy pounds. He had on bibbed overalls and a flannel shirt with the sleeves cut off exposing the long hairs that hung from his pits, matching the gray ones that hung from his chin.

My focus though was on the smaller man with the gun. He had on baggy jeans and an old tee shirt that advertised Martha White flour. He was thin and looked mean. He had beady eyes, a weak chin, and a thin mustache.

They walked to within ten feet of where we stood. I had whispered for Coty to stay. He stood by my side.

James Ernest spoke first, "Not many squirrels in those woods if that's what you're hunting."

"What were you boys doing in there?" the larger man asked.

"We're always looking for good squirrel hunting spots. We thought this would be one with the oak trees, but we were wrong," James Ernest continued the story.

"I only saw two the whole time we were in there, and they were skinnier than a rat in a box," Tucky said.

The man frowned and pointed at me, "I know who you are." He stopped there, not explaining how he knew who I was.

He then pointed toward the woods, "Don't ever come back up here again. We had better not see the sheriff up here either. If I do - he may not return. Do you boys understand?"

"Don't know why we or the sheriff would be up here again. There's no squirrel in there worth shooting," James Ernest said in his innocent voice.

The large man turned and began to walk away. But he turned and looked directly at me and said, "I know where you live and who your momma is. You want to keep her safe, I'd bet. Now get out of here."

The two men returned to their car. We began walking down the rutted overgrown section of the road, no longer navigable by car. The car turned around and headed away from us. James Ernest stopped and headed back to where the car had sat.

"What are you doing?" Purty asked. "They told us to get out of here." I noticed that Purty was shaking, and the front of his pants was wet. I didn't mention it. I thought I was going to wet myself also.

"I want to check the boot prints. See if they match the ones we found," James Ernest said.

It was a great idea. We all bent over and looked at the prints. I said, "They look exactly like the large ones."

"Yeah," James Ernest said. "We figured the prints belonged to a large man. And that guy was a large man."

We turned and walked away.

"How does he know you and your Mom?" Tucky asked.

"I have no idea, unless he's been in the store. I don't remember ever seeing him before," I said.

We walked for around a half mile in silence, all of us probably thinking about what had just happened. It reminded me too much of the Tattoo Man and how he had threatened to hurt Mamaw and Papaw if I said anything about him killing our neighbor 4 years earlier. What would we do now?

I looked over at Tucky and said, breaking the silence, "Skinnier than a rat in a box."

We all laughed and Tucky said, "It's an old saying." We all four laughed again.

We walked another mile before James Ernest led us down a steep hill toward the creek below. The terrain flattened and within a couple of minutes we were standing at the creek. Looking across it we could see the quarry road that we called Morgan Road. The other guys jumped from the bank into the water. I remembered the wallet in my back pocket. I took it out.

"How deep is it?" I asked them. James Ernest stood up and the water was up to his stomach.

"I don't want to get this wallet wet," I explained. James Ernest walked to the bank and reached up for it. I bent over and handed it to him. Just as he took it I lost my balance and fell head first into the water. We waded across the creek and climbed up the bank to the road. James Ernest handed the wallet back to me. I carried it instead of placing it back into my wet pocket.

Purty and Tucky were lagging behind us as we walked toward the store. It gave me a chance to tell James Ernest about the receipt from the storage locker I had found.

"Does it have the storage unit number on it?" he asked me.

"No. I didn't see one."

"What are we going to do about telling Sheriff Cane what we've found?" I asked.

"I'm not sure," he said.

"We have to protect Mom and Janie," I said.

"Yeah, but remember what happened when you kept everything from everyone about the Tattoo Man."

"I nearly died."

"You did. I think we have to tell Sheriff Cane what we've found and trust that he can keep everyone safe. We couldn't trust the old sheriff. By the way, I got the license plate number off that car."

"Good thinking," I said.

"So, Sheriff Cane should be able to find out who the guy is."

"What do we tell Purty and Tucky?"

"We tell them the plan and see what they think. We're still the Wolf Pack. We're in this together."

"You're right."

We got to the turn off where Purty could take the swinging bridge to his house. Before he left we told them what we thought was best. They agreed.

"Do you guys want to be there when we tell Sheriff Cane or do you want us to do it?" James Ernest asked.

"You guys can do it," Tucky said. Purty agreed.

"See you tomorrow, Purty," I yelled as he crossed the bridge.

Tucky continued with us. It wasn't long before we made it to the store. Darkness was upon us as we opened the front screen to the store. Papaw and Mamaw were standing in the store with Mom and Uncle Morton.

"You finally made it back. Did you have fun?" Mom asked.

"We sure did. More fun than a monkey in a box," Tucky said.

Later that evening, I was lying in the top bunk when I said, "We need to tell Sheriff Cane about everything."

"We haven't seen him. I guess we could suggest to Betty that she invites him for supper tomorrow," James Ernest said.

"Do you think we should tell Junior and the Bear Troop what we know?" I asked him.

"Purty and Tucky told us to go ahead. I don't know when we'll have the chance to tell the others. We need to tell Sheriff Cane, the sooner the better."

"I guess you're right."

"We'll have a meeting this weekend and tell them why we had to go ahead and tell Sheriff Cane," James Ernest said. I was okay with that.

Chapter 20

The Protest

Monday, September 23, 1963

The weekend had been busy with working at the store, church, homework, and the many fishermen we had all weekend. As much as I didn't want to go to school, it seemed like a break from all the busyness. Bernice tried to trip me again on the bus, but I was waiting for her to try. I grabbed hold of the top of the two seats and hopped over her outstretched leg. She knew better than to mess with James Ernest.

As I disembarked from the bus I was looking for Sam Hitchcock. He was nowhere in the crowd that I could see. The warning bell sounded and I headed to homeroom with Susie and Raven. The tardy bell sounded just after we had taken our seats. I looked to see that Sam was absent again. I was worried.

The bell rang, ending homeroom, I made my way up to Mr. Burns. I stood in front of his desk waiting to gain his attention. He finally lifted his eyes to see me.

"Yes, how can I help you, Tim?"

"Have you heard anything about Sam?"

"Sam....who?" Mr. Burns asked, as if he had never had a kid in his class named Sam.

"Sam Hitchcock," I answered.

"Oh, yes, Mr. Hitchcock. Why do you ask?"

"I'm worried about him. He's been absent now for over a week."

"I suppose Sam has given up on high school. Nearly every week we have a student, if you can call them that, drop out of school. I suspect that's what has happened to Mr. Hitchcock."

"But I don't think he would drop out of school. He wanted to come. His dad didn't want him to, but he did."

Mr. Burns looked down at his paper and ended the conversation by saying, "Maybe his Dad knew best."

I frowned at Mr. Burns, but he never saw it. He was busying himself with whatever was more important to him. I left and hurried to Mrs. Hempshaw's American History class. The last time we were in her class a fight had broken out and Bobby Watson had gotten a bloodied nose during a discussion of the Civil War.

We all were seated by the time the bell rang. Mrs. Hempshaw was not in the room. No teacher was in the room. We all sat there speculating as to what was going on. After five minutes, Principal Davis walked through the door.

"Turn to the chapter you were assigned to read for today," Mr. Davis said.

A girl in the front row raised her hand. "No questions at this time, please."

This response from Mr. Davis caused fifteen hands to rise in the class. Mr. Davis sighed and then said, "Okay. Okay. Put your

194

hands down. I know you're all wondering where Mrs. Hempshaw is. Because of what happened in here Friday, I had no choice but to suspend her from teaching for the time being." A groan and muttering filled the room.

"I will be filling in today, and a substitute will be here tomorrow," he continued.

Bobby Watson rose from his chair and walked toward the door.

"Sat back down, Bobby," Principal Davis demanded.

Bobby stopped and turned to face Principal Davis and then said, "It's not fair. Mrs. Hempshaw didn't do anything wrong. It was my fault, I started it. I'm leaving until she comes back."

Lenny, the boy who had hit Bobby, quickly stood and said, "I threw the first punch. It was my fault. Mrs. Hempshaw's class is my favorite. I'm leaving too." He joined Bobby by the door.

"You both will be getting a week detention and possibly suspended if you leave this room."

I was torn as to what to do. I liked Mr. Davis. He was fair to me and Sam Hitchcock. But this seemed so unfair to Mrs. Hempshaw. Raven stood up and I knew then that I had to stand also. I stood. Soon, almost the whole class was standing in support.

"You all are in deep trouble," Principal Davis declared.

Bobby and Lenny led the way through the door. The rest of us standing followed them out the door and down the hall to the stairs. We walked down the stairs and down the hallway to the front entrance of the school. We were soon standing in front of the school.

Bobby yelled out, "Mrs. Hempshaw!"

We all followed suit yelling, "Mrs. Hempshaw! Mrs. Hempshaw." Soon, everyone began chanting her name over and over, "Hempshaw! Hempshaw! Hempshaw!"

Kids and teachers were looking out all the front windows of their classrooms, wondering what was going on. I was standing there in front of the school having joined my first protest. I wasn't all too sure how Mom would feel about it, but I thought Papaw would be proud.

When the bell rang, signaling the end of the period, we all stood there wondering what we should do now. Was our display over? Should we go to our next class? Should we stay out there until Mrs. Hempshaw was reinstated? We had begun this revolution, but how far should we take it? We all talked among ourselves.

Bobby then said, "I think we should stay out here at least another period." Some of the students agreed and others didn't.

"Everyone can do what they want. I'm staying out here," Bobby said.

Lenny decided, "I'm staying here with Bobby."

Other students began exiting the building to see what was going on between periods. Word started spreading and more and more of Mrs. Hempshaw's students and former students began joining us in our protest. A few of the original protesters went to their next class but most of us stayed. Our numbers tripled during the next period. By lunchtime, most of the entire student body had joined the protest.

Susie, Rhonda, Rock, Tucky and James Ernest were all standing with us. Of course Purty wouldn't miss the fun, whether he believed in the cause or not. Even Randy came out to protest with us. He told us that Mrs. Hempshaw had always been his favorite teacher. We didn't see Sadie or Bernice or Daniel Sugarman among us. Someone estimated that seventy percent of the school was standing on the front lawn together. It was crowded.

Some of the students were smoking cigarettes. Some of them were enjoying the time outside, unaware of what the protest was even about, just wanting out of the classrooms. But most of the protesters were genuine in the protest. Some of the students walked down to the nearby ice cream shop for cones or milkshakes.

I stood there looking around at all the different students and thought of Sam. I wondered what was happening with him. Was he sick? Was he forced to drop out of school by his dad? Did he decide it was too hard fighting with his dad about continuing in high school and he decided to quit? I wanted to know. I needed to know.

The protest lasted all day. I wasn't sure what would happen the next day. I was glad when the school buses finally arrived and we were on our way home. I took my seat next to Susie and closed my eyes. I could have easily dozed off. Protesting was hard work.

That evening after supper I was sitting on the porch with Papaw, James Ernest, and Uncle Morton. Mom hadn't been too

197

happy about the protest when I told her about it. She seemed more okay with it when James Ernest told her he had joined the protest. Funny, how that worked.

"I hear there was a hullabaloo at the high school today," Uncle Morton said.

"There was," I said.

"Tell us about it," Papaw chimed in.

I went on to explain Mrs. Hempshaw's teaching lesson on the Civil War and how the fight had broken out. I then told them how Mrs. Hempshaw refused to turn in names for detention because she felt it was her fault and that she was then suspended. "Most of the students walked out of class in protest and after that period was over most of the school walked out once they heard about the suspension."

"Everyone loves Mrs. Hempshaw. She's a bit corny but she's the best teacher at the school. It's easy to learn in her class," James Ernest explained.

"Is this all hearsay?" Uncle Morton asked.

"No. I was in the class when the fight broke out and we were the ones that walked out," I said proudly.

"I can see both sides of the story. Mr. Davis felt punishment needed to be handed out due to the fight and since Mrs. Hempshaw refused to turn in the boys' names she had to be the one. But, I also understand you students feeling she was wrongly suspended. You can't just let fights break out in the schools. Kids need to be protected and feel safe at school. What happens next?" Uncle Morton asked.

"Who do you think was in the wrong?" Papaw asked.

"Originally, I'd say Bobby Watson was for charging the girl. He started it all. Between Principal Davis and Mrs. Hempshaw," I hesitated before finishing while I thought about it. "I'd say Principal Davis."

"Why do you think that?" Uncle Morton asked.

"Teachers are in charge of their classrooms, and Principal Davis can't be in every classroom, so he has to trust the teachers to do what's right. In this case, he didn't trust her decision. I think that was wrong."

Papaw, Uncle Morton and James Ernest all nodded their heads in agreement. We sat there in silence for a spell until Papaw asked, "What happens tomorrow if Mrs. Hempshaw is still not in her classroom?"

"The revolution continues!" James Ernest stood and raised his hand toward the ceiling of the porch. I stood and copied his salute. Uncle Morton and Papaw laughed.

"School was never this exciting when we were in school," Uncle Morton declared.

"I guess you have to go past the sixth grade for it to get exciting," Papaw said.

Chapter 21

Miss Hickey & the Diagram

Tuesday, September 24, 1963

I awoke before I had to. I guess the excitement of the day before and not knowing what the new day would bring had me in a tizzy. I climbed from the top bunk and saw that James Ernest was still asleep; at least his eyes were closed. I padded through the house to the back porch and peed off the porch. Coty watched me from his dog house. It was still too early for him to fool with me.

I returned to my bedroom and started getting dressed for school. It was still an hour before the bus would come, but I couldn't sleep. I kept thinking about the protest and Sam Hitchcock. I couldn't help but think something was wrong with Sam. But I had to realize Sam had told me he might drop out of school because it was too hard fighting with his dad about it. Maybe he decided to go ahead and quit.

I heard James Ernest turn over in his bed. He grunted and then said, "Why are you up so early?"

"I couldn't sleep. I'm going to fix some eggs. You want some?" I asked.

"You're going to cook? Have you ever cooked anything? Can you make biscuits?" I left the bedroom.

No, I had never cooked anything before, unless you can count putting bread in the toaster to make toast. I didn't think I could count fixing a peanut butter sandwich as cooking. I made my way into the kitchen and found a skillet and placed it on the stove. I lit the burner and placed the skillet on top. I pulled the eggs from the fridge and cracked four of the eggs and dumped them one at a time into the skillet. Some of an eggshell ended up in the skillet with the eggs. I tried to get it out with my fingers but it kept sliding around, so I left it in. I decided that was one of James Ernest's eggs. I placed two slices of bread in the toaster.

The eggs seemed to be done on one side. I figured I was supposed to turn them over to cook the other side. I looked in the silverware drawer and found a spoon and tried turning them with the spoon. The eggs yolks broke apart but I did get them turned. I wasn't sure how James Ernest liked his eggs. I decided he would get them however they turned out.

While the eggs were cooking I went outside to feed Coty and fill his water dish. He was now awake enough to greet me and get his morning pats. I went back to the kitchen to see that the toast had popped up. I took them out. They were darker than I like. I took the spoon I had gotten out and scraped the brown from the bread.

I then smelled what I thought was something burning. I went to the stove and saw that the eggs were done. I took the spoon and scraped the eggs onto two plates. I put a piece of toast on each of the plates and took them to the table. I headed for the store to get me an RC Cola to drink with my eggs. I stuck my head into the bedroom and told James Ernest, "Breakfast is ready."

James Ernest and I arrived at the table at the same time, along with Mom. I sat down at the table feeling very proud of myself for having made breakfast by myself. James Ernest looked down at his plate before sitting. He hesitated and then said, "I need butter for the toast."

"Good idea. I'll pour you a glass of orange juice," I said.

Mom stood beside the table and asked, "You made breakfast?"

"I woke up early," I said proudly. "I should have made you and Janie some eggs."

Mom looked down at the burnt, torn eggs and said, "That's okay honey, I'll have cereal."

James Ernest returned with the butter and a knife. He picked up his toast and noticed a hole in it where I had scraped the brown a little too hard. He spread some butter on it, but didn't say anything. He picked up his fork and picked at his eggs. He turned them over and saw the dark side of the egg. I couldn't scrape it off.

He tried cutting the eggs with his fork. He then took the butter knife and tried cutting the eggs with his knife. I watched him as I lifted my eggs and placed them on my toast and took a bite. It wasn't the best eggs I had ever eaten, and it was by far the worst. But it was eatable. James Ernest finally got a portion of his eggs cut and put it into his mouth and began chewing. His eyes opened wide and then closed tight. He quickly swallowed it with the help of some orange juice.

"Well?" I asked.

"I've never had black crunchy eggs before. Thanks," he said as he took the plate to the counter. He returned with a bowl of cereal. After eating my meal I asked Mom if she would make me another slice of toast.

"Me too," James Ernest said.

Soon Mom was there with four slices of toast and the blackberry jam. My favorite jam was blackberry with the seeds in it. I buttered two of the toasts and added the jam. James Ernest did the same. Finally, something worth eating, I thought.

The school bus was abuzz with kids talking about the protest and whether we would get to stand around outside the building all day again. I hoped not. I was hoping Mrs. Hempshaw would be back to teach her American History class. When our bus rolled up to the school I saw Principal Davis standing there waiting. The driver swung the door open and Mr. Davis stepped into the bus.

"Mrs. Hempshaw is back in class today. I expect everyone to return to their classes this morning," he announced. With that said he turned and left the bus and headed to the next bus that had arrived behind us. There were some groans from kids on the bus. But there were also some cheers. I was cheering.

In homeroom, Mr. Burns took the roll. But this morning he didn't even call out Sam's name. He skipped him. I wondered if some official word had come that Sam had dropped out of school, or if Mr. Burns just got tired of calling his name only to hear silence.

The bell sounded and Raven and I quickly left heading for American History class. We were anxious to see Mrs. Hempshaw. When we walked into the room other students were standing around her desk talking with her. We got as close as we could. The final bell rang and Mrs. Hempshaw told everyone to take their seats.

When we all were seated she slowly stood and walked to the front of her desk. She stood in front of us and I could see her eyes begin to moist. She turned around and reached for a tissue on her desk and turned back around to face us.

"I wanted to take time to thank you kids. Although, I can't say I agree with you walking out of class and protesting."

"Viva la revolution!" Bobby Watson yelled out from the back. Everyone laughed and began clapping.

"I do want to say I appreciate you caring about me and showing the support you did for me." She began crying. She composed herself and added, "Or maybe you just wanted an excuse to get out of school for the day." We laughed.

Lenny stood up, "We appreciate you and that you had our backs. You're the best teacher we have." We all began clapping again. The waterworks really began then. Not only Mrs. Hempshaw, but many of the girls in class were crying.

A minute later Mrs. Hempshaw said, "Our country was founded on a revolution – the American Revolutionary War. We wanted out from under Great Britain's ruling and we fought for our freedom and the right to form our own country."

We began laughing. It was just like Mrs. Hempshaw to not pass up a teachable moment. Mrs. Hempshaw then smiled and said, "Let's open our books to Chapter 4."

Later after lunch, Rock, Raven and I headed for Health class. Mr. Paxton had us for Gym on Monday, Wednesday, and Friday, but Miss Hickey had us on Tuesday and Thursday for Health. Miss Hickey was the guys' favorite teacher to look at. She was only 22 years old, with long wavy black hair, and a smile and a body that had the boys in her class smitten.

Thus far in class we had only talked about healthy food choices and exercise and what things were bad for our bodies. But today Miss Hickey said, "Today we are going to talk about and study a woman's reproductive system." I sat up in my seat.

Miss Hickey turned on her slide projector and put in the first slide. There in front of me was the body of a naked woman. Although it wasn't a real woman, but a drawing of a woman, it still was a naked woman. It had arrows pointing out certain regions of the body with strange names. Her breasts were called mammary glands. Miss Hickey first said, "Would you boys please stop snickering. Let's be adults here."

A boy from the back of the room called out, "Miss Hickey, why don't you model for us?"

He was quickly sent to the Principal's office. I was sure he would be spending the end of the rest of the week in detention, maybe the rest of the school year.

"Are there any other smart comments?" Miss Hickey asked. We all fell silent.

For the rest of the period we stared at the diagram in front of us as she threw out terms such as ovaries, uterus, vulva, fallopian tubes and other parts I won't mention. She talked about how the mammary glands were milk ducts. I had never liked milk. I could use it on my cereal, but I never drank it. Now I knew why. James Ernest would finish eating his cereal and then put the bowl to his mouth and drink the milk that was leftover. I could never do that. But I did like chocolate milk.

She talked about eggs and sperm. She talked about how the sperm travels to the uterus and fallopian tubes. I thought about the eggs I had cooked earlier that morning and how bad they were.

By the time she was done explaining the woman's reproductive system I was turning red and breathing hard. I think it was because I wanted to learn everything I could about it, but it was all so confusing. She closed the class by telling us what page the diagram was on in our textbooks and that we would have a quiz on Thursday about what we had learned today. I learned that sex was complicated and the female body was surprisingly difficult to comprehend.

"After the quiz, we'll study the male body," Miss Hickey announced as we were leaving the room.

There were a lot of boys leaving the room with puzzled looks on their faces. As Raven and I headed for Study Hall I asked her, "Did you already know all that stuff?"

"I knew how babies are made, but I didn't know all the terms and parts in my body," she said.

Susie was walking our way. I quickly dropped the conversation. The three of us walked on to Study Hall.

I sat there in Study Hall and opened my health book to the page where the diagram was. I read some of the descriptions and explanations. I then thought of Sam and the diagram faded away. I was still very worried about Sam and I needed to talk to him. I could accept that he dropped out of school if he wanted to or if he felt he needed to help his family. But I needed to hear that from him. I couldn't keep wondering and worrying about him. I would talk to James Ernest about it.

That evening we were walking to the spring to fill the two water buckets. Coty was walking by my side. "I need to go see Sam."

"He still hasn't returned to school?" James Ernest asked.

"No. I need to talk to him," I said.

"Didn't his father tell you guys to stay out of it?"

"Yes, but what if his father beat him into staying home. I need to know he's okay."

"I guess we could ask Randy to drive us to his house," James Ernest said. "But we might get run off with a shotgun."

"If he could drive us close to the farm we could walk the rest of the way and see if we could spot him away from his dad and maybe talk to him," I suggested.

"We'll ask Randy. Maybe this weekend."

"Thanks," I said.

Chapter 22

Coconut Pie and Murder Talk

Monday, July 1, 1963

We spent the morning doing chores around the lake and store. James Ernest went to the Washington's farm in the afternoon to work in his garden. A rainstorm came through around four that afternoon. After the storm passed a steady light rain continued through the evening. Mom did invite Sheriff Cane for supper.

Mamaw helped her cook fried chicken, mashed potatoes, green beans, creamed corn and two coconut pies. Mamaw and Papaw were staying to eat with us. Sheriff Cane arrived around six-thirty. Mom told us food would be ready in thirty minutes.

"It smells great. I can't wait," Hagar said.

James Ernest and I took this opportunity to ask the sheriff if we could talk to him. We led him out to the front porch. Papaw followed us.

James Ernest began telling Sheriff Cane about our trip to Blaze and Callahan Road. We took turns telling him that we had found the area and spot where we believed Thomas Back was thrown from.

"Wait, how do you know his name?" Sheriff Hagar Cane asked.

"Coty and I found his wallet up there near the spot," I said. Coty looked up when he heard his name. I pulled the wallet from my back pocket and handed it to the sheriff.

"The driver's license has the name and picture of the man we found in the creek," I added. The sheriff opened the wallet and took out the license and studied it.

"That's him alright." He then said, "There's a lot of money in here."

"Over a thousand dollars," James Ernest said.

"Whew," Papaw said. "It was probably tempting to keep that. That's a lot of money."

We nodded our heads, but didn't reply.

James Ernest told Papaw and the sheriff about the two sets of footprints we had found. I told them how the prints were different sizes, one a lot larger. "We can show you where they are," I said.

Sheriff Cane said, "With this rain they may be washed away."

James Ernest then told them about the limb with the missing leaves that we had found.

"It does sound like we have ourselves a murder," Sheriff Cane admitted.

"That's not all," I said.

"What else?" Papaw quizzed.

James Ernest told them about the two men who stopped and threatened us when we came out from the woods. I told them how the man said he knew me, and Mom, and where we lived and that I took it as a warning.

James Ernest then told them exactly what the man had said about Sheriff Cane, 'Don't ever come back up here again. We had better not see the sheriff up here either. If I do - he may not return. Do you boys understand?'

"Did he ever say anything about killing Mr. Back?"

"No, but isn't that enough?" I said, not believing what he said wouldn't confirm the killing.

"Can you boys describe the two men?" Sheriff Cane asked. We then did our best to describe the men.

"Do you know them?" Sheriff Cane asked Papaw.

"The skinny guy sounds like Weasel Wilder. I think his given name is Frank. He lives up around Blaze. Don't know if he's ever done anything except weasel people. He doesn't come around here much. The bigger guy doesn't ring a bell."

"Well, that's a start."

"I memorized the license plate number. It was Kentucky plate number 824-732, Menifee County." Sheriff Cane wrote the info in the pad he was using to take notes.

"That will help. Good job, guys. Maybe I should make you deputies. Though I wish you would have informed me you were going up there. I would have gone with you."

I looked at James Ernest but neither of us said anything. I hated to remind Sheriff Cane that he was ready to call it a suicide and be done with it.

"There are a couple of other things," James Ernest said.

Mom came to the screen door and opened it. "Come and get it. It's ready."

"Thanks, but can you give us just a minute?" Sheriff Cane asked.

"Sure, but just a minute," she answered.

After she closed the door Sheriff Cane asked, "What else?"

"After the men drove away I went back and checked the man's boot print in the dust. It was the same as the print we had found near the cliff," James Ernest explained.

"Very good. What else?"

Papaw jumped in, "We'd better get to the table. We can save it for after we eat."

"Sounds like a plan. Don't want to upset the cooks," Sheriff Cane said and laughed.

"You're learning," Papaw said.

We went to the table and sat down. It was tight around the table with seven of us there. James Ernest offered to say grace and we all bowed. Janie placed her hands together in front of her as he prayed. The plates were passed around the table. Papaw must have killed two chickens because there were four legs on the platter. I grabbed two of them. I ate like I hadn't eaten in a week. Everything was so good. I had three helpings of the creamed corn.

Mom told us that she and Hagar had decided on a spring wedding next year. It seemed like a long time away. I wondered why they were waiting so long. It didn't really matter to me. I just wanted Mom to be happy.

Mamaw said, "A spring wedding would be nice. We could decorate with pretty spring flowers."

"I like that," Janie said.

I was so stuffed after finishing off the third helping of creamed corn. But then Mamaw went to the kitchen and brought in the coconut cream pies. I knew I could make room for at least two slices of the pie. Mamaw had made them and they looked so good. I couldn't tell her how good they were because my mouth was constantly full.

After the table was cleared Sheriff Cane asked the women to join us on the front porch. I took some scraps on a plate outside for Coty. He slurped them right up.

"But we have to wash the dishes," Mamaw said.

Mom said, "The boys will help me with them later."

We all went out on the porch. James Ernest and I sat on the edge of the porch. My back was up against one of the posts. Janie was inside watching *The Lucy Show*. The sun had dipped below the western mountaintops lighting up the wispy clouds with a beautiful pink hue.

Sheriff Cane began filling the women in on what the Wolf Pack had found on our trip to the mountaintop in Blaze. Mom gave

213

us looks telling us she couldn't believe we were mixed up in another dangerous endeavor. I looked away from her condemning looks.

When Hagar got to the part where the man had threatened me and her she yelled out, "What!"

"Don't worry. I…" Sheriff Cane started to say.

"Don't worry. How can you say *don't worry*? A man threatens me and my son and you have the nerve to say *don't worry*. Is this the way you're going to take care of us when we're married!" Mom yelled.

I figured Sheriff Cane was second guessing the marriage at that moment himself. He looked pretty pitiful. Mom finally quit yelling and Sheriff Cane continued with his sentence.

"I'll probably have the two of them in jail by tomorrow evening. The boys gave me great information. I don't think it will be a problem finding them," Sheriff Cane explained himself.

Papaw looked at Mamaw and said, "One of them is Frank 'Weasel' Wilder."

"That no good skunk. He should have been in jail twenty years ago," Mamaw said.

"I'll stay here with you during the day until they are rounded up. Everyone will be okay," Papaw said.

Everyone was calmer and so I said, "You wanted to know the other thing we found."

"Oh. Yes. What is it?" the sheriff asked. He was clearly shaken by Mom's outburst.

I went inside to my bedroom and got the key. I came back and asked the sheriff to look inside the wallet again. "See that folded up paper in the right slot?"

He found the paper and took it out of the wallet. "Open it."

He unfolded the paper and saw the receipt for the storage unit. He looked up with questioning eyes.

"We believe this key that I found in the water next to the body might be to the lock that's on the storage unit," I explained.

"How do you think that?" the sheriff asked.

"I cleaned the key up and put some oil on it. It has the number 330 on it. We tried to figure out what a key with a number on it might go to. Uncle Morton suggested a storage unit and then we found that receipt in the wallet," I said looking at Papaw. Papaw nodded.

I handed the key to Sheriff Cane. He looked at it and tried to make out the number.

"I will definitely check it out," Sheriff Cane said.

"We thought maybe Tom Back was killed for whatever is in that unit," James Ernest said.

"He may have thrown the wallet down as he was being taken to the cliff to keep the killers from finding the receipt," I said.

Sheriff Cane looked dumbfounded. He was ready to dismiss the death, but now he had evidence that we had found pointing to the fact that Thomas Back, from Michigan, may have been killed here in Morgan County.

"Is that everything?" Hagar asked.

I looked at James Ernest and he said, "That's all we've got."

I looked at James Ernest and said, "Let's go and watch *The Andy Griffith Show*. I want to see what Barney is up to this week." Mamaw and Papaw left for home. Mom and Hagar stayed out on the porch for the next hour talking. I figured they were making up.

Chapter 23

Dangerous Things Before

Sunday, September 29, 1963

Randy had agreed to take us to the Hitchcock farm that evening. He couldn't do it until around seven. I figured that would give me enough time.

After church I was back in my bedroom lying on my bed thinking about a lot of different things. The thing most on my mind was the Health classes we had at school this past week. We had the quiz when we first arrived in class. I had forgotten most of the names that had been thrown around. I hadn't really studied too much. I had stared at the diagram, but that didn't help me much on the quiz.

The second half of class on Thursday we studied the male reproductive system. Miss Hickey threw around names of parts such as scrotum, testis, prostate, urethra, seminal vesicle, and others I'm too embarrassed to mention. The boys squirmed during this presentation instead of the constant giggling they did during the female presentation.

When Miss Hickey talked about how numerous boys were circumcised when they were babies and went on to describe how a doctor would cut off the excess skin, I thought most of the boys in class were going to pass out, or throw up. Many were covering their crotches as though the doctor was coming through the door with his knife. A boy, sitting two seats away, at that moment did vomit into his hat. Miss Hickey dismissed him to the restroom. It wasn't the class a person should attend right after eating lunch, which of course we had.

I looked over at Raven and Rock during the class. They saw me looking at them and they smiled back as if they knew how uncomfortable this all was for me. I wondered if they were this uncomfortable during the presentation on Tuesday, or if girls were just more mature than boys at this age.

"There will be a quiz on the male reproductive system next Tuesday. Make sure you study it," Miss Hickey announced as the bell rang.

As we were leaving the classroom Rock said, "Maybe we could study together this weekend for the quiz."

"That would be great. Timmy, you could be the model and we could take turns naming all your parts," Raven chipped in.

"That would be perfect. Susie could even study with us," Rock added.

"I didn't hear you girls volunteering after Tuesday's class," I said.

"You didn't ask us," Raven said.

"There will be no studying of my scrotum or thingy," I said. I then added, "I'm sure Purty would happily volunteer for your study."

As I walked away I heard Rock say, "Thingy". They both laughed.

"Timmy, there's a car at the gas pump," Mom yelled from the store, interrupting my thoughts. I jumped down from my bed and hurried through the store and out to the pump. James Ernest was at the Washington's making wooden woven baskets with Raven. Their baskets sold almost as fast as they could make them. We sold them in the store. The problem was that now with high school and all the other work going on they had little time to work on them.

When I got to the pump I saw that the car belonged to John and Pricilla. John and Pricilla opened their doors and got out. "Give me two dollars of gas," John said.

I hadn't seen Pricilla for a while, and I saw how big her stomach looked for such a small girl. She was now seven months along and looked like she was ready to give birth any moment. She waddled toward the porch steps. John ran to catch up and he helped her up the steps. I pumped the gas into the car, cleaned their front window, and then joined them in the store where Mom was gathering up some items for them.

"I feel like I'm ready to pop," Pricilla told Mom.

"You look awfully big for seven months," Mom said.

"I wonder if I'm having twins. They run in my family," Pricilla said.

"They ran in my family also," John told us.

"Make sure you call me if you need anything," Mom offered.

"Where are you going to go to have the baby, or babies?" Mom asked.

"We're going to have the birth at our home. We can't afford a hospital. I wanted to ask you if you knew a good midwife," Pricilla said.

"Let me ask around. I'll let you know the next time you stop in, or I'll see you at church," Mom answered. John and Pricilla had been attending our church pretty regularly. Susie and I had not been back to visit them since the racism incident.

"I know that Geraldine does it. She doesn't live nearby, but she could be here within thirty minutes. There's got to be someone in the community," Mom continued. "I think maybe Ruby has done it before. I'll ask around."

They had enough money to pay for the gas and few groceries they got, which surprised me. His pottery must have been selling.

Before they walked out John turned to Mom and asked, "Would you be interested in selling some of my pottery in the store on consignment? You would get a percentage of the sale."

Mom looked around the store and spotted a shelf that was nearly empty. "I think I could find the room. I can't be responsible if something would happen to it."

"I understand. I agree. That would be great. I'll bring a few pieces in later this afternoon if that's okay," John said, excitedly.

"That will be fine," Mom said.

"Thank you. Thank you," John said before they walked on through the door.

Mom looked at me and said, "Why don't we rearrange those items on that shelf, and move those cans up there, and then we can use that shelf for the pottery."

Mom said why don't we, but I knew she meant *me* instead of *we*. I did what she asked me while she went into the kitchen and made herself some tea. The *we* part was her telling *me* to do it. But I really didn't mind. It gave me something to do and took my mind off Health class.

Around six-thirty that evening Randy drove up and parked in front of the porch. He sauntered into the store. It was good to see him. We didn't get the chance to see him very often because of football practice, his job, and his chores at the farm. .

"Are you scumbags ready to go?" Randy teased when he saw us. We all laughed.

I yelled into the kitchen, "Mom, we're leaving!"

"Don't be out too late!" she yelled back.

We left through the screen door and I heard music and then saw Purty singing and moving in the front seat to the number one song of the week *Be My Baby* by the Ronettes.

We opened the doors and got into the back seat. Purty nodded hello as he sung, "Be my, be my baby. Be my, be my baby nooowwww."

"That's quite a singing voice," James Ernest said.

"You should sing on the radio," I said.

"Really," Purty said between lyrics.

"Yes, really," I said, and then added, "That way, we could turn you off."

"Slam," Randy said.

And just like that, the four original Wolf Pack members were back together as if it were 1960 again. The song and Purty's howling finally ended and I said, "I didn't know you were coming, Purty."

"I wouldn't miss an adventure," Purty said.

"I don't know how much of an adventure this will be," I said.

"Hey, we're back together again and we're heading somewhere. It's an adventure," Purty stated.

"Can't argue that," I gave up.

"So, where are we going?" Randy asked as he headed toward Wrigley.

"Stacy Fork," I answered.

I went ahead and told Randy the story of Sam. I then added, "I need to make sure Sam is okay. I have an odd feeling about it."

"I get odd feelings when I eat pizza," Purty said. I knew Purty would be of no help on this excursion.

We drove past the Key home. The four Key sisters were out on the porch waving at cars as they went by, ours included. Purty stuck his head out the window and howled as we drove past. I could see the girls laughing.

When we got to the intersection in Wrigley, Randy hung a right onto Route 7 and headed toward West Liberty. A few minutes later we were in West Liberty. We drove through the town and headed for Stacy Fork and Sam's farm.

Outside of West Liberty, Randy took Route 191 south through Malone and Well Station, and then turned right toward Stacy Fork. As we neared Sam's farm I explained, "We need to pull over before we get to their farm. I'll walk the rest of the way. Sam's father would probably shoot us before we could ask about Sam."

"Sounds like a friendly guy," Randy said.

"The guy was a real jerk," Purty said. I agreed.

It had been over two weeks now since Sam was in school. I was worried. Randy was getting near the farm when I saw a good place for him to pull off the road. He parked the car and everyone began getting out.

"Wait, I thought I was going to do this by myself," I said.

James Ernest looked at me and said, "No way. If Sam's father is as mean as you say, I'm not letting you go alone. Betty would never forgive if I let something happen to you."

"Besides, why did I come if I'm not going," Purty said.

"I was wondering why you came also," I said.

"That hurts," Purty said.

"We're all going," Randy said.

"Okay, but be quiet, and if I see Sam let me go to him alone," I said.

Everyone nodded their okay. We took off across a field toward the woods that surrounded Sam's farm. The woods were filled with oaks, chestnuts, and poplar trees. Squirrels scattered up and along the limbs as we made our way through the trees.

"We need to hunt here," Purty whispered. No one answered, but everyone agreed.

After fifteen minutes in the woods we were at the edge of them looking toward the farmhouse. I saw no movement anywhere. We searched the fields with our eyes looking for Sam or his dad. The truck that had been there before was not there now. The place looked to be void of people that evening.

The only movement I saw around the farm was a few chickens pecking their way across the front yard.

"Sam's father must be gone. This would be a good time to investigate," I said.

"Investigate what?" Purty asked.

"Why Sam hasn't been to school. What's happened to him? Let's go." I didn't wait for a reply. I began running across the open field toward the house.

"Wait," I heard James Ernest say.

I wasn't waiting. I was going. This was my chance. I wasn't going to waste it. I heard the guys running behind me. I ran all the way to the back of the house. Randy and James Ernest had almost caught up by the time I had made it. Purty was still fifty yards away. He walked the last twenty yards.

He was breathing hard as I said, "Sam's mother may be here. Be quiet."

I moved over to a window at the rear of the house and slowly put my head above the window sill. Inside was the kitchen. No one was inside. The kitchen was a mess. Dirty dishes covered the small countertop. The table had uneaten food covering it. I saw a line of ants marching up the legs of the table to the food supply. Flies buzzed above the table. Soon, other heads were above the window sill and looking through the window with me.

"What a mess," Randy said, stating the obvious.

"It looks like the family may have left," James Ernest said.

"But their furniture is still here," I said. I walked slowly around the house listening for sounds and to find another window. On the left side of the house I looked into the living room window. All of the furniture was also there. I continued around the house looking in each window until I found Sam's bedroom. It was in disarray. The bed was unmade; clothes were strewn around the room, so it also looked like a normal teenage boy's room, which in a way was sad.

Suddenly, we heard the crunching of gravel and the sound of a loud muffler. I looked to see the pickup pulling into the long lane toward the house. We ran to the back of the house. Hopefully, Mr. Hitchcock hadn't seen us. The truck pulled up to the front of the house. We heard the truck door open and then slam shut. I listened for a second door to open and shut, but it never came.

It worried me. If Sam wasn't home and he wasn't with his dad, then where was he? And where was his mom? I heard the front door open. We were huddled behind the house. James Ernest whispered, "Let's get away from the house while we can."

I looked around. There was an old shed directly behind the house. There was a new, sturdier shed beside it. The barn was fifty yards to the left of the house and a chicken coop attached to the barn. Randy pointed to the new shed. We turned and ran. Purty brought up the rear, still trying to catch his breath from before. Purty plopped down against the back of the shed.

"That was close," Purty said.

Unexpectedly, we heard a rap from inside the shed. I knocked back.

"Is someone in there?" I asked quietly.

"Timmy, Timmy, is that you?"

I quickly recognized Sam's voice. I noticed movement to my left. I looked to see Randy peeking around the corner of the shed toward the house. He was keeping watch.

"Yeah, it's me," I said.

"What are you doing here?" Sam asked through the slits between the wooden boards.

"We came to check on you. Are you okay? Are you locked in there?"

"Dad locks me up when he has to go away for a while," Sam answered.

"Why?" I asked.

"He doesn't trust me not to leave," Sam explained.

"Where's your mother?" I asked.

He hesitated and then said, "I – I don't know. They had a big argument one night about me going to school. The next morning she was gone. I don't know what happened to her."

"So your dad wouldn't let you come back to school?"

"He makes me work on the farm all day. Says he's making a man out of me. When he leaves the farm – he locks me in here."

"What can we do to help?" I asked.

"Noth...."

Randy turned to us and whispered, "He's heading this way." I couldn't hear Sam's answer. I started to run, but James Ernest grabbed my arm and pulled me down.

"Better stay here. If we run he'll see us. Everyone keep quiet," James Ernest directed.

I could hear footsteps getting closer. As he got closer I could hear keys jingling. We all held our breath, scared to make any noise, even breathing. Purty was huddled with his arms over his head. Maybe he thought Sam's father wouldn't see him if he came to the back of the shed, like a little kid playing hide and seek. I could hear him unlock the lock and open the door.

"Let's go, Sam."

227

I heard Sam walk out of the shed. His father then said, "Go to the barn and milk the cows and then clean out their stalls. Be quick about it. Then I need for you to do something about the mess in the kitchen."

"Yes, sir," I heard Sam say.

We heard them walk away in different directions. We waited until we knew Sam's father was back inside the house.

"Let's go," James Ernest said.

"We better get out of here," Purty said.

"I'm not going anywhere until I can talk to Sam. I may not get this chance again.'

"This could turn dangerous. We don't know what his father would do if he found us," James Ernest said.

"We've done dangerous things before," I said, as I shook free from his arm and ran for the barn.

I didn't hear any footsteps behind me. I made it to the rear entrance of the barn and carefully walked inside. It was getting late and the barn was now in shadows. It was hard to see the scene around me. I waited for my eyes to adjust to the dimness of the barn. I then saw a lantern light up ahead of me and heard the soft mooing of cows.

I slowly walked up the center aisle of the barn toward the light. I saw a stall filled with tobacco sticks. Sam must have heard my footsteps. He stood and looked my way and motioned for me to hurry. I ran to where he was and stooped down beside him.

"You shouldn't be here."

"Neither should you," I said.

Sam began pulling on the cow's teats spraying milk into the large can. I wasn't sure what to say. I knew I had to help him though.

"You should be in school."

"I'm forgetting about school now."

"You shouldn't be getting locked up."

Sam didn't say anything. He couldn't argue that point. I saw tears forming in his eyes. The lantern's light gave him away.

"What can I do to help you? The sheriff is going to be my stepfather. I can tell him what's going on."

"I just want to know what has happened to Mom," Sam said as the tears fell down his cheeks.

"Do you want to leave with us?"

"No."

"I have to stay to find out about Mom. Thanks for coming. I've never had a friend like you. But you need to leave before Dad sees you and whoever is with you. That would be bad for you guys and me."

I looked at Sam. How could I leave Sam in this predicament? But what else could I do? "Take care of yourself. I'll be back." That was all I knew to say. I turned and walked away. I went through the rear of the barn and peeked around the corner. I saw my friends still hunkered down behind the shed. I ran toward them and then past them and they followed.

We were getting close to the woods when we heard a shout, "Stop, you thieves! Come back here! I'm getting my gun!"

We sped up. Even Purty seemed to hit a different gear. We ran through briars and bushes and limbs that hit us in the face. Purty ran into a tree face first. "Ow," he shouted.

He slowly stood back up and kept running. We made it back to the car and climbed in while Randy was starting the '57' Chevy. He hit the gas and did a fishtail and then floored it as we escaped the farm. We kept looking behind us for the pickup, but it never came. I knew Randy was driving much faster than the old pickup would ever go. Randy finally slowed down as we passed through Malone.

Chapter 24

Dissecting Sam

We all seemed to relax once we saw the lights of West Liberty. I scooted down in my seat and put my head back and finally exhaled. I continued to worry about Sam and if Mr. Hitchcock had recognized us and whether he would blame Sam for us being on the farm. Hopefully he would think we were looking to steal something.

James Ernest was the first to speak when he asked, "What are you going to do, Timmy?"

"I don't know. Something has to be done. Sam doesn't know what happened to his mother. He's really worried about her." I didn't tell the guys about Sam crying. I didn't think he would want them to know.

"I think you should tell Sheriff Hagar Cane," Randy said as he was driving out of West Liberty.

"Or you could tell Principal Davis," Purty said.

Would it make it worse for Sam if we told Hagar or Principal Davis? I wasn't sure what the principal could do anyway. Like he said, kids drop out of school all the time. And he had no authority over how Sam was treated by his dad. But there had to be a law against locking your kid up in a shed.

It wasn't long before Randy pulled up to the store. James Ernest and I got out.

"Thanks, Randy. I really appreciate it," I told him.

"Anytime. It felt like the old Wolf Pack days," Randy said.

"You know you're still a member," James Ernest reminded him.

"I know that. See you two later." With that said Randy backed up and then headed for home.

It was dark by the time we got home and Janie was already in bed. Mom was watching *Bonanza*. I settled on the couch next to her. She always commented about how cute Little Joe was on the show. I liked Hoss.

During a commercial Mom asked, "What did you learn about your friend?" I had told Mom about Sam. She thought it was good that I was checking on him. What she didn't know was how dangerous it was to go see him and that we had to sneak onto the farm. I failed to mention that part.

"Did you see him?" Mom asked.

"I did, Mom. But there's a problem and I'm not too sure who to tell."

"I would be a good place to start." She had me get up and turn down the TV.

I went on and told her about how Sam was locked up in the shed and that Sam didn't know where his Mom was.

Mom covered her mouth. "I didn't know it was this serious."

"I didn't either."

"Where does he think his mother went?" Mom asked.

"That's the thing, he doesn't know if she left or his dad did something to her," I told Mom. He heard them arguing over him going back to school and he said the next morning she was gone.

"Does he think his dad may have hurt her?"

I think that was Mom's way of asking if Sam's father was capable of killing his mother. I wasn't sure how to answer that.

"I just know Sam is terribly worried about her. And he's really being mistreated. He's being treated like a slave. His Dad told him he's making him into a man."

"I think we should definitely tell Hagar tomorrow after school. I'll call him and ask him to come for supper. I'm going to pray about it tonight."

"Thanks, Mom. I'm glad I talked to you. I'm tired. I'm going to bed."

"Do you think she could have just left him?" Mom asked.

"I don't know."

"Brush your teeth before bed. And I suggest you wash those stinky pits."

That was embarrassing. Stinky pits.

As I climbed into bed James Ernest said, "I heard the conversation with Betty. I think she's right."

"I do too," I said.

"Do you think his dad is really capable of killing his mother?"

"Maybe. I'm not sure. Who knows?" I said wishy-washy.

233

"If he is, that means we were really in danger tonight. If he's killed once, he'd kill again to protect himself and hide his guilt."

I agreed with him.

"She was right about your stinky pits also."

My head hit the pillow and I closed my eyes. It didn't do any good. I knew it would be hard to go to sleep even though I was really tired. I kept thinking about Sam being locked in the shed. If I was him, I think I would run away when I got the chance. I should have suggested that to Sam. I should have told him to escape with us. I guess I did try, but not hard enough. I felt like I had really messed up. What if something bad happened to Sam? It would be my fault.

After lying there in the dark with the sounds of the outdoors coming through the window screen I finally went to sleep.

The next day I was in Biology class and Susie and I were assigned to dissect the body of a frog. Susie was not looking forward to it and I told her I would cut the frog open. I had no problem doing it at all. Each student had a partner, and we all had a frog. The frog was covered on the table by a white cloth as we neared it. I noticed that our cloth was larger than the others.

"Are you ready?" Susie asked.

"Go ahead and remove the covering." I noticed that most of the frogs had already been uncovered. Susie grabbed the end of the cloth and pulled it down and lying there in front of us was Sam Hitchcock dead. I screamed as loud as I had ever screamed.

Suddenly James Ernest was standing next to me shaking me to wake up. Mom and Janie came running into the bedroom. I was still screaming and tears were rolling down my face. I grabbed my pillow and hugged it.

"You just had a nightmare, Timmy," James Ernest said.

"You're okay. It was just a dream," Mom said.

Janie turned on the overhead light and I hid my face in the pillow. What a nightmare!

Monday, September 30, 1963

I awoke that Monday morning. I heard rain hitting the tin roof. The rainy day matched my mood. There was no way I wanted to go to school. James Ernest rose and said, "Time to get up."

I laid there with my back turned to him and looked out the bedroom window at the gray day. I had trouble sleeping after the nightmare. I had stared at the dark ceiling, and listened to the chirping of insects most of the night. I was so worried about Sam and his mother.

"Did you hear me?" James Ernest continued to nag. He finally opened the bedroom door and left me alone with my headache. I always loved the sound of rain hitting the metal roof but this morning it seemed my head was the roof and it was pounding with each raindrop.

A few minutes later Mom came into the bedroom.

"Why aren't you up?"

"I feel awful. I have a splitting headache, and I didn't get much sleep last night after the nightmare. I need to stay home today, Mom."

She reached up and felt my head. "Okay, but tomorrow it's back to school."

"Thanks, Mom. I love you."

"I love you too."

James Ernest took her place in the bedroom. He said, "Playing hooky, huh?"

"No. I really don't feel well. Will you ask Raven to call me with the homework tonight?"

"You might miss some more sex education today," James Ernest warned.

"Health class is tomorrow, not today. Besides, I don't think its helping."

"Maybe you shouldn't worry so much about it," James Ernest said as he grabbed his books and started to head out to the porch to wait on the bus. Maybe he was right.

Before he left I said, "Tell Purty not to blab to anyone about Sam. I'm sure Sam wouldn't want people to know."

"I will."

"Tell him if he does I'm going to punch him in the nose."

James Ernest laughed at me and said, "Okay."

Mom walked into the bedroom after the bus had left and gave me two aspirin and a glass of orange juice. "You need anything else."

"No. Thanks, Mom."

It wasn't long before I fell back to sleep.

I heard the door squeak and I woke up to hear the rain still hitting the roof. Mom whispered, "Are you awake?"

I rolled over and said, "Yeah. The squeak woke me up."

"It's noon, and Hagar is here. Do you feel like getting up and talking to him about Sam?"

"Okay." Mom left, and I sat up in bed. My head felt better after getting some sleep. I climbed down and got into my jeans and tee shirt. I went straight to the outhouse.

When I returned I found that Sheriff Cane, Papaw, and Mom were sitting in the living room waiting for me. Mamaw was in the store waiting on customers. It was always busy at lunch time. Truck drivers from the quarry would stop by to get sandwiches, snacks, and drinks.

We greeted each other and I found a seat on the couch next to Mom.

Sheriff Cane started the conversation by saying, "Betty said you had something important to talk to me about."

I went ahead and told him about how Sam had missed the last two weeks of school. I told him about our first encounter with Mr. Hitchcock. Papaw confirmed the rudeness of the man. I told Sheriff Cane about going to Sam's house yesterday to check on him. I told him everything that happened while we were there and how we had found Sam locked in the shed.

Sheriff Cane took notes as I told him what took place.

"It has to be against the law to lock a child in a shed. Isn't it?" I asked.

"Yes. It would be endangerment of a child. But it would be your word against his."

"It would his word against five of ours," I corrected.

"Five?"

"Us four Wolf Pack members and Sam," I said. I sighed deeply.

"There are laws protecting people from being accused of things also," Sheriff Cane explained. "Just because a person is accused of something doesn't mean he's guilty. It has to be proven."

I then went on and told him about Sam's mom disappearing, and that Sam suspects his dad may have done something to her.

"You mean he suspects his father may have killed her?" Hagar asked.

"He doesn't know. He said they had a big argument over Sam wanting to go to school and the next morning she was gone. He doesn't know what happened to her. He hasn't seen her or heard from her for over two weeks."

"I will definitely check it out," the sheriff said.

"I'm afraid of what might happen to Sam once his father knows Sam said something," I cautioned.

Papaw had been silent during our chat. But he finally offered, "Why don't you tell Mr. Hitchcock you had gotten a call from Sam's mother wanting to make sure Sam was all right. You could see what his reaction is."

"That's not a bad idea, Martin." Sheriff Cane then asked, "Is there anything else?"

"I don't think so. I'm just really worried about Sam."

"How do you always get in the middle of all these things?"

I shook my head.

"I was wondering that also," Mom said.

Mom walked Sheriff Cane out to the porch. I went into the store and asked Mamaw, "Will you fix me a baloney and cheese sandwich? I also want tomato and onion on it."

"Of course I will. You must be feeling better."

"I am. I finally got some sleep."

I went to the metal cooler and got out an RC Cola and went to the snack shelf and got a banana flip. I saw that John had dropped off some of his pottery and it was on the shelf I had cleared off. It looked good.

"Thanks, Mamaw," I said as I picked up the sandwich and headed out to the porch.

I was sitting in one of the rockers with Coty on the porch by my side. I was still eating my lunch when Clayton drove up to the store. I saw that Uncle Morton was with him. They got out of the truck and Clayton helped blind Uncle Morton to the steps. He climbed the steps and Uncle Morton said, "Good to see you, Timmy. Did you play hooky today?"

The two of them took seats also and then Papaw came out and joined us. He looked behind one of the feedbags that was sitting on the porch against the store and found two whittling sticks. He handed one to Uncle Morton and kept the other for himself. They both pulled out their Case pocket knives and began whittling, a major way to waste time and wood in Morgan County, Kentucky.

"So, Timmy, what was your hooky excuse today, splitting headache, the flu, cooties, or a broken heart?" Uncle Morton teased.

"No flu, everything is fine between me and Susie, and I haven't seen the twins for a while, so it can't be the cooties. That only leaves the headache."

Rain was still falling, so I knew that was the reason Clayton was at the store. Uncle Morton always spent a lot of time at the store whittling, carving or fishing.

I went inside and got my pocket knife and came back and began whittling myself. It helped take my mind off Sam.

Chapter 25

Secure Storage & Lucille

Wednesday, July 3, 1963

I was standing at the gas pump filling up mailman Roger Smuckatilly's mail truck. He was inside with the mail he had for us. He used to always bring us the wrong mail, but since he quit drinking moonshine liquor he had been a lot better. We still got the wrong mail every now and then but that was due to his incompetence, not his drinking, which we put up with. We liked him.

Sheriff Cane had looked for the two men who we believed had killed Thomas Back, of Michigan. He had told Mom he couldn't find Frank "The Weasel" Wilder. His parents told the sheriff they hadn't seen him in at least a month. Sheriff didn't believe them, figured they were covering for him, but there was no way to prove it.

Sheriff Cane had run the license plates James Ernest had given him and they belonged to a man named Tully Fran Musk. He apparently lived alone in Menifee County on Dog Trot Road in Cornwell, near Frenchburg. He wasn't home either and neighbors said he kept to himself and they didn't see him often. The Sheriff of Menifee County said he would keep an eye out for him.

As I pumped the gas I wondered who in their right mind would name their baby boy Tully Fran Musk. I quickly thought how much better I now liked my name, Timothy Allen Callahan.

As I was thinking about all these things the sheriff drove up to the store. He got out of his cruiser and walked toward me. The gas tank was now full and I hung the nozzle back on the pump. I met Sheriff Cane halfway.

"Howdy, Sheriff," I said.

"You know you can call me Hagar. We've had this conversation before."

"I know. It makes me feel like I'm in the Wild West saying 'Howdy Sheriff'," I told him.

He laughed and said, "Okay." He rubbed the top of my head. People used to always rub my head all the time. They had stopped as I grew older. I kind of liked that he did it.

"What's up?" I asked.

"I was wondering if you and James Ernest would like to go with me to the storage unit in Morehead to check it out."

"Boy, would I!" I said.

"Is James Ernest here?"

"He's at the Washington's working in his garden, or probably flirting with Raven," I answered. "We could stop by on our way and ask him. I'm sure he would want to go. He's been there for hours."

"I would bet there's probably more flirting going on than work," the sheriff said chuckling.

"Better go tell Mom," I said. Sheriff followed me into the store.

"I think it's only fair since Timmy found the key that he gets to see what is inside the unit. I had told him to throw it away," Sheriff Cane explained to Mom.

"Okay. As long as you know it's safe," Mom said.

"It couldn't be safer," he told Mom.

"Let me call Dad to see if he can come down and help here at the store," Mom said. She went to the phone and called. Papaw told her he would be there shortly.

Sheriff Cane gave Mom a quick kiss and we were out the door. I got to sit in the front of the cruiser, and Sheriff Cane told me I could put on the siren. I flipped the switch, the lights came on, and the siren began blaring. I saw Mom rush out the door to see what was happening. We laughed when we saw her worried face. She grinned and waved.

Two minutes later we were driving past James Ernest's garden. He wasn't working in the garden. "I guess I was right," the sheriff said.

He pulled up in front of the Washington farmhouse. Coal opened the screen door and came out to see who was visiting.

"Lordy, lordy, what have we done that the sheriff himself is at our front door?" Coal greeted. Sheriff Cane laughed as he got out of the car.

"Sounds like you got a guilty conscience about something. Should I get my handcuffs?"

Coal laughed and asked, "How can I help you?"

"We were looking for James Ernest," Hagar said.

"He and Raven are on the back porch making baskets. You'll find him around back. I think Junior is back there also."

I followed the sheriff around the house. They looked up from their work when we rounded the right corner. Junior was stripping pieces of wood from a log. Raven and James were weaving the strips around wooden basket forms they had made.

Sheriff Cane explained to James Ernest where we were going. He placed his half-made basket on the porch floor and said, "Yeah, I want to go."

Junior looked into the Sheriff's face and asked faintly, "Could I go?"

"If Coal says it's okay," Sheriff Cane answered.

Coal was standing at the back screen listening to the conversation. She opened the door and said, "Yes, you can go, but do as Sheriff Cane says."

"Yes, ma'am," Junior said.

Sheriff Cane tipped his cap toward Coal and said, "We'll be back in a couple of hours. It shouldn't take long."

We piled into the cruiser. Junior and I got in the back while James Ernest sat up front. I wished Tucky and Purty were able to go with us, but I didn't want to ask. Sheriff Cane drove out the gravel lane and turned left onto SR 711 toward Morehead.

A few minutes into the trip Sheriff Cane said, "This could all be a wild goose chase."

"What do you mean?" James Ernest asked.

"I called the storage facility and they would not confirm that a Thomas Back had rented a unit. Not without a warrant. So I had to get a warrant. We may get there and find out he doesn't even have a storage unit there."

"Did they say if they had a unit numbered 330?" I asked.

"Didn't even think to ask that," he admitted. "We'll find out soon enough."

I sat in the back and looked at the trees and farms outside the window. Cows dotted the landscape along with tobacco and corn fields. We left Morgan County and entered the corner of Elliott County for a moment and then drove into Rowan County. We drove through a small village called Elliottville, which consisted of a small country store, a gas pump and a church. It was ten minutes later we came into Morehead.

Sheriff Cane found the storage unit on a road off the main drag through town. He parked and we all got out. A small orange block building stood in front of two long rows of units inside a fence. The sign that stood in front of the building read: Secure Storage - Units by the month or year. Then it listed their phone number.

I opened the door to the building and Sheriff Cane walked in first. An elderly lady, her gray hair put up in a bun, had a hard time taking her eyes off the soap opera she was watching and slowly walked to the counter. Her show apparently was much more interesting than we were, and she was not afraid to show that we were interrupting her daily routine.

Without even looking at us she said, "What do you need?" Her eyes were still transfixed on the soap. The sheriff held out the warrant.

The music grew louder and the announcer said, "As the World Turns will continue after these short messages from our sponsors."

The lady then turned to see Sheriff Cane standing there holding the warrant out for her to take.

"What is this?" she asked.

"Ma'am, this is a warrant directing you to tell me if a Mr. Thomas Back has rented a unit here at your facility."

"Well, sir, you didn't need to bother with all that to find out. You could have just asked me," the woman said.

"I did. I called and I was told you would not give out that information without a warrant," Sheriff Cane went on to explain.

"Well, ain't that something. No one tells me anything, Sheriff," she said.

"And what is your name, ma'am," Sheriff Cane asked.

"I'm Lucille. Why are they with you?" Lucille asked, pointing at us. She especially paused and stared at Junior, almost as if she had never seen a black kid.

"They have an interest in this," he answered.

"And what interest in what?" Lucille said.

"That doesn't matter. What you need to tell me is – Does a Mr. Thomas Back have a storage unit rented here?"

"Oh, of course. Let me look real quick. My show is about to come back on." Lucille looked frantic. Her eyes went from searching through the records to the screen of the small twelve inch TV.

"Let's return to our program. Will Doctor Richards tell Mrs. Landers she only has hours to live?"

Lucille totally stopped what she was doing and stared again at the tiny screen. Sheriff Cane walked around the counter and turned off the TV. Lucille looked as though she might explode.

"This is official police business, and if you don't want to land up in jail yourself I would suggest you focus on the task at hand and give me the information I've asked for," Sheriff Cane said.

"That was plain mean," Lucille said. She huffed and then said, "He rented unit 330. He paid for a month. Is that all?" she asked angrily.

"I need the key to the unit. The warrant gives me the right to open and seize whatever is inside the unit," Sheriff Cane told her.

She looked down at the warrant again as though it would magically confirm what she had been told without her having to open it. It was still in the envelope. She turned around and lumbered over to a cabinet and lifted a key. She handed the key to Sheriff Cane and said, "I hoped this was all worth you turning my show off."

We turned and walked out of the office. I saw Lucille hurrying to the TV to turn it back on and find out what Doctor Richards would tell Mrs. Landers. It was the fastest she had moved since we walked in. I kind of wanted to know what Doctor Richards would say myself.

"That was like pulling teeth," Sheriff Cane said as we walked through the unlocked gate of Secure Storage.

As we walked Junior said, "Do you think he told her?"

"What are you talking about?" Sheriff Cane said.

"I wondered if the doctor told her she only has hours to live," Junior said.

"I was pondering that also," I said. Sheriff Cane shook his head and sighed.

We walked to the front row of units and saw that the first unit was numbered 101. We walked down the row and found that each unit went up a number. The last unit in the row was number 130. We turned the corner and went to the middle aisle. The unit on that end was 230. Directly across from it on the opposite side of the aisle was unit 330. It looked to be a small unit – maybe five feet wide. We had noticed that units varied from five feet wide to twenty feet wide.

Sheriff Cane held the key up to confirm the number matched. It had the same 330 that the key that I had found had. I was antsy to find out what was inside. I had imagined all kinds of stuff from stolen money to exotic animals.

Sheriff Cane took the key from his pocket that I had found and stuck the key into the lock. It fit. He turned the key and the lock fell apart with a yank. The door covered the whole front of the unit. With the lock removed, we were able to slide the metal door upwards to open it and reveal what was inside.

We saw three boxes sitting inside. They were all different sizes and were sitting beside each other. The two larger boxes were wooden. One was around three feet square and the other two feet square. The third box was metal and was eighteen inches long and a foot high. It was unlocked. Sheriff Cane slowly opened it and we saw stacks of twenty-dollar bills. The box was nearly full of the stacks.

"Wow," Junior said. James Ernest and I agreed.

Sheriff Cane then turned his attention to the wooden boxes. He tried to open them with his bare hands, but was unsuccessful. "I need the tire iron from the trunk of the cruiser. Will you run and get it for me, Timmy?"

"Sure," I said.

He handed me the keys and I sped through up the middle aisle and out the gate to the car. I was back within a few minutes, gasping for air.

"I didn't mean you had to literally run," Hagar said.

"I didn't want to miss anything," I managed to say between breaths. I handed him the tire iron and watched as he used it to pry off the top of the larger box. We helped him pulled the lid back.

We all looked inside.

I had no idea what we were looking at. There were brick size clear bags with greenish brown leaves of some sort inside the box. The box was close to halfway full of the bags.

"What is it? Looks like chopped up weeds," Junior said, as he peered into the box.

I looked at James Ernest and then at Sheriff Cane. I thought the same as Junior. Why would someone chop up a bunch of weeds and store them in plastic bags?

"It's marijuana," Sheriff Cane said.

"What's marijuana?" I asked.

"It's an illegal drug that folks smoke like cigarettes," Hagar explained.

"Is it like tobacco?" James Ernest asked.

"Only in the way you smoke it. They say it gives you a high that makes you do things you don't know you're doing. I don't know that much about it myself. Law enforcement has been warned that it's working its way into the area. This is the first I've seen around here."

"You think that's what's in the smaller box?" Junior asked.

"Let's open it and find out," Sheriff Cane said.

Five minutes later we pulled back the lid on the smaller box. We looked inside to find something different. Sheriff Cane picked up an envelope and looked inside. There were bottles of liquid, and paper with pictures on them of funny looking things.

"What is it?" I asked.

"I have no idea. I'll have to have this checked out."

"What does all this mean?" I asked. We had a box of money, a box of marijuana, and a box we were unsure of what it contained.

"I believe we have a drug deal gone bad." All three of us looked at Sheriff Cane. This was all new to us.

"If I had to guess, it looks like Mr. Thomas Back was killed for what was stored in this storage unit. Other than that, I'm at a loss. This case is going to take some investigation, and hopefully finding 'the Weasel' and Tully Musk will give us some answers."

"What happens now?" James Ernest asked.

"I need to call in the state authorities and find you guys a way home. I'm going to be here a while. Let's lock the unit and make some phone calls."

After locking up we went back to Lucille's office. She was not happy to see Sheriff Cane back. "I need to make a couple of phone calls."

"I don't think I can allow you to do that," Lucille said while smiling as though she was teaching the sheriff a lesson.

"Then I guess when I do make the calls I'll have to let the Feds know about the illegal drugs you have stored in your facility. They'll search every square inch of this place," Sheriff Cane informed her.

She picked up the desk phone and slammed it on the counter for the sheriff to use.

His first call was to Mom. He told her someone needed to come to Morehead and pick us up. She told him that Papaw was at the store and he would be there as soon as he could. He then called his office and directed them as to whom to call. He told us he would have to stay with the unit until they took the drugs and money into custody.

"Did the Doctor tell Mrs. Landers?" Junior asked Lucille.

She huffed and ignored his question.

It wasn't long before Morehead cops were surrounding the Secure Storage facility. Lucille looked terrified. She was on the phone calling her boss, her friends and her relatives.

Nearly a half hour later, Papaw was let through the boundary the cops had set up. He collected us and we headed for his pickup. We took turns telling Papaw about what we had found and all that had happened.

Chapter 26

"Where is Mrs. Hitchcock?"

Tuesday, October 1, 1963

School, I had school again – today. I knew I couldn't play hooky two days in a row. I knew the only reason I got to stay home yesterday was because Mom felt sorry for me because of the nightmare I had. I knew she wouldn't feel sorry for me two days in a row.

I got on the school bus and saw right away that Bernice the skunk was staring at me. As I went past her she said, "Why didn't you do us all a favor and stay home again?"

"The only thing sick about him is his face," Delma chipped in.

"His face," Thelma said, and started laughing.

Janie, my sister, took up for me and said, "Leave Timmy alone. He had a bad nightmare."

Oh no. I knew what was coming next.

Bernice quickly said, "Timmy had a bad dream and got to stay home. Poor Timmy, I didn't know he had a dream, poor thing. I take it all back." The other kids on the bus began laughing as the school bus began rolling again. I looked at Susie, and even she was grinning along with them. Riding the bus was such fun.

During homeroom Mr. Burns announced to the class that he was glad to see that I was back at school. At least he didn't mention my dream. The bell rang and I was on my way to Mrs. Hempshaw's American History class. We walked in to see a small gray tent pitched in front of her desk. We all took our seats. We wondered where our colorful teacher was. Soon we heard singing in the tent. Mrs. Hempshaw was inside the small tent humming *When Johnny Comes Marching Home.* She crawled out of the tent wearing a Union soldier's uniform and carrying an old musket. She sang:

"When Johnny comes marching home again

Hurrah! Hurrah!

We'll give him a hearty welcome then

Hurrah! Hurrah!

The men will cheer and the boys will shout

The ladies they will all turn out

And we'll all feel gay

When Johnny comes marching home."

She asked us to join her in singing the Civil War song. We did. We all sang the first verse again. Kids were singing out loud and we were pumping our fists as we sung. She was the greatest. She explained that the song was sung by both sides during the war and was quite popular at that time.

After lunch I had Health class with Miss Hickey. She had moved on from sex education to caring for our bodies. I felt as though I needed to take the sex education part over again. I was clearly still confused. Caring for our bodies was boring, but watching Miss Hickey show us how to care for our bodies clearly helped keep me awake. What a wonderful teacher.

As we were finishing up Health class Sheriff Cane was turning onto the lane to Sam's family farm. Sheriff Cane told James Ernest and me about the visit that evening. He said he pulled up to the farmhouse. Mr. Hitchcock was in the barn when he heard the car drive up. In the cruiser with Sheriff Cane was the truant officer, Mr. Mick Johnson.

As Sheriff Cane and Mr. Johnson were getting out of the cruiser Sam's dad came out of the barn.

Mr. Hitchcock looked annoyed at the disruption and made it known. "I'm not sure why you're here, but I've got work to do."

"I'm sure you do, but first we need to ask you a few questions. This is the school's truant officer Mick Johnson," Sheriff Cane introduced.

"I don't have time for this nonsense. The boy ain't coming back to school. He's dropped out, and it's none of your business."

"Sir, it is my business. You need to fill out a form and sign it to make it official. You can't just take him out of school without informing the school of his intentions. There are laws," Mr. Johnson tried to explain.

"You can have your laws. I'm telling you both now: He ain't coming back to school. He had no business starting high school in the first place. It was him and his mother's idea. Stupid."

"By the way; your wife called me yesterday and asked me to check and see how Sam is doing. Could I see him?" Sheriff Cane asked.

Mr. Hitchcock looked at the sheriff, his eyebrows burrowing his face into a squint. "Sam's busy," he said.

"I've had some reports..," Sheriff started to say when Mr. Hitchcock directed; "I think it's time you two got off my property. You're trespassing. I don't see a warrant. Git!" Sheriff Cane told me that evening Mr. Hitchcock was treating them like two old stray dogs.

"You have until the close of school tomorrow to come in and sign those papers or you will be arrested," Mr. Johnson said.

"And I'm telling you that you have two minutes to get off my property or I'm getting my gun," Sam's dad threatened. Sheriff Cane and Mr. Johnson headed for the car.

Before getting into the cruiser Sheriff Cane turned back toward Mr. Hitchcock and asked, "Where is Mrs. Hitchcock?"

"I'm getting that gun."

Sheriff Cane said he saw Sam looking out a barn window in the hayloft. "I'll be back with that warrant, Mr. Hitchcock. You can count on it." Sheriff Cane got into his cruiser and backed into the yard, turned around and then left.

Susie got off the school bus with Janie, me and James Ernest. Susie and I were going to do homework together. We hadn't gotten to spend much time together lately. We had a lot to talk about. We walked into the store.

Mom was in the store waiting on Mrs. Sugarman. Mud McCobb was drinking an Orange Crush near the cooler.

"This sure is pretty," Mrs. Sugarman said while holding up a piece of pottery, a water pitcher made by John James. "I'll take it."

"It really is nice," Mom told her as she rang it up along with her other groceries she had gathered. I went over and grabbed the bags and carried them to the car for Mrs. Sugarman.

"Thank you, Timmy. That's very nice of you. Good day," she said as she started her car. I waved goodbye and then went back into the store.

"We're doing homework together," Susie was telling Mom as I walked in.

"That's good," Mom said.

"I doubt if much homework gets done. You two will be making eyes at each other," Mud said.

"Don't you have some rocks to move or bait to waste up at the lake?" I asked. Mud was one of my favorite fishermen and I loved teasing him. He teased right back. He was a truck driver for the quarry.

"I think you meant to say: Are you catching fish this evening?"

"No. I said it right. Where's your right arm, Louis Lewis?"

Louis Lewis also drove a truck for the quarry and also fished with Mud. You would swear they were married. They were always together.

"He had a late delivery. He'll be here shortly. I'll have some chicken livers," Mud said. Fishermen were always using raw chicken livers for catfish bait.

"At least you'll have something to snack on," I teased.

Susie and I finished our homework around six and Clayton came to pick her up. Mamaw and Papaw had come down to the store. Mamaw was in the kitchen cooking supper. It smelled so good. It smelled like meat loaf and mashed potatoes.

Sheriff Cane came for supper and that was when he filled us in on his visit to Sam's farm.

"I used your trick, Martin. I told him his wife had called asking about Sam."

"What did he say?" Papaw asked.

"He gave me this strange confused look. I definitely think he had something to do with her disappearance."

"You think he killed her?" I asked.

"I didn't say that. He could have sent her away. She could be gone to visit her mother. There are numerous reasons she could be gone."

"One of those reasons could be that he killed her and buried her in the corn field," I said.

"Timmy, we're eating," Mom scolded me.

"I'm sorry, Betty. I shouldn't have brought this topic up at this time," Sheriff Cane apologized.

When everyone was finishing up Mamaw asked, "Who would like a dish of cherry dumplings?"

What! I thought I could smell cherries. "I would. I would," I cried out.

"That goes without saying," Mom said. Everyone knew that my favorite thing in the world to eat was Mamaw's cherry dumplings.

We all had dessert and then I asked, "What will happen now about Sam?"

"I'll wait to see if he comes in to sign the school's papers. If he doesn't come in by tomorrow evening then I'll get a warrant on Thursday for his arrest and to search his property," Sheriff Cane said.

"Couldn't happen to a more deserving guy," Papaw said.

James Ernest and I at the same time said, "Amen."

"Do I hear preaching going on in there? I thought that was my job," Pastor White said as he passed through the living room and entered the kitchen. He was carrying baby Marie. Miss Rebecca was right behind him with Bobby Lee.

"We didn't mean to interrupt your meal," Rebecca apologized.

"We were done and just sitting around the table talking police business," Mom said as she got up and walked over to take Marie away from Pastor White.

"Aren't you the most precious thing?" Mom cooed over her namesake. The baby had dark hair and big blue eyes. Her smile could melt any heart. I was sure she would grow up to look like Miss Rebecca.

James Ernest and I followed the men out to the front porch. The sun was setting over the western mountaintop. It would soon disappear. Louis Lewis and Mud McCobb came around the store with a stringer of four nice catfish.

"Looks like you won't starve tonight," Pastor White said.

"The good Lord provided," Mud said.

"That's the only way you caught them," I said. The men laughed.

"The good Lord didn't provide Mud with anything. I caught all four of them," Louis informed us.

"I'm waiting for the Lord to provide me that big one Morton lost earlier this year," Mud said.

"That fish is still in there. No one's been able to catch it yet," Papaw said.

Chapter 27

All Good Points

Thursday, October 3, 1963

I woke up thinking about Sam and his father. Hagar told us the night before that Mr. Hitchcock had not come in and signed the papers officially pulling Sam out of school. Sheriff Cane was going first thing that morning to get a warrant to arrest Sam's dad and search the property. I wanted to be there so bad, but I knew I couldn't, no matter how much I begged and pleaded. I wanted to see his face when Sheriff Cane slapped the handcuffs on him. It was all I could think about before finally drifting off to sleep. I was thinking about it again that morning as I awoke.

I got on the bus and saw that Bernice was busy bullying a young boy behind her. I slipped past her. He looked up at me with pleading eyes. I mouthed, "I'm sorry." I headed for Susie.

The bus stopped at the Tuttle lane and Sadie and Purty got on. Bernice turned around leaving the boy relieved. Sadie quickly took the seat beside Bernice while Purty stopped a row in front of Bernice and held up his arms. What was he doing now?

"Did you guys hear the TV news this morning?" Purty loudly said. The bus driver turned around to hear the news. Everyone on the bus fell silent to hear the news.

"What news?" Bobby Lee called out.

261

"There was a lawsuit filed yesterday. The skunk wants his stripe back, Bernice!"

Every kid on the bus burst into laughter. In the rear view mirror I even saw the driver laughing as he turned back around. Sadie was sitting next to Bernice and couldn't stop laughing.

Bernice was almost at a loss for words. She finally managed to say, "Very funny, Purty. What kind of stupid name is Purty?" But the damage had been done. Purty was high-fiving everyone as he went to his seat. One small girl even got up and hugged Purty. Never had Purty been a hero to so many. No one was paying Bernice's words any mind. Bernice sat silent for the rest of the ride to school.

School was boring again today. Even Mrs. Hempshaw was solemn for some reason. The only bright spot of the day was Health class. Miss Hickey was fun to stare at. I was anxious to hear about Sam. As soon as school was out I saw Mom standing outside the school waiting on me and James Ernest. Janie was by her side.

"What's up?" I asked. James Ernest, Susie and Raven were with me.

"Hagar was shot," Mom said as she began to cry. "He's at the hospital. Let's go."

"I'll see you later," I said to Susie. She and Raven turned toward the bus. We walked to where Papaw was waiting for us in his pickup.

"What happened?" I asked before jumping into the bed of the truck.

"Hitchcock shot him," Mom said as she closed the passenger door. Janie was riding in the front. James Ernest and I looked at each other.

Papaw was driving fast north on SR 519 toward Morehead. Apparently Sheriff Cane had been taken to the Morehead Hospital. James Ernest and I couldn't talk to each other due to the speed in which Papaw was driving and the noise it made in the back. We sat with our backs up against the cab of the truck.

We jumped from the bed when Papaw stopped in front of the emergency room entrance. He continued to the visitor's lot. Deputy Sonny Hughes was inside waiting for us.

He said, "They've taken him into surgery. The doctor told me it looked as though he had lost a lot of blood, but they felt he would make it."

Mom sighed in relief, but the worry never left her face.

Papaw entered just as Deputy Hughes said, "I'll take you to the waiting room and explain everything to you."

The hospital had given us a private waiting room. We all took seats. Janie stayed close to Mom's side.

Deputy Hughes began, "We arrived at the Hitchcock farm around one-thirty this afternoon with the warrant. Mr. Hitchcock had posted a large sign at the entrance of his lane. It read: No trespassers. All will be shot.

"The sheriff called the office and had the secretary call the state police. Two state policemen arrived around two. We discussed what we should do. It was decided that since we had the search

263

warrant we would continue onto his property and arrest him. As we neared the house we saw Mr. Hitchcock and his son run from the barn and into the house.

"One of the state patrolmen went around to the back of the house in case they tried to escape through the back door. The sheriff asked the other patrolman to stay by the car and give cover. Hagar and I slowly walked toward the house. Hitchcock yelled from the front window, ""Stop, turn around, and leave. Another step closer and I'll shoot. Get in your fancy cars and leave."

""I have a warrant here for your arrest, Mr. Hitchcock. Come out with your hands up,"" the sheriff told him.

""I'm not going anywhere. This is my property. Get off it,"" Hitchcock said.

""That's not going to happen, Mr. Hitchcock. We're not leaving without you in the back of that squad car."

"Two shots were fired, both by Mr. Hitchcock. One of the shots hit the sheriff in his stomach. I was able to help him back to the car. We then radioed the station. They called for an ambulance and we met it halfway to West Liberty. They brought him here."

Mom was crying. So was Janie.

"I knew that man was no good," Papaw said.

"What's happening now?" James Ernest asked. That was what I wanted to know.

"From what I've heard, it's a standoff. He's demanding everyone leaves or he's going to kill his son and himself."

"What?" I cried out.

264

"We believe, now I don't have the facts to back it up, but we believe he killed his wife and he knows we're closing in on him and he's not willing to spend his life in prison."

"But why kill Sam?" I said.

"He's desperate. It's anyone's guess whether he would do it or not. The state patrol has left his property, but they still have it surrounded. He won't get away. He's really got no options other than to surrender or do what he's threatened," Deputy Sonny told us.

"But you've got to do something to save Sam. He's innocent in all of this," I begged.

"It's now up to the state police as to what they will do. It's their call."

I saw Mom sitting there with her head bowed. I knew she was silently praying. I settled into the chair I was sitting in and looked around the room. Papaw looked angry. James Ernest was in deep thought. Janie had her head in Mom's lap. Deputy Hughes got up and left the room, I figured he left either for coffee or to place a call.

Papaw got up and said he was going to call Mamaw and let her know what had happened. Mom motioned for me to come and sit beside her. I did. She wrapped her right arm around me and held me tight. It was quiet, almost a suffocating silence. I wanted to open a window and let some sound in, but I knew the hospital windows wouldn't allow it.

I was so thankful when Pastor White and Miss Rebecca walked into the room. Mom quickly let me go and stood to hug

Miss Rebecca. "I am so sorry," Miss Rebecca said with tears flowing down her cheeks.

"How is he?" Pastor White asked.

"In surgery, they say they think he'll make it, but he's lost a lot of blood," Mom said between sobs.

Mom and Miss Rebecca huddled together and Pastor White asked me to fill him in on what had happened. James Ernest and I told him all that Deputy Hughes had told us. Papaw entered the room and greeted the newcomers. Papaw told us that Mamaw was relaying the news to the community. I knew it would only be minutes before everyone heard the news. That was the one thing the community was great at.

"Where are the kids?" Mom asked.

Miss Rebecca told us, "Coal is watching them. Bless her heart. She is the sweetest person on this earth. She told me not to worry one bit, not one hair on my head. And I'm not. I'm sure Bobby Lee is playing with Mark Daniel and Junior."

Mom nodded in agreement. We all felt that way toward Coal and the whole Washington family. They were good people, as were most of the people in our community.

A few minutes later Susie's head popped into the room, followed by her parents, Monie and Clayton. I was so happy she was there. She took the seat next to me and we held hands. James Ernest told the story of how Hagar had been shot for those who had just come in. After fifteen more minutes went by, Susie and I decided to take a walk to the cafeteria and see what they had. Mostly, we wanted to get out of the waiting room for a little while.

As we walked down the empty hall Susie said, "He'll be okay."

"Who?"

"Sheriff Cane."

"I believe so. The doctor said he probably would be fine. I hope so."

"Who else were you thinking about?" Susie asked.

"I keep thinking about Sam in that house with his Dad who is threatening to kill him. He must be scared to death."

"Wouldn't you think he could escape the house?"

"I don't know. His dad could have tied him up. I mean he had Sam locked up in the shed. He must not care anything about Sam. What if he does kill Sam and then himself? I keep thinking I could have done more. I keep thinking I need to go there tonight and try to get him out of there."

"Tim, I now know for sure you have gone crazy. There are numerous reasons that would be wrong."

"Like what?"

"Are you kidding? Like for instance, you could get killed. You would be messing with a state police operation. You have no way to get there. Your Mom is already going crazy with worry over Sheriff Cane, and you want to add to it? Even if you did get there, how in the world would you get past his dad and the police and get him to safety?"

"Well, I didn't think that far into the plan. You make some good points. I guess I'll need to talk to James Ernest."

"You are impossible."

We roamed around the cafeteria for a little while. Nothing looked that appetizing so we headed back up to the waiting room.

We had been there for hours. The clock on the wall showed it was nine-thirty. Pastor White took his family home around eight and asked for someone to call them when we found out anything. He prayed with us before leaving.

The minute hand on the clock stuck ten o'clock. The door opened and the doctor walked in with a smile on his face.

"He is going to be fine." A deep exhale was felt in the room. "The operation was trickier than we first thought. Without going into details at this time I'll say we had to do more repair than we anticipated. But it all went well. He'll be out for most of the night. You are welcomed to stay here or come back in the morning. No visitors at his time. Sorry."

Mom told us to go home. She asked Mamaw to take Janie home. She told me and James Ernest to stay home from school tomorrow and tend the store. She said she was spending the night there at the hospital. She hugged everyone goodnight and sent us home. Papaw said he would be back tomorrow and pick her up. I kissed Susie goodbye, and she and her family left.

Since Papaw drove home slower, James Ernest and I were able to sit in the back of the pickup and talk on the way home. I told him about wanting to rescue Sam from his father. James Ernest looked at me like I had lost my mind.

"We wouldn't be able to do it, plus it is way too dangerous," he said.

"You're the one who snuck into each of the Boys from Blaze's bedrooms without them knowing it until you woke them up and scared them to death. You sneak around in the woods in the dark all the time. I know you could do it. Don't tell me you can't."

"But the police are taking care of this."

"They're not rescuing Sam. They're going to let him die if his dad decides to pull the trigger."

"How would we even get there? I know Martin isn't going to take us," James Ernest said.

I thought about it and then said, "Mom's car is out front. You can drive."

"I don't have a license."

"But you can drive. I need to save Sam!"

Chapter 28

A Real Shame

Thursday, July 4, 1963

I was told later that Deputy Sonny Hughes was watching Frank 'Weasel' Wilder's parents' home at noon. The thinking was he might come home for the holiday. A car drove into the driveway. Weasel got out. As soon as he saw Weasel enter the home, he left to go call Sheriff Cane.

A half hour later the two police cars pulled up to the front of the house. Sonny took the back, and Sheriff Cane went to the front door and knocked. No one answered. The car Weasel had driven up in was still parked in front of the house, blocking his parents' car in. They knew the Wilders were in the house.

"We know you're in there. Open the door, or I'll have to bust through it."

Finally a haggard-looking woman with stringy brown hair with gray roots opened the door. "Sorry, I was using the toilet." She held out her hand for the sheriff to shake. He looked at it and declined. "Can I help you, Sheriff?"

"I would like to speak with your son, Frank."

"That would be fine if he was here. But I'm afraid I haven't seen him for a few months, as I told you once before, I believe. Could you please stop harassing us, especially on this day that we celebrate our freedom? It seems we don't have as much freedom as I thought."

"Mrs. Wilder, we saw him drive up and enter a few minutes ago."

"That wasn't him. We haven't seen..."

Deputy Hughes walked around the corner of the house with Weasel in handcuffs.

"He was trying to weasel his way out the back door," Sonny said.

His mom looked shocked to see him. "What a surprise!"

"Ma'am, you are either blind or a liar," Sheriff Cane said to her.

"You can't say that to me."

"I can take you to jail for accessory if that would be better," Sheriff Cane told her.

She quickly closed the door on Sheriff Cane and her son. Hagar walked over to Weasel and said, "Let's have a talk."

An old couch sat on the front porch. Sheriff Cane had Weasel take a seat. Sonny sat down in a plastic-webbed lawn chair. The sheriff remained standing.

"Do you know the whereabouts of Tully Musk?" the sheriff asked.

"Never heard of him," Weasel answered.

"Weasel, let me spell it out for you. We have a dead body. We know you were with Tully, and we know Tully killed the person the body belonged to. You can help yourself a great deal by answering my questions. If not, you will be charged with the murder,"

"I didn't kill the man," Weasel quickly said.

"Who said it was a man?"

"You did."

"No, I said a person."

"I just assumed it was a man. Not many women get killed."

"We found the body in a creek," the sheriff continued.

"I haven't been near Licking Creek in months," Weasel said.

"How did you know it was Licking Creek?" Sonny said.

"You guys are confusing me. This isn't fair."

"This is your last chance. Where is Tully?" Sheriff Cane asked.

Weasel looked down at the rotting floor boards of the porch and stared for a bit. He then said, "He has a woman out on Dead Possum Road. He's stays there most of the time."

"What's her name?"

"She goes by Tadpole. That's the only name I've heard her called. Sort of looks like one – a tadpole. She's big on top with no bottom."

Sheriff Cane told the deputy later he knew Weasel was not the smartest person in the county, but he had no idea he was a borderline moron. He then asked Weasel, "Do you know what type of gun Tully used to shoot the fellow?"

"He didn't shoot the guy. He threw him off..." Weasel stopped talking.

"How do you know he didn't shoot the victim? He threw him off what?"

Weasel looked defeated. He shook his head from side to side. He then looked at the front door and said, "Tully told me he threw the guy off a mountain."

"That's better, Frank."

Weasel sat up a little straighter by being called Frank instead of Weasel.

"Did he tell you why he threw him off the mountain, Frank?"

"Tully told me he was trying to make a deal for some drugs. The man didn't like the deal. Tully was trying to make the guy tell him where the drugs were. Tully told me he took him to the top of the cliff and dangled him over the edge. The guy had a change of heart and decided to accept the deal. As Tully attempted to pull the guy back up he lost his grip and the guy was gone. He said he didn't mean to kill the man. He was just trying to scare him and it worked, until he dropped him," Weasel explained.

"That is a shame. He didn't mean to do it, but yet, he did it. And with the man dead Tully had no idea where the drugs were."

Weasel shook his head and then said, "Yep, it was a real shame."

"Where were you when this happened?" the sheriff asked.

"I swear I wasn't there. I had nothing to do with it. I was here at the house with Mom. Just ask her."

"She lies. I think she would say anything for her little boy," Sheriff Cane said. "Let's go."

273

"Where are we going? Where are you taking me?" Weasel asked, as Deputy Hughes pulled Weasel up from the couch and led him to the backseat of his cruiser.

Fifteen minutes later Frank 'Weasel' Wilder was sitting in a jail cell in West Liberty. Sheriff Cane and Deputy Hughes rode together on their way to Dead Possum Road to find a woman named Tadpole, or the killer named Tully Fran Musk.

Sheriff Cane knew of a small country grocery near Dead Possum Road and planned to stop there. Ten minutes later they entered the store and bought soft drinks, a snack cake, and a Zero candy bar.

Sheriff Cane introduced himself to the man behind the counter. He handed him a five dollar bill.

"I'm Stanley Profit," the counterman said. "I know who you are, Sheriff. Everyone in the county does, I suppose."

"Sorry I haven't stopped in before now. This is Deputy Sonny Hughes."

"Glad to meet you, Stan."

"Stanley, please. I never go by Stan. I hate that name. Makes me feel like I should stand up every time someone calls me Stan," Stanley told them. Hagar and Sonny laughed. Stanley didn't.

Sheriff Cane took a long drink from his bottle of Pepsi. Sonny took a bite of his Zero bar. "Are you closing early tonight for the 4th of July?" The sheriff was making small talk.

"No. It's just another day for me. I'll watch the fire flies this evening. That's enough celebrating for me."

"That's a great way to do it. Have you seen Tadpole lately?"

"She was in here yesterday, I believe it was. She was with that no count boyfriend of hers."

"Who is that?"

"He goes by the name of Tully. It must be a nickname," Stanley said.

"Did they walk here?"

"No. It's too far for her to walk. She's a lazy woman. That would be about a half mile walk. No way she'd walk that far."

Sheriff Cane finished his Pepsi and handed Stanley his bottle.

"Let me give you your nickel," Stanley said.

"Just keep it. It was nice to meet you."

Deputy Sonny gave him his bottle but took the nickel for the bottle refund. "Have a nice Fourth."

"You too, Deputy."

Sonny got into the passenger seat and Sheriff Cane got behind the steering wheel. "I guess we now know where to go," the sheriff said.

Sheriff Cane drove slowly down Dead Possum Road while keeping an eye on the odometer, measuring the half mile. The first house they came to was seven-tenths of a mile from the store. The house was a small white ranch with a tiny porch attached. The paint had fallen off most of the rotted wood siding. There in the gravel driveway sat Tully's truck. Sonny spilled out of the car and headed toward the back of the house. Sheriff Cane went to the front door.

Before he knocked, a woman with short red hair and a round face opened the door. Her nickname fit her to a tee. She had big bosoms and a large stomach. She was then slender from her waist to her feet. The sheriff later said he wondered how she kept her pants up.

"How can I help you, Sheriff?" Tadpole said through the screen door.

"I would like to talk to Tully Musk."

"Let me check and see if he wants to talk to you. Sometimes, he's not very talkative... moody, you know."

She yelled out, "You want to talk to the sheriff?"

"Not especially," Tully yelled back.

"Tell him I would really like to talk to him," Sheriff Cane said.

"He wants to talk to you."

"Hold on. Let me put some pants on," Tully yelled back.

"He was relaxing in his drawers," Tadpole explained.

A minute later Tully Fran Musk appeared at the screened door.

"What's this about?"

"Would you please step out on the porch so we can talk?" Sheriff Cane asked.

Tully opened the screen door. It squeaked. He walked out onto the porch with no socks or shoes on.

Sheriff Cane reached behind his gun and pulled out his handcuffs.

"Hey, wait a minute. I thought you wanted to talk," Tully complained.

"I do. But first I need to arrest you for the murder of Thomas Back. Please turn around."

Deputy Sonny Hughes came around the side of the house with his gun pulled. Tully turned around and said, "I didn't kill anyone."

Tadpole opened the door and started to come out. "Please stay inside," Deputy Hughes told her.

"He was here with me," Tadpole said, with her hands, stomach, and boobs pressed against the screen.

"When was he here with you?" Sheriff Cane asked.

"Whenever he did it, I mean whenever it was you think he did it. He's always here with me. We're in love, true love."

"You can visit him in jail," Sonny told her.

The handcuffs clicked around Tully's large wrists and they led him to the cruiser.

Tadpole made her way onto the porch and screamed, "He was here with me! I love him! Don't take my love away!"

As Sheriff Cane drove away from the house he told Tully, "Nice being in love. Isn't it?"

Tully looked out the window and said, "I wouldn't know."

As they passed the store Tully said, "Who did you say I killed?"

"A man named Thomas Back from Michigan," Sheriff Cane answered.

"Who says I killed him?"

"The evidence."

"What evidence?"

"Evidence from the crime scene and a witness," the sheriff told him.

"There was no witness. I mean - I didn't kill anyone."

Later, they led him down the hallway to a cell next to the cell that held Weasel. Tully took one look at Weasel and said, "I thought you were a weasel, not a rat."

Chapter 29

A Second Shot

Thursday, October 3, 1963

I gathered up my flashlight, my rifle, and my pocket knife. James Ernest took only his pocket knife. James Ernest gathered up the keys to the car from Mom's dresser. We were fortunate she didn't keep them in her purse.

We got in the car and James Ernest started it. He checked the gas gauge. We had half a tank. He checked all the mirrors.

"Will you drive, already?"

"If I'm going to drive I'm going to be safe. I don't want to get picked up," he said.

"Who's going to pick you up? All of the police are either at the hospital or the Hitchcock farm."

He backed up and then turned onto SR 711 and headed toward Wrigley. We drove through West Liberty and continued toward Sam's farm.

"What are we going to do once we get there?" I asked.

"This is your idea. What *are* we going to do once we get there?"

"We need a plan,"

"Genius," James Ernest mocked me.

"Okay. You need to park far enough away from the farm that the state police don't see us. We can go through the back woods and across the corn field. The corn will give us cover. We'll sneak up to the house and I'll keep watch outside while you go in and get Sam."

"That's your plan?"

"Yeah. What do you think?"

James Ernest shook his head and sighed deeply. He then said, "It's as good as any. It may not go quite that easy."

"Why?" I asked. Sounded like a good plan to me.

"They may have the entire property surrounded. They may see us. The doors and windows may be locked. He could be tied up to something. His dad may be right next to him. His dad may be awake and may shoot me."

"You worry too much," I said.

James Ernest began laughing. "I can't believe I let you talk me into this."

"I can't believe you did either," I said.

"It's not too late to turn around," James Ernest said as he stared straight ahead at the road he was driving down.

"The only reason I agreed to do this is because I remember when you and Susie were kidnapped and I couldn't stop looking for you until I found you. I figure you feel the same way about saving Sam," James Ernest said.

"I do. I know I haven't known Sam all that long, but I know Sam is good and deserves to have a good life. If we don't save him he may not have any life."

"You're a good person, Timmy."

"Thanks, but I'm only doing what you've taught me," I said.

"Don't blame this on me," James Ernest said. We both laughed.

I wasn't sure what I was getting us into. As we neared the farm I began to have second thoughts. What if this all went terribly wrong and James Ernest, or I, or both of us got shot or killed. What if I got Sam killed trying to rescue him. I began thinking the state police was handling it. Why would a fourteen-year-old boy think he knew better than them? I didn't think I knew better. I just thought I knew a way to maybe save Sam from his father. We had to try. I knew I wouldn't be able to forgive myself if I let Sam's father kill Sam.

It was almost midnight by the time James Ernest pulled the car off the road before we got in sight of the farm and the state police. We got out and I got my stuff from the back seat. We turned toward the farm.

"I'm sure the police have the front and sides covered. I'm not sure they would have the back of the property covered. It looked to be deep woods back there," James Ernest said. "That would be our best bet. That field was still in corn. It would be easier sneaking up to the house through the corn."

I agreed, because that was my plan. We headed west across an open tobacco field. I tripped a few times on the cut off tobacco stalks in the field. I didn't want to use the flashlight until I had to.

Friday, October 4, 1963 –Just after midnight

We made it to the woods and turned south and slowly made our way toward the Hitchcock farm. There was a full moon, but it was covered by deep clouds. The moon would have helped us to see but would have made it easier to be seen.

The woods were spooky in the middle of the night and not easily navigated. Teaberry plants, blackberry vines, and holly bushes littered the forest floor. Small trees blocked our way much of the time and we had to find our way around the obstacles. And it was dark. I couldn't see much of anything. I kept waiting for my eyes to adjust to the darkness, but I guessed it was hard to adjust to total blackness, which it seemed we were in.

James Ernest kept plodding along and I followed as closely as I could. I had worn shorts and a tee-shirt. I knew my arms and legs were now covered with scratches. I could feel blood running down my legs. At least I was hoping that's what it was. James Ernest had been smart enough to wear bibbed overalls and a long-sleeved shirt. I wondered why he didn't tell me to do the same.

We seemed to be getting deeper and deeper into the woods. I wasn't even sure we were going in the right direction. I was depending on James Ernest's sense of bearing. Suddenly, I heard a scuffling up ahead. James Ernest stopped. We then smelled it. I knew what it was. A skunk had sprayed another animal. We could hear the other animal bounding through the woods. The problem was - the odor didn't go with him. We were headed right into the aroma.

I held my nose and James Ernest motioned for us to go west. He said, "The wind is blowing a little to the east. Let's get away from it."

I quickly agreed to us getting away from the smell. We made our detour. It took us further away from our destination, but was well worth it. In the distance I could hear coyotes howling. It began to our south and then we heard howling to the west. I hoped they weren't communicating between each other about fresh prey walking through their territory – meaning us.

In my last four years of adventures I couldn't remember feeling the fear that I felt at that time. It had to be a combination of things. Knowing we would soon be making our way into a dangerous situation, knowing we were already in a dangerous position with possible coyote attacks, the smell of skunk circling around us, the blackness and most of all – the uncertainty.

I stopped. I was actually frozen with fear. I felt like the world was caving in around me. I couldn't speak. I heard the hoot of an owl and nearly jumped out of my skin. James Ernest stopped when he noticed I wasn't following him. He retreated to my frozen spot.

"What's wrong?" he whispered.

I couldn't speak. I stood there shaking like a leaf in an autumn storm.

James Ernest put his hand on my shoulder and began to pray, "Father, I know you're here with us. I know you understand our fear and hesitation. I ask that you lead us either back to the car or onward to rescue Sam. I pray that Your will be done. I pray for Your protection upon us. Give us strength and wisdom in what we're doing. I pray for all this in the name of Jesus. Amen."

My shaking slowly went away. I thought about telling James Ernest that I felt we should turn around, but then my thoughts went back to Sam instead of my own fear. I thought of the fear he must be going through. He had to have heard his father tell the state police he would kill his son and himself if they came onto his property again. I knew Sam was wondering when he would draw his last breath.

My fear went away. I looked toward my best friend and said, "Let's go save Sam."

I stumbled through the woods on a mission. James Ernest continued to lead us. He turned to the east and I followed. "The cornfield is right up ahead," James Ernest whispered. The woods began to open up. I now didn't have to follow the path he had made. I was looking ahead at the corn when I tripped over a rise and toppled over it onto the ground. My rifle jammed into the ground, and I hurt my left arm when I fell. James Ernest came back again.

"What happened?"

"I tripped over some dirt, I think."

James Ernest looked at the spot where I was lying. He swiped some leaves off the ground to reveal fresh dug dirt. I turned on my flashlight, trying to hide much of the light. We both knew what it was - the grave. I was lying on the grave of Mrs. Hitchcock. I quickly turned the flashlight off and rolled off the dirt.

"C'mon," James Ernest said as he jerked on my hurt arm. I didn't scream, although I wanted to. We were quickly at the edge of the cornfield. James Ernest broke two of the cornstalks and bent them over. I knew he was marking the spot where Mrs. Hitchcock's grave could be found. We then headed into the field walking as quietly as possible through the corn. The only sound I could hear was the sound of my beating heart. I hoped the patrolling police couldn't hear it.

It was only around five minutes before we made our way to the other side of the field. Standing fifty yards away was the shed in which we had found Sam. I wondered if he was in it or in the house. I was hoping he was in the shed. We were now at a tricky point in our mission. We had to cross the open yard to the shed without being seen.

We were hoping the state police had not secured the back of the property. But we weren't sure about that fact. James Ernest whispered, "Our best bet of not being seen is to crawl on our bellies the rest of the way. It would be harder for them to detect us." Which meant it would be harder for the police to see us crawling than running across the yard.

"Ready?"

"Let's do it," I said.

James Ernest led the crawl into the grass. I followed, although it was hard with my arm hurting and with having to drag the rifle along. I wondered how many nightcrawlers I was crawling over and if I was interrupting them.

When we were nearing the shed, a light came on at the edge of the cornfield. I froze like a deer in headlights. James Ernest continued to the shed. The shed hid him from the light. James Ernest whispered, "Keep crawling."

I kept crawling until I was beside him.

"Do you think he saw us?" I asked.

"No. I think he just turned it on to do something. He never did point the light in our direction."

I rapped on the side of the shed and waited for a reply. There was nothing. I couldn't be sure he wasn't in there asleep. I rapped a little louder and whispered, "Sam. Sam. Are you in there?" There was no answer.

"I guess it's on to the house," I said.

It wasn't very far to the house – maybe thirty feet. We got down on our stomachs again and crawled to the back door of the house. James Ernest reached up and tried the door knob. It opened. Apparently it didn't have a lock or Mr. Hitchcock didn't feel the need to lock it. A lot of homes in Morgan County didn't even have locks.

This made it a lot easier to enter than having to find a window to crawl through.

"Stay here and keep watch." He took his shoes off and left them with me. He then asked me, "Can I take the rifle? I might need it."

"Sure," I said, hoping he wouldn't need it.

"Is it loaded?" he whispered.

"Yes, but the safety is on," I whispered back. He slipped the safety off and entered the house.

What had I done? My best friend in the whole world was risking his life to save a friend I hardly knew. I should be the one risking my life, not James Ernest. I quickly took off my shoes and with hesitation I entered the kitchen door. I had my flashlight in my left hand, even though it wasn't on. I had my pocket knife open and in my right hand.

I slowly made my way across the wooden floor. I hoped no one could hear me. I couldn't hear James Ernest. It was as quiet as a tomb. My heart was beating through my chest. My breathing quickened. I started down the hallway toward the front of the house where the living room was. Halfway down the hall I noticed a faint light coming from that room. I thought it must have been from a lantern. I saw the form of a man sitting back in a chair. I knew it was Mr. Hitchcock.

It looked as though he was keeping watch out the front window, but his head was tilted and he looked to be asleep. As I neared the living room, two figures popped out from around the corner and scared me to death. I let out a scream. Mr. Hitchcock woke and still being drowsy he said, "Who's there? Is that you, Sam?"

James Ernest quickly said, "It's the police. Put your gun down." He then pushed both Sam and me to get us going. We ran down the hall and into the kitchen and then through the back door. A shot rang down the hall just after we had turned the corner.

We didn't bother crawling. We picked up our shoes and ran with all we had across the yard and into the cornfield. As quickly as we ran, floodlights came on all around the house. We saw state patrolmen rushing the house from all directions. They had been in the barn, in front of the house, in the woods at the other side of the house, and in the cornfield where we had seen the light.

Then from inside the house - we heard a second shot!

Chapter 30

The Questioning

We hunkered down in the cornfield and watched the action from the edge. No other shots were fired. We knew what had happened. Sam sat by my side and with the floodlights covering the house. I could see tears cascading down Sam's face.

"I can't believe you guys came back to get me. I didn't know anyone had friends like that," he said as he cried.

"I knew I was going to die," he continued as he wiped the tears away.

"Dad told me there was no getting out of his mess. He promised me he was going to take me with him to Hell. He told me Hell would make a real man out of me if he couldn't. He told me that Mom thought she was going to Heaven when he killed her. He said she looked down the barrel of the gun and said, 'I'll be in Heaven with my Savior. Where will you be?' He then told me he shot her.

"He told me it was all my fault. He said I wouldn't listen to him and went to high school. He said they wouldn't have argued about it if I had just listened to him and stayed home to work. He said I killed her, therefore, he was going to kill me."

I didn't know what to say. I put my arm around his shoulder and let him cry. James Ernest told him, "Your Mom is in Heaven.

Someday you'll see her again. You're safe now. And Sam, none of this was your fault. I'm sorry about your mother."

It wasn't long after that we saw the police searching around the house. James Ernest stepped out from the cornfield and yelled out, "We're over here."

They pointed their guns toward him and slowly came toward us. James Ernest held his arms high in the air.

"Are you Sam?" one of the policemen asked.

"No. He's right here with us." Sam and I stood and walked out of the cornfield and faced the uniformed officers.

"I'm Sam. These two friends saved my life."

The rooster was crowing by the time the officers stopped questioning us and took the body of Sam's father away. The second shot was what we had thought; Sam's dad had killed himself. We were severely scorned for our interruption of a police operation. We were threatened of having charges brought against us.

I sat there during all their ranting and raving and thought, *We saved my friend. Do whatever you want.*

I also thought about what Mom would say. She was at the hospital with Sheriff Cane and here we were being threatened with all kinds of stuff.

"How do we get ahold of your parents?" the Chief finally asked me.

"We have no father and our mom is at the hospital with my future father-in-law, Sheriff Cane."

"Sheriff Cane is marrying your mother?" he asked.

"Yes. Next spring," I answered. He sighed.

"Who should we call to come get you?" he asked.

I gave him Papaw's telephone number and told him, "Make sure you tell him to bring someone else with him who can drive Mom's car back home."

He started to say something else but then just turned around and left.

We were finally sitting alone. James Ernest looked at me and said, "That went well. Don't you think?"

We both laughed.

The chief came back over to us a few minutes later and said, "Your grandfather is coming to pick you up. He's bringing Clayton with him."

"Thank you. Where's Sam?" I asked.

"He's being questioned by others."

"We forgot to tell you something," I said.

"What did you forget?" he asked.

"We're quite sure we found Sam's mother's grave," James Ernest answered.

"Where?"

"We can show you," I said.

The chief motioned for two patrolmen to come with him and we led them through the cornfield to the spot where the broken stalks were. We then headed into the woods and found the spot.

"It's right there. I stumbled over it last night," I said, pointing to the hump.

The two men the chief had brought along proceeded to wipe the pile of leaves from the fresh dug dirt.

"It sure looks like it. This is a big help."

I felt like he almost thanked us. But he didn't.

As we walked back toward the house through the cornfield I asked, "What will happen to Sam?"

"They will probably see if he has any relatives who will take him in. If not, then they will see if anyone else wants to take him in," he said.

"Can we see him before we go?" I asked.

"Yeah, sure. This way."

He led us over to the spot where Sam was being kept. I hugged him. James Ernest hugged him.

Sam looked at the chief and said, "I'd be dead if they hadn't risked their lives for me."

I asked Sam to keep in touch and let us know where he ends up. He said he would. He said he hoped to come back to high school. We told him that would be great.

Papaw and Clayton arrived on the scene walking down the lane. The chief met them and thanked them for coming to pick us up.

"Do we even want to know what they've been involved in?" Papaw asked.

The chief simply said, "They saved their friend's life. Take them home."

Clayton shook his head as he turned back up the lane. We told them the short version of our escapade on the way to the truck.

Papaw didn't seem to have any words.

"We saw Betty's car off the side of the road. I guessed you drove it here." Papaw said to James Ernest.

"Yes, but I drove it very safely."

"Why didn't you just drive it back home instead of calling us?" Papaw asked.

"The state police didn't seem to be very happy with us. They wanted to throw us in the pokey as it was," James Ernest said.

"That might learn you something," Clayton said.

We arrived at the pickup. Papaw dropped Clayton off at the car. James Ernest handed him the keys and followed him to the car. I hopped into the front with Papaw.

As we drove home Papaw said, "What are we going to tell Betty? She already has enough worries with Hagar."

"We could forget to tell her about it," I offered.

"She'll find out about it later on," Papaw said.

"The longer, the better," I suggested.

"I think you're right. We'll wait until Hagar is out of the woods to tell her about you guys being in the woods," Papaw said smiling. It was nearly nine o'clock.

When we got to the store Mamaw was there tending the store. We had to tell her the whole story. I was pooped.

"I heard part of it on the radio," Mamaw said.

"What?" I said.

"Your names and everything. Are you two plumb crazy?" Mamaw said.

The phone started ringing. We knew it would ring all day. Mamaw took the calls while James Ernest and I took care of the store.

Later that morning Mom called from the hospital. She had watched the news report on the TV in the waiting room. She was shocked when she heard our names as 'the two teenagers who made a daring rescue to save a friend of theirs.'

Waiting to tell her wasn't going to work. Mamaw assured her that we were fine and were there watching the store. Mom told Mamaw that Hagar had made a good recovery and was now awake and able to talk to her. Mom said the doctor had come in and asked him how he was and Sheriff Cane had told him, "I'll be better, doc, as soon as I am able."

When Mamaw told us what he had said, we all laughed.

Chapter 31

Celebration

Thursday, July 4, 1963

We had closed the store early to celebrate the Fourth of July. Some of my cousins from Ohio had come down to visit and we all were sitting on the porch at Papaw's farm. The Washington family came over. Clayton had brought his family over. Homer and Ruby were there. Robert and Janice had come.

Two of my aunts had made the trip from Ohio with their families. Aunt Ruth and her husband Joe were there with their kids Joe Junior, Jenny and Judy. Janie was so excited to see Judy again. They were the same age and had been great friends when we also lived in Ohio. My Aunt Helen had come down with her husband, Bill, and her stepson, King.

The adults stayed on the porch and talked while most of us kids played kick ball and Red Rover and other games. It was a terrific evening. Sheriff Cane was there with great news of the arrests of Tully Musk and Weasel Wilder.

I was so happy that the drama from the killing of Thomas Back was over with, and I hoped nothing else would threaten our family or friends that year. Boy, was I wrong.

After dark, I sat with Susie on the grass and watched the men set off firecrackers and fireworks. James Ernest and Raven were sitting next to us. I wondered if the nightcrawlers were taking time to watch.

Chapter 32

Summary

Friday, November 22, 1963

Susie, Raven and I were sitting in study hall. I didn't really have much to study, or at least I didn't feel like studying anything at the time. Susie and Raven both were working on an English assignment.

I began thinking about the past summer and fall. It had been such an eventful few months. The Bear Troop was formed and on our first adventure wading Licking Creek we had found a body that had been thrown off a cliff. His name was Thomas Back from Michigan. He had been trying to sell drugs to Tully Fran Musk and Frank 'Weasel' Wilder when it all went south. Tully ended up killing Mr. Back by throwing him off the cliff.

It was determined at the trial that Weasel wasn't involved with the murder but did cover it up. Tully's lawyer tried to convince the jury that the death was an accident. They didn't buy the defense. Tully was sent to prison for a long time. Weasel was given three years for his part in it. The one box of drugs was marijuana. The other box was LSD. The drugs were destroyed. The money in the wallet that Coty and I had found that had led Sheriff Cane to the drugs was given to me as a reward.

I decided to split the money with the members of the Wolf Pack. It was only fair. We each received around two hundred dollars. We all either had or opened up savings accounts with Mr. Harney at his bank and deposited the money for college, or something else.

Sam Hitchcock was taken in by his Aunt Sara in Lexington. She was his mother's sister. She had never married and was happy to be able to offer Sam a place in her home. He had written to me a few times telling about his new high school and the life he had there. He seemed very happy and very thankful for his friends, me and James Ernest.

He was planning to visit one day during Christmas break. I couldn't wait to see him. I was so happy for him.

Sam's mother was dug up and both of his parents were now buried, but apart. Sara wanted her sister buried in Lexington away from the man who had ended her life. Mr. Hitchcock was buried in a small public cemetery in Ashland, Kentucky, where his family was from.

Sheriff Cane spent a week in the hospital. He was cleared to go back to work in late October. He was now as good as he was before the shooting. He and Mom are happy and still planning their big spring wedding. Neither of them was very happy about our decision to rescue Sam, but they said they understood it.

The school welcomed us back with mixed emotions. The students thought we were heroes. The teachers and Principal Davis never acknowledged it so as to not encourage that type of behavior. But Principal Davis, one day, took James Ernest and me aside and told us it was very brave of us to do what we had done, and he was very proud of us. To me, that was better than anything else.

I thought of John and Pricilla who had their babies two weeks ago on November the 9th. Ruby and Geraldine helped with the births at John and Pricilla's home. They had a son and a daughter. Ruby said the births almost killed Pricilla. Geraldine said she wasn't sure Pricilla would live through it or not, but she did. They named the twins Ken and Barbie.

No one could believe it. I guessed Pricilla hadn't grown out of her doll stage and wanted her own Ken and Barbie dolls. John told me and James Ernest that he couldn't change her mind. He said he would end up calling them by nicknames.

The bell rang and we headed for Science class with Mr. Castle.

"I am so glad it's Friday," I told Raven and Susie as we headed for our last class of the week.

"This is going to be so boring," Susie said.

Chapter 33

The Shock

Friday, November 22, 1963

We were waiting for the bell to ring ending the school week. Mr. Castle had talked about the solar system non-stop and then asked us to read about it the last ten minutes of class. I was watching the second hand on the clock go slowly around the face.

Five minutes before class was to end Principal Davis interrupted the classes to make an announcement, which happened a lot on Fridays. Usually it was to announce sports events on the weekend, or other activities, or to recognize someone for what they had accomplished.

"I'm sorry to bring you sad news this afternoon," Principal Davis began. I could tell that Mr. Davis was having a hard time speaking. "President John F. Kennedy was shot and killed at 12:30 this afternoon in Dallas, Texas."

The End

Dear Readers

By your buying and reading this book I know you must be glad I changed my mind and decided to continue writing the series. Thank you so much.

Thanks to all the readers who asked me to continue the books, for all of you who said how much they missed them.

Despite the wants, I couldn't see continuing the series. But after a two year break I missed writing them so much. I tried writing other books. I even tried writing another series. But each time I found myself wanting to write about Kentucky and the Wolf Pack. I wanted to write about the people I loved and missed. I hope you missed them also.

I apologize if I've hurt anyone's feelings over the subject matter in this new book. One of the reasons I had wanted to end the series when I did was because the boys were getting older and I wanted to keep their innocence intact. With the boys now in high school I feel I need to write about what they would be going through in their life. As we all did growing up.

I know, I questioned a lot once I got to this high school age. I questioned if God was real. I questioned the Vietnam War. I had lots of questions about sex and no answers. I've always wanted the books to portray real life, but then throw in enough fictional adventures to make the stories fun and interesting to readers. I've wanted the books to bring glory to Jesus. I pray I've done that.

I hope you're not offended by the talk of sex in the book. I tried to keep it clean with a touch of humor. Thank you for your continued support and I hope to have another in the renewed series out soon.

Blessings,

Tim Callahan

email: timcal21@yahoo.com   website: www.timcallahan.net

Short Stories

Read readers, I originally had planned to write a book of short stories about the characters from Kentucky Summers. I never finished it and probably never will.

Therefore, I decided to include some of them at the end of each book in the Kentucky Summers 2 series. Instead of being told through the eyes of Timmy, they are told through the eyes of the character that the story is about.

I hope you enjoy the first three.

Bonus ~ Three Short Stories

1

Purty

Love of Nudity

I'm not sure why I love being naked. I've been this way since I was born. Maybe I loved the feeling as soon as I slipped from my mother's stomach and entered this new world. Mom says I would take off my clothes and diaper whenever I could as a baby. She told me she would leave me in the bassinet and go into another part of the house and return to find me with my diaper slung into a corner and a big smile on my face.

I was potty-trained very early in my development. I'm thinking I figured that as soon as I didn't need the diaper any longer for bodily functions, the sooner I could go around without any pants at all. What would I need pants for? They were no longer needed to catch my doo-doo or pee-pee. I remember being very disappointed every time Mom would pull pants over my legs. I didn't understand the need of them.

When I would manage to escape from my clothes and get natural my brother Randy or my sister Sadie would rat me out.

"Mom! Mom! He's naked again," Randy would scream as I ran through the house trying to get away from my mother's clutches.

"Mom! Mom! I can see his little wee-wee again, Mom!" Sadie would yell out.

When Randy and Sadie were gone from the house or at school, Mom would sometimes give up and let me run around in the house buck naked. I felt so free and happy when she would do this. It was like we had a secret between us, and maybe an understanding. I was allowed to be free of garments when we were alone as long as I wore those garments when anyone else was around. I think Mom just gave up trying to keep clothes on me and compromised.

It was so much easier to let me roam the house free than to fight me. At least she would finally get some peace and quiet during those times. Those were happy days.

Those happy days ended when I had to start school myself. I found out quickly that Mom was right when she told me the teacher would get angry at me if I took off my clothes in school. We lived in Morehead when I started my schooling and I went to a small elementary school with Randy and Sadie. In 1st grade I sat in the back row of our classroom. The first day of school was a hot September day. I was hot and miserable sitting there. Of course the school didn't have air-conditioning and the teacher, Miss Patterson, had opened the windows to let in some air. All it let in was hot air.

Miss Patterson had turned to write the alphabet on the blackboard. By the time she turned back around I was sitting in my desk chair completely disrobed with my clothes at my feet on the floor. It took her a moment or two to figure out what all the snickering around the room was about. When she finally saw me sitting there, she shrieked. I mean an actual, literal shriek!

She ran to the back of the room to where I sat and quickly gathered up my clothes and grabbed me by my arm and half-drug me to the restroom. "Put your things back on and come back out here when you're done. You are in big trouble, Mr. Tuttle!"

No one had ever called me Mr. Tuttle before. I felt like a grown-up, at least I did until I got taken to the principal's office. Miss Patterson left me seated outside Principal Harp's office while she went into his office, which I soon learned, to rat me out. When she came back outside his office to fetch me, I was

303

standing with my pants and underwear around my ankles in the process of disrobing again. Another shriek!

Upon hearing the shriek, Principal Harp ran to Miss Patterson's aid and saw me standing there giving him a good example of what I had been ratted out for. I guessed there was no getting out of the punishment that was to come. I received a stern lecture and warning and three firm swats from a wooden paddle on my now-clothed behind. At that moment I was happy to have been not naked.

I now knew that Mom was right.

This, of course, wouldn't be the last time I would get swats or get in trouble for being naked in public. One day while in the grocery Mom heard an announcement over the address system, "Would the mother of a young naked boy that we found in the fruit section please come to the office!"

I heard laughter coming from all over the store. What was so wrong if I was able to make folks laugh?

Any time we would go to a swimming pool or the ocean on vacation I would end up naked. I was found hanging upside-down naked on the monkey bars at the playground while Mom was having a conversation with other mothers. The little girls' screams ratted me out that time.

First grade was endless trips to the principal's office for more swats and constant teasing from my classmates and older kids. Randy and Sadie ignored me at school. It wasn't that I was hardheaded, I just loved being free from clothing.

By second grade I had finally realized that I would have to keep my pants on at school. I only had a couple of further incidents at school.

Growing up was hard when I was constantly wanting to be nude. I would study the National Geographic magazines that Dad received and see all the African tribal people that were shown naked in the publication. Apparently no one told them they had to get dressed. I was so envious of them. I wanted to be a member of an African tribe. One day in school we were assigned to write a report on "If we could be anything in the world other than ourselves what would it be and why." I wrote about how I wanted to be a naked African native. I explained how I then could be naked all the time and no one would care. I wrote about how I could walk around naked, swim naked, eat naked, go to bed naked, go to school naked, play naked and go to the grocery naked.

I got a D-minus on my fantastic essay.

I also saw my uncle's Playboy magazines, and I saw famous statues and paintings that were filled with nudity. Apparently people thought those were okay for everyone to see, but it wasn't okay to actually see a live boy naked. It really was confusing.

When I get old and make out my Will there is one thing I will make clear in it. I will want to be placed in my casket completely nude. They can place flowers over my 'not so' privates if they must. I don't want to go into eternity burdened from clothing. I'm hoping that in Heaven we will be wearing the long white robes like I've seen portrayed. It looks as though they will be so easy to slip off over my head.

Delma

"Salt in their Wounds"

Wednesday, June 28, 1961

My twin sister, Thelma, and I pushed our way to the front of the reporter. The reporter noticed us and asked, "Do you know the missing boys?"

"Yes, we do. We know them very well," I answered.

"We know them all extremely well," Thelma said.

"Are you sad they haven't been found so far?" the reporter asked.

"We'll miss three of the boys," I said.

"What about the fourth one?" the reporter asked.

I paused and then said, "Won't miss Timmy so much."

"Won't miss him at all," Thelma said.

"Isn't Timmy the boy that was the hero a couple of summers ago?" the reporter asked with a surprised look on his face.

Just as Monie grabbed Thelma and me by the collar, I said, "One man's hero is another girl's weirdo."

"You girls get back in the house!" Monie screamed. She nearly lifted each of us off the ground by our collars as she directed us back inside the store.

The Wolf Pack - Timmy, James Ernest and brothers, Randy and Todd, nicknamed Purty - had been missing for a couple of days. They had gone off on a day adventure and had not returned. The community and families were panicked and beginning to expect the worst. Apparently Mom felt we, 8-year old girls, had accosted the reporter from the local TV station when he arrived at the store to do a report on the lost boys.

We were greatly insulted to have been treated in such a way in front of rolling cameras. "You embarrassed us in front of the whole world. We were just answering his questions," I tried explaining. We huffed and puffed inside the store complaining about how our freedom of speech had been taking away.

"That's not the only thing that's going to be taken away if you two don't hush up right now," Monie told us angrily.

"Nothing more important could be taken away than what you've done - our dignity," I called out.

"Yeah, my dig-no-ty," Thelma echoed with a different pronunciation.

"I'm going to get a switch and take away some of the hide from your butts in a minute," Monie told us.

Thelma and I marched to the couch and dropped to a pouting position.

The women were gathered in the kitchen fretting and worrying about the boys possibly being trapped in a cave that may have caved in. They went over other scenarios that could have happened. Truth was no one knew where the boys were.

I looked at Thelma and said, "Do you think Timmy is dead?"

"I don't know. We can only hope."

I smiled and said, "Yeah."

Thelma looked up at the ceiling and then seriously asked me, "Do you think Timmy would go to Heaven?"

"I don't think so. God probably only wants the best people in Heaven – like us."

"Could you imagine us having to spend all of eternity with Timmy?" Thelma said.

"God probably has different neighborhoods up there," I thought out loud. "We would probably be in the fancy neighborhood with big mansions and servant angels. If Timmy makes it into Heaven he would be in the badest section in an old cabin with no doors or windows."

"We would never see him. He wouldn't be allowed into our neighborhood."

"I wonder what else we would have in Heaven. I bet we would both have a pony, all white with pearly teeth," I declared.

We sat on the couch imagining what Heaven would be like when we got there. Nothing was out of question when it came to our golden rewards we would be given. No one that knew our family could understand how Thelma and I could have come from the same family. We didn't understand it either. It was like when a son turned to crime and the community made comments about how they couldn't figure how he came from such a good family, or a famous - talented star came from a dirt poor family from the deepest holler. Some things in life were hard to sort out.

Because of one incident, we had made up our minds to despise Timmy. Timmy had always been nice to everyone except us. But now he had two enemies – Thelma and I. This is what had happened to fester such hate.

When we were almost four we went to the store one summer day with our family. When Daddy pulled into the gravel parking lot we saw Timmy standing on the store porch and I had told Thelma, "He's kinda cute." Thelma nodded her head.

Our family emptied from the truck and started up the steps with Thelma and me lagging behind. Timmy held the door open for Mom, Brenda, Dad and then Susie. Timmy's eyes were squarely on Susie.

Timmy said, "Hi, Susie," and then closed the screen door behind him and followed Susie into the store leaving Thelma and me on the porch wounded. Timmy acted as though he hadn't even seen us behind our sister, Susie. He held the door open for them, and then he shut it right plumb in our faces.

"Well that was mean!" I shouted. Timmy may not have even heard us due to the laughter inside the store.

"That was so rude."

"He must be the rudest boy in the world," I told Thelma.

"He is the rudest boy in the whole world," Thelma echoed.

Timmy had no idea the twins were behind Susie, but that action was the thing that began the twins' hatred for Timmy. Everything he did from then on was multiplied into greater dastardly deeds in the eyes of the twins giving them great fetter to fuel their thinking. One simple misunderstanding of Timmy's closing of a door would forever ignite that extreme dislike on the twins' part. Timmy was very much unaware of what started it all. It all mainly came out of two girls' jealousy. A boy they thought was cute had closed a door in their face to talk to their sister.

The girls' dislike for Timmy even turned to downright meanness. They baked a celebration cake when they held out hope that Timmy had died on the cave adventure. They teased his inability to say certain words correctly; they told him no one loved him except a dog. In school they mocked everything he said or did, making some of his day's miserable.

Tucky

The Key Family

My birth certificate shows my name as Kenny Tuck Key. We, my twin sister Rock and I, are the middle children of our family. There are three older and three younger children than us. We now live in a small shack on the bank of Licking crick. Some folks call it Licking River, but it ain't no bigger than a crick and even smaller than most. We could stand on the back porch and throw a line into the water and fish if it was deep enough in this spot, but it ain't. We can wade in and catch crawdads and minnows - and tadpoles in the spring. On down the crick are deeper holes where we catch bluegill and rock bass for food.

I'm a member of the Wolf Pack, an all-boys club, along with five other guys and a dog, Coty. I have had the most fun and best adventures I've ever had in my twelve years on this green earth because of the Wolf Pack. They poke fun at me, due to my mountain, backward upbringing and probably due to all of our family's names.

My mom is named Winona, which is pretty normal, but my dad's name is Buck Key. He named all the kids so our first name could be combined with the last name to form another meaning. My oldest brother, who should be gone from the house by now, is named Monk Key. The next oldest is Chuck Key. My older sister is Sugar Cook Key. She probably gets the most teasing. We call her either Sugar or Cookie most of the time.

My younger siblings are named Chero Key. My dad says we have some Cherokee Indian blood running through our veins. My next youngest sister is Adore Key, as in A Door Key. I think dad was running out of names for girls when he came up with it. Mom calls her Dorie. I sometimes call her Dorkie. Our

310

youngest brother is named Luck Key. Mom had said she was done bearing children at seven, but somehow Luck came along, so he was lucky to be here and we were lucky to have him, thus the name. My twin sister's name is Rock Key.

Our small house only has two bedrooms. Mom and Dad sleep in one with Lucky. The four girls sleep in the other, and Monk, Chuck and I sleep anywhere we can find to lie down, usually the living room. When it isn't deathly cold outside I like to lie on the back porch and fall asleep to the sound of the water and the frogs croaking on the banks of the crick.

Our house doesn't have electric or running water. We get water from the crick to wash our pants and shirts and get baths, or if it's warm enough we skinny dip in the crick and wash off. There's a spring nearby to get drinking and cooking water.

Since I brought up cooking, this is what the guys tease me about the most - roadkill. My dad and us boys have always hunted for our meat. We eat squirrel, rabbit, deer, raccoon, possum, groundhog, and turkey – most anything we can find in the woods and fields. But sometimes meat is hard to come by and Dad has never passed up fresh meat we've found along the side of the road. As long as its stomach isn't bloated up and the maggots haven't already taken up residence we snatch it up and take it home.

"No use wasting perfectly good meat. The crows and buzzards can find food elsewhere," Dad would say as we put it in a burlap bag to take home. We live on the bank of the crick, but we also lived right up close to SR 711. When dad would hear a thump or a car slam on its brakes, he would send two of us boys out in different directions along the road to look for the fresh kill. The Wolf Pack teased me constantly about our family appetite for roadkill. I took the teasing because I knew it wasn't normal fare, but I and my brothers and sisters had been raised on it. It was sometimes that or go without. And sometimes it could have turned into weeks.

I was sitting near the water watching what Timmy, my best friend, called Jesus bugs skate on the top of the water when Mom rang the supper bell. I got up and saw most of my siblings scampering toward the house. I walked through the back porch door to the kitchen and asked, "What's for supper, Mom?"

"Chuck found a groundhog earlier today, so I made a nice stew and some fresh biscuits," Mom answered. "Help yourself."

I found the pot of stew in the middle of our table, which was only big enough for six to sit around. Usually we boys would eat in the living room or out on the porch. I picked up a bowl and dipped the stew from the pot and grabbed a couple of biscuits and made my way to the raggedy flowered couch.

I knew we were poor. A lot of folks were poor in Kentucky. All you had to do was look at our torn bibbed overalls that we all wore or look at the sagging shack we lived in to know we were poor. I didn't know any other way of living. Eating roadkill and eating it any place I could find to park myself was just as normal to me as cooking up a store bought roast and sitting at the dining room table to eat it was to other families with some money.

But this evening Rock decided to make an issue out of it.

"Mom, Kenny and I get made fun of because we eat roadkill," Rock spurted out as most of the family ate around the table.

"Who makes fun of you?" Dad asked.

"Some of the kids at school do."

Dad huffed and Mom said, "Well, you need to pay them no never mind. They can do as they please and so will we."

"Maybe you two should stop going to school. I'm not sure why you want to go anyway," Dad said, his voice showing some anger in it.

"We're always teasing each other about all kinds of stuff. They don't mean nothin' by it," I said from the couch, trying to calm the rising storm Rock started.

I wasn't much for going to school when Timmy and Susie suggested it, but I had gone to check it out and I now liked going. I wasn't able to go every day. I had to help Dad and Mom a lot of days and couldn't go, but I went on days I could and now liked it. I liked learning different things and liked learning to read

312

and write. Rock went more than I did, and I knew she loved it. I didn't want Dad stopping us from going.

Mom took my side. "Now, Buck, there's nothing wrong with the kids learning to read and write and being able to add figures. I would like for more of them to go. It would be better for them to be able to find good jobs one day."

"I don't want them forgetting where they come from and getting' too high-for lootin'. Just because we're poor don't mean we're not as good as other folks. You kids remember that," Dad warned us.

"I don't think most of them think that. We've made a lot of good friends at the school," I said.

"It's mostly Sadie and Bernice that tease me," my sister explained.

"Sadie and Bernice don't have the sense God gave roadkill," I challenged.

"You're probably right. Sadie thinks she's better than everyone," Rock said.

"Isn't she the sister of the boy who runs around naked as a jaybird?" Mom asked. Everyone laughed. Mom was talking about Sadie's brother, Purty. He loved being naked and wasn't afraid to get that way every chance he could. He was also a member of the Wolf Pack and provided our club with most of its humor and entertainment.

Mom added, "Seems as though they've got some strange ways in their family too."

Mom was right about that. Most of the families in the community had some quirk in their family. The Perry family had the twin girls who bugged everyone to death. James Ernest didn't talk for years and his Mom and Dad left him behind and then died in a car crash. He now lived with Timmy and his family. Timmy's father was an alcoholic before dying a couple of years ago. I can't even name all the oddities of Purty's family, the Tuttles. The most normal family seemed to be the Washington's – and they were black living in an all-white community. So they had very different problems.

But, even with all the strangeness and difficulties most everyone loved and cared about their neighbors. It was a great community of farmers and mountain folk – like us.

As I was eating my groundhog stew and biscuits I heard brakes and then a 'Ker plunk'. I quickly laid my bowl on the floor and hurried out the door. I stood on the porch and looked up and down the road to see what had been hit. I was sure it wasn't far away by the closeness of the sound. I was almost sure the sound came from up the road. I began walking and searching the ditch lines as I went. It wasn't long before I saw a dead deer lying in the ditch. Jackpot!

Anytime we could get deer out of season it was a good day. It meant fresh meat for a couple of weeks and good deer jerky. What a treat! I needed help dragging it back to the house so I ran back. I told my family about our good fortune and then finished eating my stew. Monk and Chuck went with me to get the deer after we had finished our meals. When we got it home we hung it up in a tree and bleed it and then gutted it into an old wash tub. Monk and Chuck hauled the guts away while I began removing the hide. Dad opened the door and made his way to where I was working and watched me for a while.

"You're getting mighty good at that," Dad said.

"Lots of practice, I guess."

"It seems to me that you have all the skills you need to get by without having to go to school," Dad told me.

"I probably do, Dad, but I enjoy learning things about the world. I want to learn to read and write good and be able to do some math. I think it could do some good in the future."

"I haven't needed those things."

"I know. And you've done a fine job of taking care of our family. But the world is changing and I'll need to know things to get a good job."

"A job? Why would you want to work for someone your whole life?"

"Maybe I won't. Maybe I'll start my own company."

"Like what?"

"Like......guttin' and skinin' deer for city folks."

Dad laughed and then I laughed. He spit tobacco juice on the ground and said, "Maybe you're right. But sometimes I think I should have kept us deep in the hollers of the mountains."

Monk and Chuck returned with the empty tub. Dad looked at them and asked, "You boys ever gonna get a job?"

"No way," Monk quickly answered. "Why would we do that?" Chuck followed.

Dad nodded his head and smiled. I figured he figured at least he had raised two boys correctly.

The End

Made in the USA
Lexington, KY
27 April 2018